ZOMBICIDE INVADER
TERROR WORLD

There, coming out of the darkness – the light hit the serrated triangles of the creature's teeth first, then the fishlike mouth that housed them was already splitting apart to make room for the bite.

The Xeno latched onto the man in the rear, and before he could do more than glance over his shoulder, his left arm was completely torn off his body. Those terrible teeth clamped down on the corner of his neck and ripped a hole large enough for its barbed tentacles to slither inside.

The man managed a single horrific, piercing scream as he died, one that his companions echoed, powered with adrenaline and shock. It was clear from their reactions that this was the last thing they'd expected to find when they crash-landed at the distant mining outpost.

More Zombicide from Aconyte

Zombicide Invader

Planet Havoc by Tim Waggoner

Zombicide

Last Resort by Josh Reynolds

All or Nothing by Josh Reynolds

Zombicide Black Plague

Age of the Undead by C L Werner

TERROR WORLD

CATH LAURIA

First published by Aconyte Books in 2023

ISBN 978 1 83908 201 6

Ebook ISBN 978 1 83908 202 3

Cover art by Rafael Teruel

Distributed in North America by Simon & Schuster Inc, New York, USA

Printed in the United States of America

9 8 7 6 5 4 3 2 1

ACONYTE BOOKS

An imprint of Asmodee Entertainment Ltd

Mercury House, Shipstones Business Centre

North Gate, Nottingham NG7 7FN, UK

aconytebooks.com // twitter.com/aconytebooks

To everyone who believes that someday,
space travel – and all of its wonders
and horrors – will be a reality.
And also, for my mom. Hi Mom!

CHAPTER ONE
Ix-Nix-Six

"You are about to do the inconceivable."

The voice over the comm unit fell flat. Ix-Nix-Six wasn't sure if it was because his hivemate was disconcerted, or because his ship's acoustics were so different from other, normal Caridian vessels. Their people almost never traveled in cramped quarters such as these – the Seethe were accustomed to traveling en masse, each ship large enough for an entire hive's worth of voyagers, no ship ever traveling by itself.

The Glorious Hegemony was a single unit, united in their goal of spreading Caridian influence across the universe. Small ships like the one Ix-Nix-Six sat in now were generally only manufactured as escape pods, and even then, most of them were designed to hold up to fifty Caridians. This one would carry no more than ten, and right now it was only carrying one. Six.

"It has been done before," Six replied, his mind occupied with the future even as his ungues moved smoothly over the control panel before him. Caridians, insectoid by morphology, had lost their nimble third set of legs in the distant past of their evolution, but they made up for it somewhat by developing extra claws on the pretarsal segment of their front limbs. It made operating the switches and knobs he'd specified to be included in this ship a bit of a challenge but far from impossible.

The comm crackled slightly. "Not by a reputable member of the Seethe."

"Our spies are considered very honorable, as you well know," Six responded.

"But not *reputable,*" his companion pressed. "Their work is a necessary evil which forever taints them in the eyes of Caridian society. You are throwing away all of your respectability, not to mention a great deal of your hive's fortune, on this fool's venture."

"It's mine to do with as I wish." A fact that stuck in the palps of many of his fellow Caridians, but which was backed up by a millennium of tradition. Ix-Nix-Six was the heir of his small but lucrative hive, and custom dictated that he could do whatever he wanted to with his fortune. It was simply that the custom for most hives was to share their wealth directly back into the Seethe.

Not so with Ix-Nix-Six. Six, having long ago decided that the life of an explorer and scholar was more to his taste than a future as another faceless soldier slaughtering at the Seethe's command, funneled his wealth into the pursuit of scientific discovery, instead. He'd built a laboratory on his home planet, that now housed some of the finest minds in the whole of the Seethe, pursuing everything from alternative fuel sources to cloning technology.

Being permitted to reinvest his income back into research was truly rare, but Ix-Nix-Six liked to think that the wealth of knowledge he had provided the Seethe with more than paid for his occasional foray into more personal ventures. This ship, for example, which he'd spent over a decade and millions of credits on, was the result of very careful planning, and not a little bit of wishful thinking.

Even tradition might not have been enough to get him permission for his very unorthodox plans for his hive's fortune if not for the support of the queens, the Caridians' ruling class. Every time Ix-Nix-Six was challenged over his strange ideas and unharmonious streak of independence, the queens firmly sided with him. Rumors swirled about their indulgence of him, about whether or not he had some sort of hold over the entire leadership cohort of the Glorious Hegemony. Absurd! But he couldn't deny that their steady support was as surprising as it was welcome. They must love science and discovery just as much as he did.

How fortunate I am, Ix-Nix-Six reflected as he slowly tuned back in to the lecture he was *still* getting from his conservative and decidedly chatty hivemate.

"... must understand that your conduct among the aliens could be ruinous for our people if..."

"I will make it clear to the Galactic Coalition that I am acting completely independently from the Seethe," he assured his lab's second in command. Ix-Kik-Par would be in charge of overseeing all the lab's employees and experiments while Six was gone. Yet another breach of orthodoxy, but one that was tolerated since the Ix line had a history of success in their scientific ventures. Tolerated, as long as it benefited the Seethe. "No one will have any reason to associate my actions with you or the Glorious Hegemony, Par."

"They will anyway." Par's voice was noticeably gloomy, the usually brisk buzz of his mouthparts clicking at a much slower rate than usual. "Species like humans love to extrapolate vast knowledge from limited data. Show them one hive ship, they will assume all hive ships are just like it. Have you read their data file on us? It's positively insulting."

It was very basic, Six agreed. But humanity, and the Galactic Coalition at large, couldn't be faulted for that, not really. There had been very few interactions between the Seethe and the Coalition so far, and most of them had ended in violence.

The trick, Six thought to himself as he primed the ship's subatomic fissure generator, would be to get them to listen to him before blasting him and his ship into nothingness. He was, after all, about to send himself deep into Coalition space. He would have no allies there, no backup. He was doing this on his own, and the consequences would be borne solely by him. If he returned triumphant, he would be welcomed back to the Seethe. If he died…

Well. Six would travel along that tunnel when he got to it.

"You could just bypass them completely," Par said, not for the first time. Or the fifth. "Take the wormhole straight to Sik-Tar; there's a weak spot in the continuum there already. You could investigate the planet on your own, away from the Coalition's prying eyes and puny weapons."

"Sik-Tar is in Coalition space," Six replied as patiently

as he could manage as he began to input the password to let him access his wormhole generator. Extra layers of caution were a good thing, when it came to breaking apart the space-time continuum. "Even if it is very distant from the epicenter of it. I would rather go with the chance of gaining allies as a result of my forthrightness than sneak into a restricted area and hope they think me too small a prey to chase down." Which they probably would, given the remoteness of Sik-Tar and the red dwarf star it orbited, but Six had his own reasons for wanting to make himself known to the Galactic Coalition.

A blue spark flared to life in front of Six's ship, magnified by his viewscreen. It began to expand, growing from seed to flower to a revolving, unspeakably intricate mandala in a matter of seconds thanks to the kilotons of fuel that Six was pouring into the fissure generator. Travel by wormhole was something his people had perfected generations ago, but it was still a costly measure. Every second holding this tunnel open spent another year's worth of Six's accumulated credits in the cost of fuel.

"You really think they're going to have something useful to offer you?" Par droned on. "They're all such primitive, selfish creatures, so afraid of anything new and superior. You'll be lucky if they don't pop you onto a dissection table and take you to pieces just because they can."

Not even his desultory cautions could bring Six's mood down, though. Par might be right. Six could be heading to his death right now, or the wormhole might collapse unexpectedly, or any of a dozen things could occur and render all his careful planning useless.

It was a risk he was willing to take. Sik-Tar called to him like a nest mother to her nymphs, using a song that meant nothing to everyone else in the universe. It was a song tailored to Six, and he could no more stop listening to it than he could survive outside of his exoskeleton. The song was a part of him now, and he could no longer abide its distance from him.

He was going to Sik-Tar. Light and glory willing, he wouldn't be traveling there alone.

"I'm going in," he said, his mandibles quivering with excitement. "Wish me good fortune."

"May you not get sucked into a rift in space-time and deposited a billion years in the past, you complete and utter idiot."

"Thank you!" Six double-checked his end-coordinates, then fired up his impulse engines and eased his ship into the wormhole.

He felt the barest sensation of stretching, just for a moment – like every cell in his body was being pulled far beyond its physiological limits, so that he was in one place far behind him and another far ahead of him all at once. He couldn't breathe, but it didn't matter. Atoms didn't need to breathe. He couldn't see – light was nothing but another form of energy, just like him. He couldn't… he couldn't…

He couldn't *stop!* Oh dear, oh dear…

Six cut the throttle to the impulse engines as fast as he could, but not before the klaxon keen of his ship's warning system filled the cabin.

"You are intruding in Coalition space," his comm system conveyed.

Goodness, they'd wasted no time in finding him. He'd truly chosen the perfect exit.

"This is a restricted area. Cease all engine output now, or we will fire on you. You have five seconds to comply. Four. Three."

"Oh." Six shut the engines down entirely, letting his ship drift. On his viewscreen, he could see the symbol that was his ship – a small ultraviolet star – being surrounded by a whole host of yellow stars that were much, *much* bigger than him. "Well." He opened a channel on the frequency he knew Coalition ships used. "Hello! I am Ix-Nix-Six, chief researcher for the Ix Hive. I come–"

Every alarm on his ship began to peal again as one of the Coalition vessels fired close enough to singe his hull.

"–in peace," he finished. "I officially request to be taken to your leader so that we might discuss my–"

"How did you get into this restricted zone?" the Coalition commander interjected. Hmm, what was that tone? Low, with a certain amount of buzz to it even though humans were biologically incapable of making that sound… ah, *anger*, that was it. "This system is off limits to all non-Coalition spacecraft."

"Is it? I'm sorry, I didn't know that," Six lied. "As you can see, I've only just debarked here. I would like to–"

"Do you have sensor deflectors? A cloaking device?"

"Nooo, I don't. I–"

"Then how did you get here?"

"Through a wormhole, of course," Six said, surprised that they even needed to ask. Didn't they know anything about the technology of the Glorious Hegemony? He was sure it was in their file on his people. Maybe it was considered an… how did they put it? *Urban legend,* that was it. As if no species could possibly be more advanced than the mishmash that made up the Coalition. Six resisted the urge to clack his mouthparts with derision.

There was a long silence. "You need to come with us," the voice on the other end of the comm finally said.

"I would be delighted to come with you!" Six replied. "Send me the coordinates and I'll–"

"You will activate your autopilot and follow on visual. Maintain impulse engine power only. If you try to flee, we'll destroy your ship."

"Oh. All right." Six input the appropriate commands into the computer, then sat back in his chair, a little deflated. It wasn't that he'd been expecting a welcome party, exactly, but… was it so difficult for the Coalition to believe that he came in peace? He only chose this particular landing site because it increased his chances of making contact, not because he wanted to sabotage anything!

Besides, it was such a remote place, just a few odd habitable planets around a distant yellow sun. What was so important about the PK-L system, anyhow?

CHAPTER TWO
Dizzie Drexler

Shrouded in silence, Dizzie watched from their perch on the rim of the spindly communications tower as the drab, mustard-brown expanse of sky was suddenly penetrated by a needle of white light. It coalesced into a ship: an oblong, Hades-class military frigate that was trying, and clearly failing, to control its descent. It shivered as it approached the ground, barely managing to lift its nose up to horizontal before it smashed into the runway at high speed, yet somehow managed to keep from rolling over or breaking apart. Dizzie watched it slide to a halt between two of the station's outbuildings, finally settling in a cloud of dust.

As the grime of the ship's inelegant landing dissipated, two sets of stairs extended from its body, one in the front, one in the back. Seconds later a group of armor-clad people trooped off it, looking wobbly but also very well armed. They headed in the direction of the main hangar at a meandering pace, gawking at the damage all around them.

This was more than could be explained by a crash landing or ten. The exterior of the main building of PK-L7's mining colony looked like it was ground zero in a war.

You have no idea.

Two of the newcomers loitered near one of the destroyed hangars, hands tight on their guns as they looked around. Neither of them saw the danger that lurked in the shadows of every ramshackle outbuilding and ragged hole in the ground, but Dizzie did. There, coming out of the darkness – the light hit the serrated triangles of the creature's teeth first, then the protrusible, fishlike mouth that housed them. Its bifurcated upper lip was already splitting apart to make room for the bite.

In three, two, one – bam.

The Xeno creeping up out of the blackness latched onto the man in the rear, and before he could do more than glance over his shoulder, his left arm was completely torn off his body. His armor might as well have been paper for all the good it did against those terrible teeth, which clamped down on the corner of his neck and ripped a hole large enough for one of its sets of barbed tentacles to slither inside, slip-sliding through its victim's blood before they latched on to the trembling viscera. The Xeno had a long, rounded head, reminiscent of an octopus, but its dark eyes were more alien than anything found in Earth's oceans could ever be, and its powerful limbs had no trouble securing its human meal through his death throes.

The man managed a single horrific, piercing scream as he died, one that his companions echoed, powered with adrenaline and shock. It was clear from their reactions that this was the last thing they'd expected to find when they crash-landed at the distant mining outpost.

That one's just a worker, mid-sized... they haven't seen anything yet.

His companions fired on it, destroying their comrade's killer, but by then the other Xenos had appeared. Hunters surged up through the ground, built like the worker but twice as large. Fast and frenzied, they killed indiscriminately, and didn't even seem to notice the barrage of bullets hitting them until they were so shredded, they could no longer move.

For a few moments it looked like the humans would be able to hold their own. Then, in the very center of the flailing group of people, up came–

The Tank. Huge, hulking, with incredible strength and a quad of thick, muscular tentacles jutting from its back in addition to the cluster that emerged from the bottom of its mouth, this Xeno was one of the most formidable Dizzie had ever seen. They watched breathlessly as it whipped its appendages around, grabbing anyone within reach and dragging them over to be finished off by its deadly, devastating claws.

The newcomers fought back, of course. Their weapons were decent, and fear made them fierce, but there was no way they would be able to keep this up for long. They were about to be slaughtered to a man, when all of a sudden–

"Dr Drexler?"

Dizzie sighed and paused the augmented reality recording they were watching, then removed the headset and put it down on their desk. "What's up, Corinus?"

"You, um." Dizzie's grad student, Corinus Lifhe, looked as abashed as a Centauran ever could. That wasn't very much – their faces, three bony plates descending from broad on top to a tiny point of a chin, didn't offer a lot of flexibility of expression. Corinus had small amethyst-colored eyes that didn't give anything away, but his third eye – the soft spot between where the top of his third plate connected with the small set of horns most Centauran males sported – was pulsing at a rapid pace. It was a clear giveaway to anyone who knew the species that he was uncomfortable. "Sorry, but the program that monitors your heart rate set off an alarm. I thought it was best to pull you out of the simulation before you… um."

"Before I get security set on us again. Yeah, thank you." Dizzie groaned as the soreness from sitting in one position for a long time caught up with them. They rolled their shoulders out and twisted their neck until something cracked, then ran a hand through their poufy brown hair in an effort to counter the tamp-down effect of the headset. "I still think that's a shitty rule. We're not even working with real Xeno DNA, just simulations! There's no chance of exposure or infection. It's ridiculous for them to monitor us like this."

Corinus shrugged in understanding. "Too many–"

"Empusas," they said together with a sigh.

Infiltration by the alien Empusan species was an ongoing problem for the Coalition, and one they tried to counter by constant biomonitoring in all their in-house labs. Any rapid shifts in heart rate, adrenal stress, even vocal volume, meant security was required to check it out. Dizzie had set the biomonitoring alarms off five times over the past two years – they were becoming kind of infamous for it.

Dizzie kicked their feet up onto the edge of the desk, then grabbed the nearest datapad and pulled up the latest round of atmospheric computations gathered from probes in the PK-L system. It was all good stuff if you were an atmospheric physicist or interstellar climatologist, but Dizzie was neither. They were a biogeneticist, following in the footsteps of their hero, Dr Vivian Rigby. Her groundbreaking research on Xenos was what had inspired Dizzie to become a scientist in the first place.

Unfortunately, Dr Rigby's brief but fascinating body of work wasn't likely to be expanded on anytime soon. Dizzie couldn't count the number of requests they'd made for an expedition to PK-L7, aka Hellworld, or its nearby sister-planet PK-L10, aka Penumbra. They wouldn't even have to touch down! Hell, they didn't even have to put landers or probes onto the actual surface if the powers-that-be were so worried about it – simply being able to take readings from orbit would inform so many latent questions about Xeno physiology, habitat, biochemistry...

They were turned down every time. It didn't matter how many layers of security Dizzie put into their proposed expeditions, they were always met with a consistent "not only no, but hell no" from the Galactic Coalition military brass and the Guild honchos who funded them.

Corinus must have sensed Dizzie's bad mood, because he dropped down from his formal standing position to a more casual all fours and padded over to her, emanating an aura of calm and tranquility. Tall and elegant, with relatively short limbs compared to their torso, Centaurans were the pacifists of the galaxy. Their telepathy gave them the ability to avoid conflict rather than battling it out for space and supremacy like so many other species did. For a Centauran, fighting was always a last resort, and they preferred to keep everyone in their immediate vicinity in a level, pleasant mindset if possible.

Dizzie was positive that they would have been kicked out of the Coalition Science and Technology Institute years ago if not for Corinus's timely intervention on their behalf, offering to work with them on Xenos research. That didn't mean they had to like being *handled* by their damn grad student, though. "Knock it off."

"I don't mean to offend."

You never do.

Some of the sarcasm must have gotten through, because the corners of Corinus's mouth twitched, a sure sign he was upset.

"Reel it in, please," Dizzie said with a sigh. "You know it's rude to read other people without permission."

"I truly can't help it sometimes," Corinus said, ducking his head. Dizzie reached out and scratched the smooth pink skin just in front of his soft spot, a Centauran gesture of understanding and friendliness.

"I know," Dizzie said. "It's fine. I'm just… I'm so frustrated. We're coming up on five years on this project, and it feels like nothing has changed from the moment I got here. Atmospheric research is all well and good, but it's not *enough*. The Xenos are more than a simple case study on the kinds of shit that can go wrong in space – they're an existential threat to the Galactic Coalition, to the Guilds, to the entire galaxy!" Corinus nodded his head in agreement. "What are a few small risks in the face of gaining knowledge that could lead to the difference between entire planets living and dying?"

"The risks must not be negligible, or surely your superiors would allow study to occur."

Dizzie snorted. "Now I *know* you're bullshitting me. You understand how my 'superiors' think better than I do." They tilted their head a little and tapped a finger against their bottom lip. "I wonder how much of a nudge from a Centauran it would take to get somebody in the chain of command to take us seriously."

Corinus's healthy pink skin took on a pallid tinge. "I – to do so would be an enormous ethical violation on my part, and leave me in a position of extreme pain from having compromised my personal morals so extensively, but if you insist upon it I shall – I suppose I could–"

"Oh shit, no!" Dizzie dropped both feet down to the ground and reached out toward Corinus, not quite close enough to touch but hopefully close enough that he could sense their sincerity. A Centauran's telepathy wasn't touch-based, but direct contact did strengthen its transmission. "No, god, I was just joking! I would never ask you to compromise yourself like that for me. You shouldn't do that for *anyone*, no matter who's asking. That's bad-touch stuff."

Corinus blinked in confusion. "How does touching enter into it? You know that my people don't have to–"

"It's another joke, a bad one. Never mind me, OK? I'm

just…" Dizzie dropped their hands and looked back at the augmented reality headset. "I'm just in a mood. We know the Xenos are dangerous – they're *so* dangerous. What we're still not sure about is where they originated, and how. The aliens that became the Xenos – they were on PK-L7 long before they started becoming monsters. So, what turned them into mindless killing machines? Was the mold on the planet already, too, or was it imported somehow? Does the Xenium act on the mold, or vice versa? What's the link to Xenium in the first place?" They shook their head. "We just don't know, and in this day and age, knowledge is power."

'Mm," Corinus agreed. "Maybe that's why no new expeditions have been launched to the PK-L system."

Dizzie frowned. "What do you mean?"

Corinus lowered his voice. "You know there's been talk of unsanctioned visitations gone awry – smugglers pursued onto Penumbra, military ships crash-landing in the system. Then there was that footage that leaked about nine months ago of devastation wrought by Xenos on a landing party."

Right, the "Havoc" recordings. Supposedly, they were video evidence of a violent Xeno encounter with Coalition troops from a long time ago. The way the encounter had been described sounded like the Xenos in question could even be an entirely new subspecies. Dizzie was still pissed they hadn't been able to get their hands on a complete copy before it was too late. They'd only caught a few snippets, but those had been downright captivating, and a hundred percent terrifying, too.

"The military said it was all faked, and the footage was suppressed very quickly," Corinus continued, "but my advisor is of the opinion that the recordings were genuine. Incidents that could be accidental, or… could be a front for something else. It's not wrong for me to mention this," Corinus added quickly, "since I didn't learn it through my telepathy."

"No, I know that." He'd learned it because he had good ears and was a huge gossip, that was how he'd learned it.

People thought Centaurans looked so innocuous, so ethereal as to be almost cute, more like something out of a kid's dream than a scary alien, but they could only afford to be cute and kind because they made it their business to know everything that was going on around them. *Everything.*

"If those incidents *were* deliberate," Corinus continued, "the idea of Coalition military or private contractors acting on behalf of the Guilds, only to fail so dramatically… There is power in *not* allowing someone else to succeed there, under the circumstances."

Dizzie nodded slowly, working it through. "Sure, I can see that. You don't want someone else to figure out what you yourself couldn't hack, which gives you a vested interest in ensuring there are no more exploration attempts unless you're the one making them.

"But!" Dizzie jabbed a finger at Corinus. "But, but, but! *We're* on the side of the establishment!" They gestured around the lab. "Our research is funded by the Coalition Science Consortium and the Energy Guild. You'd think they, of all people, would be keen to find a way to get Xenium into their hot little hands. I want to make that happen for them!"

"Maybe it's more dangerous than even we know," he offered.

"I'm sure it is, but..." Dizzie sighed. "It just feels like such a waste. I'm *sure* we could mitigate the risks enough to make it work out, but the Galactic Coalition doesn't even trust its own people." They idly patted the console beneath their hand. "I guess our research will stay theoretical in perpetuity."

Corinus made a mournful honking sound. "If I could use my ability in this way for you, I would."

Dizzie shook their head. "Don't worry about it. Hell, if you were to actually use your ability to get us an expedition, no doubt a bunch of people would take note of the change of heart in the brass and strap us down on an exam table to make sure we weren't–"

"Empusas," they said together.

Dizzie grinned. "So, let's forget about it for now. How about we do some – actually, can you get me the–"

"Of course," Corinus said, trotting off to the other end of the lab to download the latest round of data from the server. As soon as it was in their in-lab computer, Dizzie would feed it into their custom program to see if there was anything to be gleaned from another layer of atmospheric processing. This time they were doing comparisons with half a dozen moons around the largest planet in the Chronos system to cross-check for particle similarities.

The primary goal of their research was to find new sources of Xenium in Coalition space, but after scanning over three thousand, seven hundred individual planets, moons, and various satellites over the past five years, they had come up with exactly zero positive atmospheric correlations.

Dizzie propped their head up on their hand as they stared at the empty graph in front of them. Were they even looking for the right things? Was their data on particulate Xenium correct, or had Dr Rigby made a mistake?

No, surely not. Dizzie didn't believe it. Besides, they'd found similar particles on both planets in the PK-L system, which was far better than a single data point's worth of information. The science was sound; it was just that they were looking for a needle in a giant, universe-sized haystack. There were so many places out there that were as-yet unexplored, with no satellites or probes nearby to gather information with. There could be Xenium on dozens of planets, and no one would even know because they hadn't proven interesting enough in other ways for anyone to explore yet. Uninhabited planets, planets that were hostile to carbon-based lifeforms, planets that–

Ping.

Dizzie stared at their datapad. Um… what? This datapad – everything in this lab, in fact – was supposed to be completely separate from the institute's larger communications array. Their work, boring as it was right now, was also extremely secret. So how had a message gotten through?

They shut down the particulate identification program and warily opened up the messaging app, ready to grab the nearest electric pulse generator and zap this pad to hell if they'd picked up some sort of infiltration virus.

Priority One Message, read the top of the screen.

Oh damn. Oh *daaaaaamn.*

Priority One messages were the purview of the elite members of the Galactic Coalition – reserved for the heads of the guilds and the military elite only. They could penetrate any firewalls set up to prevent communications because they had *built* the firewalls. And now they were sending a message to Dizzie!

They tried not to get too excited as they read further, but some of their emotion must have leaked through because Corinus abandoned what he was doing and trotted over immediately. "What's going on?"

"I'm not sure yet."

Dr Drexler, you and Dr Lifhe are hereby required to attend a special briefing in the Dark Room in fifteen minutes. You must bring no devices, ensure all implants are turned off, and inform no one else of this meeting.

Compliance with these directives is required.

That was it. There was no official signoff, but there didn't need to be. The fact that the message had made it onto the datapad in the first place was sufficient evidence of its senders' origins.

"Oh, wow." Dizzie read the message a second time, their sense of excitement rising along with their curiosity. "This is…" It could be a lot of things, but Dizzie had a good feeling about this summons.

Corinus, on the other hand, seemed to be taking it the opposite way. "Oh no," he whispered, blinking so fast his small amethyst eyes looked blurred. "What could they possibly want with us? Have we done something wrong? I'm positive that I haven't done anything wrong, have you?"

"I'm sure it's not that type of summons," Dizzie soothed, checking the wording over again. "There's nothing in here about punishment. They wouldn't bother warning us about it over the secure message system if they were going to kill our funding or, y'know, kill *us*."

"That's not funny!"

"I – sorry." Dizzie looked more closely at their research assistant. "What's wrong? Why are you so worried about this?"

"Because I didn't know about this message until right now!" Corinus swayed back and forth on all fours, shaking his head. "I'm not in the Coalition's direct hierarchy! Everything they have to say to me has to go through my advisor first; that's the *rule* for dealing with all Centaurans in Coalition territory. At the very least, Dr Yoche should have reached out to me telepathically to inform me we were about to be summoned into a private meeting, but he hasn't! Why not?"

"Maybe he just found out too," Dizzie offered. "Maybe he's already in the Dark Room and can't reach out to you."

"That's against protocol!"

Dizzie frowned sympathetically. This was the thing about working with Centaurans – their instinctive caution and immutable sense of "follow the leader" made them excellent backup in a lab like this, where the safety precautions were myriad and only one person could call the shots.

These same traits made them bad at handling surprises, though. Centaurans didn't believe in being surprised – they were powerful telepaths, after all. If anybody should see bad news coming from a light year away, it was them.

"It's going to be OK," Dizzie assured Corinus. "No, really, it is. The Centauran treaties with the Coalition are rock solid. I bet you anything that Dr Yoche is waiting for us in the Dark Room right now. If whatever we're going into involves some major decision-making, he'd *have* to be there, because nobody else can order you around here but me. Right?"

Corinus nodded, his fluttering eyelids gradually slowing down. "Right."

"Exactly. Because the Galactic Coalition isn't run by stupid people." Greedy people, people who put profit before almost everything else sometimes thanks to the Guild influence, but not stupid ones. "And they don't want to make trouble if they don't have to. So, let's go into this with an open mind, OK?"

"Yes."

Corinus wasn't swaying anymore, but he didn't sound very assured either. Dizzie paused before getting up. "Do you want to take one of your shots?"

The shots were a combination sedative and chemical blocker, the ultimate calm-down drug for a Centauran. They were also a closely kept secret, only meant to be used in the most extreme situations. Dizzie only knew about them in the first place thanks to Dr Yoche's insistence that Corinus have access to them in the lab, which meant Dizzie had to know what they were.

"No." Corinus shook his head, sounding stronger now. "No, it's fine. I'll be all right. We should leave now if we're going to get to the Dark Room on time."

Dizzie glanced at the chrono on the datapad and swore. "Yikes, yeah. Let's go."

They led the way out of the lab, locking it up tight with a biometric key, a retinal imager, and a password that no one but Dizzie would ever think to put together. Hopefully the people calling this meeting wouldn't ask for data that Dizzie needed to look up.

Dizzie and Corinus's lab was located in the Torus, a massive circular space station the size of Earth's moon. It floated in orbit around C-Prime, the capital world of the Coalition, and was almost as old as the first Martian colony. The Torus was one of the headquarters of the Galactic Coalition, favored when diplomacy was required because it was in more neutral territory than anything closer to the Terran system. The Torus was bright, clean to the point of sterility, and filled with dangerous technology that was designed with both function *and* form in mind. *Look at our weapons arrays, look at our defensive capabilities…* It was the ultimate showpiece for the Coalition, which it badly needed right now.

The Galactic Coalition was holding itself together – barely – but between outcry from the human-first Upholders and sabotage from the alien-first Safekeeper factions, there was a lot of uncertainty floating around as to how far the Coalition's authority really spread. The Guilds were working with the Coalition, because the Guilds favored stability over insecurity any day, but when it came right down to it, Dizzie was sure they'd turn on a dime if it meant a bigger profit. There had been multiple protests against the Coalition's stances on… basically everything, both on C-Prime and the Torus this past month. Dizzie was willing to bet that the Guilds had something to do with it. They were the type to test the waters before deciding to poison them.

Those were thoughts for another day, though. Right now, they had to get to a special meeting. Their lab was located in the outermost end of one of the Torus's enormous spokes, while the Dark Room was at the very center of the station. If they had to walk to the Dark Room, it would take close to half an hour to get there. Fortunately, each spoke had its own hyperloop transport. Dizzie led the way into the pill-like transport and snapped the door shut. "Ready?"

Corinus nodded, already buckling himself into one of the adjustable harnesses. "I suppose."

"Great." Dizzie followed suit, then pressed their palm to the control panel. It lit up green, but before they could give it a location directive, the transport leapt forward. "Whoa!" Dizzie exchanged a startled glance with Corinus. "I guess it knows where we're going."

"Or it's malfunctioning and about to smash us into paste on the other end of the tunnel," Corinus muttered.

"Or that, sure."

The transport picked up speed until the image outside the windows was so blurred it might as well have been an opaque wall instead of transparent steel. They slowed down just as quickly, g-forces distributed across the transport and through the tube so well that passengers hardly felt anything at all inside. Total time in transit: twenty-four seconds. Dizzie couldn't help but be a little impressed, despite having been riding the transport every day.

We can do anything we set our minds to. Travel a thousand miles an hour in a space station, fly ships faster than light with jump drives, make peace between alien races for the benefit of all. Surely we can come up with an expedition to the PK-L system that satisfies the safety requirements without being a total waste of time and money.

That was a question for another day. Right now, they had – shit, less than a minute to get to the Dark Room. Lucky for them, the transport had bypassed Torus's central hub and stopped right outside the secretive chamber itself, just over the station's engines. Dizzie felt the thrum of those engines here in a way they didn't in the lab, because it was too distant for the vibrations to travel. They liked it – it made the station feel alive, less like a floating box and more like an organic habitat.

They stepped out and walked down a short hall to a dark, wood-finished double door. Dizzie raised their hand to knock, but the door opened before their knuckles made contact. *OK… this is weird now.* They looked over at Corinus for confirmation of said weirdness, but their grad student was already entering the room, practically sagging with relief as he walked over to his mentor, Dr Pelobar Yoche. The Centaurans gently tapped their foreheads together, the way close friends would, and Dr Yoche motioned Dizzie in to join them. Carefully shutting the door behind them, Dizzie did so.

The only other person they recognized there was Torus Station's research director, an astrophysicist named Melissa St Paul. She was a heavyset human woman, and she looked as bright as any star in her virid green jacket and neon blue boots. Everyone else at the table was considerably more subdued, except for the…

Caridian? What the hell?

What was a Caridian doing in Galactic Coalition space? Last Dizzie knew, they were avoiding Coalition territory in favor of expanding in less-contested directions. Dizzie completely ignored the other people at the round table in the center of the windowless room in favor of getting a better look at this surprising newcomer.

Dizzie had only ever seen pictures of Caridians before, and even then, those ones had been independents, not associated with the… oh, what did they call it… the Seethe, that was it. The others had been insectoid in appearance, four-limbed like this one was with the antennae and all, but their outfits had been… casual, if there was such a thing when it came to Caridians. Vests and simple pants, loose overcoats, that sort of thing.

This Caridian was wearing a pale blue, full-length suit similar to an EVA suit, but far less bulky. Their feet were shod in form-fitting slippers, and they had no visible harnesses anywhere for weapon attachment. Their compound eyes were larger than Dizzie had expected, and the way the overhead light shone off them as they tilted their head made the bulging orbs look almost rainbow patterned.

Beautiful. Dizzie wasn't used to thinking of other beings as beautiful; their mind didn't save much room for the contemplation of something as subjective as physical beauty, consumed as it was with experiments and hypotheses and data. Beauty was the hallmark of a perfect equation, or a particularly efficient algorithm… but in this case, Dizzie remembered that beauty could also be a physical, palpable thing.

"Dr Drexler?"

Dizzie snapped their head back to Dr St Paul, who was giving them a look of irritation that probably meant they'd had to call out more than once. "I'm sorry, yes?"

"If you and Dr Lifhe would be seated, we can get this meeting under way." She gestured to the two empty chairs on their side of the table. One of them was directly across from the Caridian, and Dizzie claimed it instantly.

Covert messages, special meeting rooms, and an inexplicable alien presence? Dizzie grinned broadly. They couldn't *wait* to hear what all of this was about.

CHAPTER THREE
Corinus Lifhe

The buzz was incredibly distracting.

Corinus liked to think he didn't have the same god complex as the rest of his species. Centaurans, as a people, far preferred to keep themselves out of the way of aliens. It was safer not to become drawn into their posturing and grandstanding, their petty wars and conflicts. Centaurans, thanks to their telepathy, were well positioned to maintain their neutrality in the galaxy, and they went to extreme lengths to do so. No alien had ever stepped foot on the Centauran home world; none of them were even entirely sure where it was. All attempts to pry it out of Corinus's people had been doomed from the start.

When you could sense your enemy coming from a light year away, did they even qualify as an enemy? Or were they merely an annoyance to be avoided?

Centaurans didn't completely ignore the larger universe, though. To be overly confident in their telepathic defenses would be the height of irresponsibility. It was overestimating their own abilities that had gotten them noticed by the

Thassians in the first place, *curse* those ever-hungry bounty hunters. Ever since that first contact, the Centaurans had maintained a presence among the powers-that-be as scientists, researchers, and engineers. They used these positions to gather intelligence, anything and everything that would allow them to avoid future conflict, and they learned to read the minds of every sentient species in the galaxy.

Except for Caridians. Even for an alien, their minds were… strange. Multifaceted, like their eyes, and the surface thoughts that Corinus could sense, usually shallow as a petri dish in other species, were as deep and intricate as an ocean in this being. There was no penetrating these thoughts, no looking within. All there was, was what he could see, and all he saw and felt and knew was a heinous *buzzing* sensation, like there were a hundred people shoved into this creature's head and all of them were trying to speak at the same time.

"Don't keep trying. It's no use."

Corinus relaxed and anchored his mind on the steady, familiar feel of Dr Yoche's.

"*We will have to listen more with our ears than our minds for the duration of this meeting,*" Dr Yoche went on. "*But it is vitally important that we do so. Pay attention now.*" Thus chided, Corinus refocused on the scene playing out in front of him.

There were two unfamiliar humans, one with the bearing and mental signature of someone who had grown up within the rigid structure of the last surviving Martian colony, the other with a freer, blowsier feel to his mind that was nevertheless military in nature – an Earthling. There was also a Thassian, male, taller than everyone else in the room even while seated, his face serene but his mind constantly edged with thoughts of death and killing. Corinus checked the insignia on the collar of his suit – ah, of course. A high-ranked member of the Thassian Mercenary Guild. No wonder he was so attuned to violence.

The familiar humans were the science director for Torus Station and, of course, Dizzie. Only Corinus, and Dizzie, from what he could glean from their mind, felt truly curious about the Caridian sitting across from them. What did everyone else know that they didn't?

"Focus, Corinus."

Dr St Paul spoke first. "I'm sure it doesn't need to be said, but I'm saying it anyway – what we discuss in this room goes no further. There will be no messages, no media posts, no hints or references or anything else that might compromise the secrecy of this meeting. Understood?"

"Absolutely," Dizzie said, and Corinus nodded as well. Dr St Paul checked in with Dr Yoche, who inclined his head in agreement.

"Dr Lifhe is a remarkably adept telepath," Dr Yoche said. "He is perfectly capable of hiding all knowledge of this meeting from anyone who might be curious."

"Good." Dr St Paul sat back and gestured to the Earthling Coalition general, who cleared his throat. The Martian commander remained silently at attention as the Earthling Coalition general spoke.

"Six weeks ago, one of our patrol ships made contact with a Caridian ship in a place we didn't expect to find it. After a brief... miscommunication, we learned that Ix-Nix-Six here traveled into Coalition space with the express purpose of carrying out a scientific mission, one that we're inclined to let him proceed with." He cleared his throat again. "I'll let Mr Six tell you the rest of it himself."

The Caridian's mouthparts widened, like they were hinged. Corinus repressed a shudder as he stared at the gaping, feathery maw. Was that a... smile? An attempt at conveying harmlessness? It was *not* successful.

"Six alone is sufficient, general," the Caridian said. His voice was actually quite pleasant, like a human chorus singing all at once with one prime voice rising slightly above the others. "And yes, I was greatly fortunate to find a receptive audience for my request, as soon as I assured them that I meant no harm with my sudden appearance."

"How did you appear so suddenly?" Dizzie asked, completely disregarding the looks the other humans gave them for interrupting. Personally, Corinus was glad they asked – he was curious as well, but didn't want to open himself up to criticism. "If I recall, Caridians don't use jump drives."

"Not as such," Six agreed. "We prefer to travel long distances via what you call Einstein-Rosen bridges, otherwise known as–"

"Wormholes!" Dizzie sounded thrilled.

"Correct. Our command of them is not quite as precise as we would like, however, and when I emerged from this one, I quickly determined that I was somewhere I wasn't meant to be."

There was something about the alien's demeanor as it

said this part, something glib that echoed in the buzz of its mind, that struck Corinus as a lie. He gently pushed the impression toward his mentor and was rewarded with a warm burst of approval.

"As a happy result of this mishap, though, I was able to enter into negotiations with the Coalition very quickly," Six went on. "As stated, my goal in your space is purely one of scientific exploration. There is a planet approximately five-point-six parsecs from our current location that is of interest to the Caridian people."

The general reached forward and placed his palm on the tabletop. An image sprang up from it, a distant view of the star system that the alien seemed to be referencing. It was a sparse section of space even for, well, for *space*. The only star of any note there was a red dwarf, and in close proximity to that was a tiny… surely that was too small to be called a planet! A dwarf planet at *best*.

"This," Six said, waving a clawed hand through the image to enlarge and focus on that tiny speck, "is a planet my people call Sik-Tar. That is one of the ways Caridians say 'signal', and that is what this planet is broadcasting."

No one said anything for a moment, all eyes – and minds – trained on Dizzie and Corinus. There was a pageantry at hand here that bothered him, like everyone else already knew the answers and were just waiting for them to catch up.

Why, though? What did a distant, unnoticeable planet have to do with the two of them? Corinus was desperate to speed this up, but he didn't dare go poking at too many minds with Dr Yoche right there. It would make it seem like Corinus didn't trust Dr Yoche to keep him informed.

Dizzie was more inclined to play along with the charade. They had a tolerance for putting up with ridiculous human machinations that Corinus had found impossible to match. "And what is that signal transmitting?"

"It's a distress call," Six said. "A distress call that has been going off for more than a thousand Coalition-standard years."

Corinus blinked rapidly. "So long?" he asked, breaking his silent vow to let Dizzie do the talking. "And your people still haven't answered it?"

"A thousand years ago, Caridians didn't have the technological expertise to make a journey like that," Six replied. "Using impulse power, it would have taken us several hundreds of those years to reach the planet, and there was no guarantee that we would find anything there worth the time and expense of such a long journey. Once the technology to reach Sik-Tar more quickly became available to us, new avenues for the assimilation of knowledge and resources also opened up. The Glorious Hegemony decided it was better to pursue more profitable ventures.

"Our people do not make a habit of exploring for the sake of it," he said, a flatness in his buzzing tone that indicated disapproval. "The Seethe only mobilizes when it sees something it knows will benefit it. Sik-Tar has always been dubbed too much of a risk to be worth the trouble."

"What changed your mind?" Dizzie asked.

"While the Seethe on the whole has no reason to investigate this distress call, over the course of my lifetime

I have personally amassed enough resources to take on the venture myself." Six's mandibles clacked excitedly. "I was given permission by our queens to embark on such an exploration, provided I could persuade your peoples to grant me access to your space. The Seethe has no desire for an interstellar incident to result from satisfying my personal curiosity, after all."

Dizzie glanced at Dr St Paul. "Has the Coalition ever been interested in this place?"

"Before now, we were barely aware of its existence," the director replied, steepling her fingers as she stared at the hologram of Sik-Tar. "This area is technically Coalition space, but apart from basic stellar mapping we haven't done much out there. There was never any reason to – no known sentient species live in that quadrant, and basic scanning shows no resources worth our time to go after. *That,* at least, has changed thanks to your research, Drs Dexter and Lifhe."

She pulled up a new file, and a string of numbers appeared next to the projection of Sik-Tar. "Look familiar?"

Dizzie nodded. "Those are proportions of atmospheric gases. Nitrogen, oxygen, methane, nitrous oxide… the usual suspects for a planet capable of sustaining most types of life that we're aware of."

"Indeed." Dr St Paul swiped a hand along the numbers until she got to the end of the list. "Plus a number of unknown trace substances that weren't important enough – or didn't *seem* important enough – to track down. We didn't have references for these last three elements until we did a comparison with your recent findings on the atmospheric compositions of PK-L7 and PK-L10. And this one?" She tapped it, and the final number glowed bright green. "That's–"

"Xenium," Dizzie said breathlessly. They glanced at Corinus, excitement clear in their face and thrumming through their body.

Corinus felt rather breathless himself. Could it be that they'd inadvertently assisted in the discovery of another source of Xenium? This was the sort of find that could make a scientist's reputation for life!

"In an even higher proportion than what you've measured in the PK-L system," Dr St Paul added. "Which makes Sik-Tar of immediate interest to the Coalition."

The Thassian suddenly snorted. "Just like a human," he said, the elegant arch of his high forehead making him seem like he was looking down on all of them. "And all those *infected* with your greed. You only give something a second glance when it is either profitable or persecutable."

Corinus bristled, both at the insult to Dizzie and the insinuation that he and his advisor were anything like a human – because to be fair, most humans *were* like that – but quelled at the sense of warning he got from Dr Yoche.

"If we're so offensive to you, you don't have to be here," the Martian commander finally snapped, his jaw working like he wished he had something to gnaw on. "We brought you in as a courtesy, Leader Pavul, and we can disinvite you just as fast."

"And provoke war with the Thassian people? I think not."

"Here you are talking about *us* like we're the greedy ones, when your entire culture is consumed with selling itself for goods," the Martian continued. "How many of you are mercenaries, huh? How many of you fight in our battles and hunt down our enemies because your own planet doesn't satisfy your bloodlust anymore? Talk about greed – you blackmailed your way into this meeting in the first place, don't think I don't know how you found out about Ix-Nix-Six, and if you–"

"You were not going to share the information willingly, that much was clear!" Leader Pavul said. "An opportunity like this must be extended to everyone involved equally, or else it is no opportunity at all!"

"Gentlemen," Dr St Paul said, setting both hands down flat on the table. The holographic image disappeared. "We're getting off track. No matter how we got to the point where we are now, the fact is, we're here. Let's stay focused on the objective." She looked back at Six. "If you would continue, Six."

"I would be most pleased to, director." Six's antennae dipped in what might have been a nod or a salute. "I have taken the liberty of asking for a Coalition-sponsored expedition to Sik-Tar to be assembled. I will personally provide for the cost of the fuel to both get there and return, in exchange for the assistance of able researchers in uncovering the source of this signal and its significance to my people. For your help, I and the Seethe at large will forgo all claims to any natural resources on Sik-Tar that are not entwined with the source of the signal."

Meaning that any Xenium found on the planet is the Coalition's for the taking. Corinus knew what he and Dizzie were doing here now. They were the closest thing the

Coalition had to experts on Xenium, even though they'd never so much as seen it in person before.

"Your presence in particular, Dr Drexler, is non-negotiable," Six went on. "Upon reading a selection of your papers since my arrival here, it is clear to me that you are ideally positioned for a venture of this sort. If there are volatile chemical compounds to be found on this planet, I don't want to accidentally endanger anyone through my ignorance."

Dizzie blinked for a moment like a confused Centauran as they were caught off guard. "I'm flattered you think so, but you should know I've never been involved in elaborate fieldwork before." Corinus felt a smidgeon of resentment accompanying that statement, one he knew well.

"But you are willing to make the journey, are you not?" Six pressed. "As I said, if you are not a member of my team, then I will be less inclined to pursue this course of action. I feel it is imperative that I have full Coalition support before making the very expensive journey to Sik-Tar."

The writing on the wall, as humans sometimes put it, was clear. There would be no trip to Sik-Tar without Dizzie. That would mean no chance at the Xenium there for as long as it took the Coalition to actually make a decision about sending a team out there themselves to research it, which, given their inability to agree on almost anything, could take years. Corinus already knew that he and his fellow Centaurans wouldn't be part of any such investigation on their own. There were far too many risks involved.

If Dizzie said no, though, they would be destroying their career. Not that there was any chance of Dizzie saying no.

Corinus could feel their excitement growing with every second. Just as the director opened her mouth to take the decision out of Dizzie's hands, Dizzie spoke up.

"I would be honored to be a member of your team." Their voice was strong and clear, approbation on full display. "I promise I'll perform to the very best of my ability on this venture."

Six's mandibles clacked so quickly it could have been applause. "Wonderful! I'm very glad to hear that. I think we might also–"

Dizzie held up a hand, white lab coat falling halfway down their forearm. "I do have a condition, though."

Anger swelled up in the other humans in the room – understandable given Dizzie's insistence on making a demand despite their status as an underling. Corinus was surprised to feel apprehension from Dr Yoche, though.

"Please speak it," Six said.

"I must insist on including Dr Lifhe in the expedition." They gestured to Corinus, and now it was his turn to blink rapidly. He was confused, he was surprised, he was a little horrified… and also rather pleased. "Dr Lifhe has proven himself to be an excellent researcher for as long as we've worked together and will be instrumental in helping me discover the source of the Xenium. I worry that I might not be able to fulfill my role in the mission without him," they went on, blithely ignoring the discomfort on the other humans' faces.

Surprisingly, it was Leader Pavul who spoke up first. "I am in favor of this. Having another non-human as part of the crew will improve my trust in the expedition."

"Another non-human?" Dizzie asked. "You mean Six?"

"I mean the protector that I will be assigning you and this mission on behalf of the Thassian people, and our interests," Leader Pavul said.

"Oh." Dizzie's momentary confusion lightened. "That would be great! I've never spent much time with Thassians before; our specialties don't intersect much. I'm sure we'll have the chance to learn a lot about each other."

"You will be fortunate to learn from one of our most exemplary protectors," Leader Pavul said. There was something in the way he said it… Corinus didn't know why, but all of a sudden he felt like a bug had crawled down the middle of his back.

"This is all dependent on Dr Lifhe actually wanting to go to Sik-Tar, of course," Dr Yoche interjected. "Which is not something I will require or even encourage him to do. The decision is solely up to him."

"Of course," Dizzie agreed. Corinus could tell they were doing their best to control their emotions, to not let them leak out and influence Corinus. It was an admirable attempt, but he could still sense the excitement and beneath it, the anxiety that surrounded this potential voyage, all those emotions now centered on Corinus. If he said no, Dizzie would be devastated.

He couldn't do that to them.

"I'll go," he said, and the burst of happiness from Dizzie was almost enough to drown out the resignation he felt from Dr Yoche. "It is an unparalleled research opportunity."

If he said it enough, he might even be able to ignore the fact that it was also an unparalleled danger.

"Wonderful!" Six's antennae practically danced, and although his thoughts were as opaque as ever, Corinus was quite sure that the alien was feeling... satisfaction. "Now we have only to finalize the last two members of the crew, and then we can leave for Sik-Tar."

Corinus was taken aback. "Surely an expedition of this scope requires a significant planning period?" he said. "We need to think about equipment, supplies, logistics–"

"All taken care of!" Six said.

"We'll ensure that you have everything you need for an extended stay," Dr St Paul said, her calm, measured tone matched by the serenity of her mind. Corinus focused on her so that he could borrow some of her composure. "You'll get a chance to review the supply lists, of course, but speed is of the essence for all of us. We don't want word to get out about a potential new source of Xenium, especially when the element has proven so unpredictable." The director stared at both of them, her demeanor going from calm to stern. "Proper containment protocols must be followed at all times; do you understand me?"

"Of course," Dizzie said. "We'll make sure everyone understands."

"Good." Dr St Paul turned to the Martian commander. "As for the last members of the team, they're being provided by Mars. We're still working out the... details on them. The two of them are–"

Dr Yoche unexpectedly spoke up. "As Dr Lifhe is the subordinate scientist on this mission, I am comfortable ceding the decision-making from here on out to Dr Drexler. Dr Lifhe and I will begin a census of his laboratory and determine what to do with his current experiments, if that's all right with you, Dr Drexler."

"Of course," Dizzie said, happy to let them leave for Corinus's sake and just as happy to stay and learn as much as they could for their own sake. "It's fine with me."

"Go ahead," Dr St Paul confirmed. Corinus followed his advisor's lead, inclining his head to the assemblage before turning and leaving on his hind feet. Once the door closed behind them, though, Dr Yoche fell to all fours with a sigh. His mind was shielded, a trait that all Centaurans mastered in their youth, but Corinus didn't need to use his telepathy to see that his elder was unsettled.

"Shall we..."

"No words," Dr Yoche said gently, shaking his head. "Not here. Let's go to your lab and get started." The lab had similar shielding to the Dark Room.

"Surely we can speak like this."

"Not. Here," Dr Yoche reiterated, and now Corinus started to get concerned. Who was going to be able to hear them if they spoke telepathically? There were no other Centaurans on Torus Station, and no Kolbani here either. Obedient as ever, though, Corinus kept his silence as they were picked up by the transport, as they sped back out to the end of the spoke where Corinus and Dizzie's lab was, and as he unlocked the door to the office beside it and ushered his mentor through.

They couldn't meet in the far-more-secure lab, unfortunately. According to the rules governing the Torus, Corinus couldn't enter their lab without Dizzie – ostensibly because they were the senior scientist, but also because the humans who ran the station weren't *quite* as trusting of Centaurans as they could have been. It was galling to be singled out like that, but Corinus's interest in Xenium had been encouraged by Dr Yoche, not only because it was a useful mineral, but because *someone* needed to keep track of what the human scientists knew about it. Research was research, whether you were looking into crystal microstructures or people's minds.

Only after the door was firmly closed behind them did Dr Yoche begin to speak, his words sounding as wary as his thoughts.

"We don't know what Caridians are capable of," he said bluntly. "They possess no outward indicators of telepathy, but that doesn't mean they don't have it. I had no success reading Ix-Nix-Six's mind. Did you do any better?"

"Not really," Corinus said apologetically. "Just a general feeling, here and there. Nothing at all comprehensible in terms of words."

"I don't like that," Dr Yoche said gravely. "And I don't like that the Coalition was so quick to agree to allow this Caridian access to a planet they've never been concerned with before."

"But they didn't know about the Xenium…" Corinus tried to protest, but it was weak. To him, the Coalition's actions made sense.

"All the better that they didn't know about it! What has Xenium proven to be other than a lure and a curse?" Dr Yoche shook his head and began pacing across the office, his eyelids fluttering with anxiety. "Your research is as comprehensive as it can be, but there is still so much we don't know about this element. It has wrought wonders and terrors, and I'd say the balance of that tips on the side of terror. The Xenos who spring up wherever Xenium has been found are killing machines, and none of you, apart from whoever the Thassians provide for the expedition, have any experience as fighters. If worst comes to worst... I fear for your life, Corinus."

Corinus swallowed hard, his throat clicking dryly in a way that reminded him of Six. "I don't have to go," he said, changing his mind as easily as he'd originally agreed to go, in the face of his advisor's warning. "I could stay here and keep running the experiments and... and..."

But he knew he couldn't. There was no way he'd be allowed to keep the lab going without Dizzie. *They* trusted him, but the people in charge of the Torus didn't. If he didn't go along on this mission with Dr Drexler, he'd lose his access to the lab and lose his utility to his people.

No. He had to go. "I think I'll be all right," he said, trying to sound convincing. "After all, there is a tremendous potential to learn so much, which can't be ignored with this mission. Not only about the Xenium, but about the Caridians themselves. You heard his description of the Seethe, the Glorious Hegemony. They are many, and they are powerful, and there are valuable secrets at work here."

Dr Yoche nodded grimly. "I suppose. How did such an identifiable signal of theirs get so far from their territory, when he already admitted that their species didn't have the technology to make the trip at that time? What is the nature of this signal? What wavelength does it broadcast on? Could this be a ploy by the Caridians to establish an outpost in Coalition space, with our unwitting assistance?"

"I don't know," Corinus admitted.

"We can't know," Dr Yoche said. "Not the way that we're used to knowing, not with our telepathy. Not yet, at least. You may learn how to decipher his mental noises, but it will take time and familiarity. I don't like it" – he closed his eyes for a long moment – "but I suppose you're right. The benefits to our people to understand both the Caridians and Xenium are worth the risks of your participation."

He leaned in close to Corinus, nudging their faces together in a Centauran embrace. "Do not make yourself vulnerable to the Caridian in any way," he said firmly. "You must first and foremost prioritize your own survival on this mission – ahead of everyone else, even Dr Drexler."

Corinus reared back, but Dr Yoche grabbed him by the back of the neck and pulled him in close again. "I know you are close to them, but you must not give in to your softer emotions. Nothing is more important than the survival of our people. Is that not correct?"

"It is," Corinus whispered. "Of course it is."

"Of course." Dr Yoche nodded. "Only those who remember their role in the greater good are permitted to remain in the company of aliens, Dr Lifhe. Your loyalty has come under question several times recently."

Corinus was shocked. "But why? I've never done anything to betray our peoples' best interests!"

"You haven't shared all the information about PK-L7 and your research that you could, either." Dr Yoche sent him a quelling thought even as Corinus began to object. "And I understand why. I told them that you are a thorough scientist and will not present any information to our ruling council that you can't be sure is correct. Nevertheless, it's easy to feel your attachment to Dr Drexler. You admire them greatly."

"I… yes, but…"

"They are your tool."

It wasn't true, though. Dizzie was so much more than that – they were a brilliant scientist who was capable of looking at the world in an expansive way, opening Corinus's mind to possibilities he'd never have seen otherwise. To think of Dizzie as nothing more than a tool for him to use to gain covert information felt wrong.

He knew that wasn't what Dr Yoche wanted to hear, though. "They are my tool," he agreed.

"You will protect yourself above all others on this journey."

"I will put myself first."

"You will discover as much as you can about the Caridians and their intentions toward this part of space. If necessary, you will sabotage this mission to ensure that they don't gain a foothold in our space."

Corinus whimpered. "*Sabotage?*"

What, ruin an experiment or get someone else hurt or even… or even… get them killed? Maybe get himself killed in the process? Was he not supposed to put his own life first? How could he do that if they all died on distant Sik-Tar?

"If you can't promise to do this, you will not be allowed to go," Dr Yoche said, his mind and tone equally implacable. "I hope with all my heart that it won't come to such lengths, but if it does, we need to be able to trust that you'll do the right thing."

Of course they did. "I will do everything you ask," Corinus assured his mentor. "I promise. Nothing will escape my notice, and I'll learn everything I can about Ix-Nix-Six without putting myself at undue risk. And if the worst comes to the worst, I will make sure that–" Corinus's eyelids were fluttering so fast now the room looked shrouded "–that the alien doesn't get the chance to bring any harm to Centaurans."

Dr Yoche bumped their foreheads together in approval. "Excellent," he congratulated Corinus. Warm approbation flooded his mind like a hot bath, and Corinus sighed and closed his eyes, taking the time to enjoy the sensation. "Your behavior is exemplary, as usual. I'll make sure you're rewarded properly for this when you return, Dr Lifhe. Perhaps it's time to negotiate for your own lab, hmm?"

Corinus hmm'ed back, ignoring the sick pit of doubt that had opened in his second stomach. If he was lucky, he wouldn't have to do anything other than what he'd already planned on – conducting experiments on Xenium with Dizzie.

If he was really lucky, this expedition would be nothing but a… what did Dizzie call it? A "wild goose chase".

For the first time in his scientific career, Corinus earnestly hoped for poor results.

CHAPTER FOUR
Protector Divak

Three weeks later

"Incoming!" The scout relayed the warning just in time for Divak and the rest of her squad to shelter behind their plasma shields as the grenade sailed over the wall toward their position. The antique technology, which was the type that worked best in this place, exploded a moment later, spewing fire and thunder in a twenty-foot radius around it. The edges of that fire singed the toes of Divak's boots. She grinned, baring all her sharklike teeth in pure satisfaction.

Guerrilla warfare was the sort that Divak liked best – small forces battling each other in unsteady terrain, every corner you could turn a source of dread and doubt, every second you survived another opportunity for someone else's death. As chief protector of Leader Pavul's top-performing squad of mercenaries, Divak's services were in high demand. The Thassian Mercenary Guild charged a fortune from all lesser species who sought to have those proficient in the arts of war settle their petty disputes for them, and Divak was the best of the best.

Currently, she and her squad were working for Coalition forces in an effort to root out a knot of Upholders, foolish "humanity-first" activists who had decided to begin their own independent colony on Dossa Nine. The Coalition had been willing to ignore their political leanings as long as they kept paying their taxes, but after their leader broke the neck of the last Coalition representative to set foot on the planet, the desire to indulge them vanished. These humans needed to be put in their place.

Unfortunately, the city the Upholders had settled in was built among massive sheets of multicolor volcanic glass, impregnated with compounds that made scanning it and locating the Upholders from a distance difficult. The glass itself was the colony's biggest export, and useful enough that destroying it all via an orbital attack was considered unprofitable. The only thing for it was infiltration – sneaking into the city, discovering the location of the Upholder leaders, and making examples out of them so that the rest of the population fell into line.

That was much easier said than done. Divak couldn't have been more pleased.

"Send up the bat," she said to her second in command, her tail twitching in anticipation. Trooper Tavul reached into the utility belt in the middle of his suit and pulled out a small, heat-shielded drone. Even protected from thermal viewing, it wouldn't last very long against the Upholders' entrenched firepower, but all they needed to know was where to direct their other weapons.

Trooper Tavul threw the bat into the air. It spread its long, webbed wings and flew in the direction the grenade had just come from. Divak watched the feed from its eyepiece – her battle map was becoming more precise with every bat they flew. *Closer, closer...* Bullets whizzed out of the air toward the tiny drone, but it managed to dodge them.

Almost there.

The bat reached the outermost wall of the Upholders' hideaway, sending back images of two heavy-duty, multi-barrel machine guns mounted in either corner of the blockish fortress, with a stationary rocket launcher backing them up in the middle. Divak grinned again – that weapon had blown the legs off one of her troopers two walls back, but it appeared that now they were too close for it to work effectively. She counted nine, fifteen, twenty-three humans – that supported the information the Coalition had given her. All adults, it seemed.

Too bad. There was something about destroying the young of an invasive species that left her feeling like she'd really accomplished something.

A second later the bat was blasted into oblivion, but Divak had already made her gameplan. She transmitted her battle map to the rest of her squad's computers, then highlighted the sheet of glass in front of them. "Troopers Morve and Kilar, I want this wall destroyed. I want it done loudly, but it also needs to be done slowly – it must take at least five minutes to break through. If they're still firing on you by the time you're done with that, begin on the next one. One of you needs to work the plasma beam to cover our approach.

"Troopers Tavul and Ahkta, get as close as you can to the inner wall and release your snakes. Fling them over the wall if you have to, but I want them in there and drawing fire.

"And I…" Divak flexed her fingers with anticipation. "I'll be on cleanup duty. Tavul and Ahkta, join me in there when your job is done. Go."

Her troopers didn't verbally acknowledge her orders, but they all moved immediately to do her will. Naturally – they were well trained. Divak waited for the first set of charges to be placed on the volcanic glass wall, then moved ten feet to the right so that she was just on the edge of the blast zone. She activated her armor's mirror feature and waited for the explosion.

BAM! The demolition was highly targeted, but still noisy enough that she could use it in her ruse. Extending her claws and straightening her tail, Divak leapt up until she was clinging to the lowest part of the radiant, rainbow-hued glass wall. She flung herself over it and landed easily on the other side, as silent as a slither.

Divak hunched against the wall and waited to see if she had been noticed. A few more grenades from the Upholder stronghold were lobbed over the barrier she'd just scaled, but none came her way. Excellent.

The second step in breaching this fortification was using their plasma beam. Its light was even better than the thermal explosives at blinding cameras and sensors. Divak crossed the gritty, glass-covered lane between her and the next barrier in a single bound and up, up, and over it she went.

Her armor's claws, tipped with plasteel, chipped a purchase into the glass like it was nothing. Fragments fell to the ground below, rainbow shards that some species might call pretty. Divak appreciated the colors because they made hiding easier – when the light from the nearby sun hit these walls just right, like it was now, they reflected it like mirrors. Her armor mimicked the effect perfectly, and once again, Divak avoided her enemy's notice as she scaled their staggered wall fortifications. The only thing left between her and the Upholders was their final wall.

"Snakes are out," Tavul said. "Tracers on."

Divak watched the snakes fan out from her troopers' positions on the battle map. Each one left a glowing trail, and she watched as they turned and twisted and, in some places, became knotted together as they tried to penetrate the enemy's defenses. Hmm, that was inconvenient. They did better on the ground, perhaps…

Ah. One of them had found a way through. Now another followed it, and another, and another. The snakes, tiny creatures more like leeches than serpents, had been cast out of the blood pouches where her troopers had stored them. Without the warm bath of their bloody home to pacify them, they went immediately on the hunt for more of their ideal living conditions.

In this case, these snakes had been trained to detect and home in on *human* blood sources. The screams that emanated from inside the compound fed Divak's soul as only a successful hunt could.

"Aaaahhhh!"

"Oh my god, *what is it?*"

"Get it out of my – it – my *neck,* it's in my neck, I ca-ca-n-n-n–"

Gunfire erupted within the compound. Divak waited to see how fiercely they would fire upon themselves before adding herself to the mix.

Trooper Tavul was not so patient. Through her eyepiece, Divak saw his symbol climb over the final wall, perhaps fifteen meters to her left. A second later, she heard the hiss and gurgle of his death as an Upholder who had retained some of their sense saw and fired upon him.

He was a poor hunter after all. It was a shame – she had been thinking of adding him to her harem when she earned the right to form her own mercenary troop. That was the highest right of a leader among their kind, and Divak's ambition would tolerate nothing but the best for herself.

Eventually the gunfire came to a stuttering halt while the screams multiplied. Satisfied that her odds were good, Divak climbed the final wall and landed inside the open interior of the Upholders' fort.

It was complete chaos. Humans, none of them in good power armor, lay scattered all about. Some of them were trying to fire on the snakes, but the creatures were so thin it was almost impossible to shoot them down. They couldn't burrow through metal, but too many of these simple fools had left their heads or hands exposed.

A centimeter was all the space a snake needed in order to dig into the blood they desperately craved, swimming through their host's internal waterways until they reached the heart, where they would nest and lay their eggs. By then the host was paralyzed by the toxin the worms secreted – easy pickings for an ambush hunter like Divak.

Speaking of… there went the first one, down with

a stunned look of agony on his face. Divak pulled her chainsword from the magbelt across her back, catching the rainbow light reflecting off the walls with the blade and reflecting it up on her own power armor. She wanted the humans to see her coming, wanted them to know the bringer of their ends.

I will be the last thing you see, you little–

A faint shuffle of feet behind Divak, careful and deliberate among the mess of screams, propelled her into a roll. She grabbed the dying human off the ground and extended him out behind her like a shield just as a barrage of bullets flew from the weapon of the man standing ten feet away.

The only mildly human thing about him was the top portion of his face. Everything else – his mouth, the lower part of his nose, all of his neck – was mechanical.

An android. No, a cyborg. This was a cyborg – she could still hear the beat of his human heart, bolstered by machinery but not entirely replaced. Not impossible to infect, but not as easy a target as the others here, who had shoddy, hole-ridden power armor as their only, and poor, defense between them and the snakes.

He was out of bullets, too. She could hear his minigun click as it ratcheted over and over on empty. He tossed it aside a second later. Divak had to keep him from going after another gun. She threw the paralyzed human at him, snapping the perforated man's neck in the process. In the time it took the cyborg to catch and drop his former Upholder, Divak closed the distance between them.

Her chains on her blade had monofilament edges that

could penetrate power armor given enough time, but her target was the soft tissue. The snakes would do her job for her if she could only get this creature to bleed long enough for them to home in on it. It had to be soon, though – they only lasted ten minutes outside the blood bath.

He brought a heavy cutter up to intercept hers, inhumanly fast. *Of course he is. He is worthier than all the rest of them.* Worthy of a fight, of honing Divak's skills with his life. When he came at her, she blocked, but slid back almost a foot from the force of the blow. *Strong.* But he reacted with the speed of a striking serpent, able to counter her every move well enough that Divak couldn't get close enough to draw blood.

"You won't win this fight, alien." His voice was monotone, but there was true emotion in those human eyes of his. "Just like I will kill you here, someday the Upholders will destroy all of the alien life that pollutes the galaxy."

Divak bared her teeth in a fierce smile. She wasn't going to lose this fight. Her life would not end in a useless conflict on a wasted world. She was going to survive to run her own mercenary group, to take many mates and brood many hatchlings. Taking him on directly wasn't the way, though. He had too much strength.

There was more than one way to descale a fish, though.

Divak suddenly disengaged and leapt away from the cyborg. In the seconds it took for him to recalibrate and follow her, she sliced the arm off one of the recently paralyzed humans and swung it in a wide arc that encompassed the cyborg, particularly targeting his face.

He grunted and wiped his eyes clear. "You think defacing

the dead will frighten me? I will burn your body to ash and scatter it across the – *tthuuuh*."

He abruptly stopped talking as first one, then another tiny snake made their way up his armor, following the blood trail to the living, breathing human they craved. They carved their entrances, one through each eye, and tears of blood appeared in their corners as the snakes burrowed deeper.

"You–" The cyborg grimaced, his cutter still fixed on her, even as he wavered on his feet. "You fight with – no honor – alien scum..." He collapsed a second later, those bloody eyes taking on the same stunned look that everyone else here shared.

Divak stood over him in triumph. She hoped he could feel how little she thought of his pathetic attempts to intimidate her. "Take your due, *human scum*," she spat, then sliced down quick and hard with her blade and cut his head clean in two.

There was still enough left of him to identify the body with.

Ahkta leaped over the inner wall and joined her a moment later, surveying the killing field with satisfaction. "Your strategy worked well, protector."

"It was over too soon," Divak said with real regret. "But more interesting than it might have been thanks to the machine here. Start removing and bagging heads, and we will–"

"Protector." Kilar interrupted Divak. She would have tail-slapped him if he'd been within reach. The audacity, to take the initiative of contacting her before she'd sent the all-clear signal. "Forgive this lowly trooper for the interruption, but you have a high-priority communication coming in from Leader Pavul."

"Ah." Divak always silenced all her computer's communication abilities for the duration of the fight, except for those that connected her to her squad. Someone had to maintain the role of outside liaison, though – usually the weakest, least useful fighter. That was Kilar, all right. "I will speak with him."

"Putting him through for you, protector." Her screen went blank for a moment, and Divak took herself a few feet apart from Ahkta to take the call. A second later, Leader Pavul's dark gray visage filled her screen from side to side. He wasn't much to look at, apart from his eyes – they were the blackest red Divak had ever seen, the color only appearing as a faint gleam.

"Protector Divak. You are finished in your current mission, I'm sure."

"Our objective was accomplished," Divak confirmed. "My second in command is taking heads right now."

"Good. While your squad cleans up, you will return to the field where you parked your ship and await retrieval there. You have a new mission."

Divak's eyebrow ridges raised. She didn't voice the question on her face, but she didn't need to. Leader Pavul inclined his head slightly. "Time is of the essence, and there is no one I would sooner trust this mission to than you."

Well. Divak preened at the compliment. "Who do I need to kill?"

"Perhaps no one." Leader Pavul hissed out a chuckle. "It

isn't that kind of mission. I see that you're disappointed, but the opportunity for your ascendance to the rank of leader with the successful completion of this mission is nearly assured."

That put a different smell on the situation. Divak felt her curiosity rise despite herself. What was she about to get into?

"I'm sending a contract to your personal computer on the requirements," Leader Pavul went on. "I want it read and signed off on by the time you're picked up."

"Understood."

"If for some reason you must decline, send word immediately." The undertone of *you'd better not decline* was clear, but Divak had no intention of draining the waters of her future for any reason.

"I will not decline."

"Good." Leader Pavul ended the communication, leaving Divak back on her open line with Trooper Kilar.

"What did he want, protector?"

Anger surged through Divak. "Know your place and hold your tongue." She contemptuously cut her connection with him and turned to Ahkta. "I'm being called to another mission."

Ahkta paused where he was slicing through necks with his chainsword and looked at her, open admiration gleaming in his red-star eyes. "Our leaders honor you, protector."

"Indeed they do." She was glad he'd noticed. "Finish out this contract and wait for word from me in the home system before taking another. You may use my credits to sustain yourself and our squad in the meantime."

Ahkta's eyes widened. Divak held her breath. If he allowed her to command him while she was gone, it was an implicit acceptance of her offer of officially taking him as a mate when she returned. It was both a promise and a challenge. Would he accept it?

"I will do as you direct, protector. We will wait for your return on Thassia's second moon."

Hot satisfaction flooded Divak's veins, almost as good as the heat of battle. "Excellent," she crooned. "I will look forward to it." Then she turned and climbed up the wall again, careful to wave her tail in an alluring way as she vanished from Ahkta's view.

She read up on the new contract as she made her way back to the landing zone. By the time she got there, Divak was equal parts annoyed and excited. Annoyed, because this looked like it was going to be the most boring excursion of her adult life – a trip to a tiny planet in the middle of nowhere, herding a bunch of fur-faces around while they poked at stones. Ridiculous. A waste of time when she could be fighting battles and improving her status, for as much as an Earth month *on site*. Travel time was included, but left "unspecified." She didn't like anything being unspecified in a contract.

The excitement came from the knowledge that her current leader had deemed this long, dull assignment sufficient reason to elevate her status. After all, Divak had much glory in battle already – this would bring her a new kind of glory, the glory of reaching the height of Thassian culture. Not to mention, if the aliens actually *did* find Xenium there, it would be a simple thing to enrich herself with it as well. Thassians valued cleverness, and procuring a healthy helping of Xenium for herself and Leader Pavul on this mission would show that she was very smart indeed.

Divak stood beside her ship and sent out the coded signal Leader Pavul had provided her with. Less than a minute later, a ship appeared in the bright yellow sky above her – a ship like nothing she had ever seen before, longer than a caravel but less blocky. This ship was shaped like a flying insect, with a large bulb on the front end, a smaller bulb at the back, and a slender segment in the center. It looked unreasonably delicate, but seemed to handle the landing without issue.

Ah, yes. There was the other reason that Divak was excited for this mission. *New prey.* She had never met a Caridian before – they were barely known in this galaxy – and she was eager to evaluate one for herself. Would they prove as challenging a prospect as the Pelnar of Dramon Six? Or would they be as easy to kill as the twenty-three humans she'd just left behind?

A door opened in the front part of the spindle, and a ramp descended. Divak hissed with disdain. A ramp? What kind of species did they think she was? She walked over to the Caridian ship and jumped up into the entrance, completely ignoring the insulting ramp.

The first person to greet her once she was past the airlock and in the main cabin was not, as she had hoped, a Caridian, but rather a human. They were wearing no armor – ridiculous, not to acknowledge the weakness of their form and guard themselves against it – but a dull, Coalition-standard, gray and black jumpsuit instead, along with decently thick boots but no weapons to be seen. They had a wild shock of brown hair that protruded from the top of their head, and bright brown eyes with an amber gleam to them that spoke of, if not ferocity, at least liveliness.

"Welcome aboard, Protector Divak!" they said in an annoyingly chipper voice. "Leader Pavul told us we could pick you up here, but I hadn't thought you'd be so…" The human took in the state of Divak's power armor. "Fresh from a job."

Behind and to the left of the human, a Centauran with the petal-pink skin and purple eyes of their kind shivered all over, nostrils flaring.

Yes, smell my success. Read the triumph in my mind, little one. Centaurans, pacifists though they were, had their uses, but they were easy to distract.

"Where is Leader Ix-Nix-Six?" Divak demanded.

"I am here," a buzzing voice said. Divak turned to the helm of the ship and watched a chair swivel to face her. Here, then, was the Caridian. Would he be a challenge, or a trifle?

Divak's heart slumped within her as she got a good look at the alien. He seemed tall, a fact confirmed as he pushed to his strange, knobbed feet, but too slender to take a blow well. The exoskeleton could work as a form of armor, of course, but it wasn't as good as actual armor, which he wasn't wearing. Lazy. And those eyes! Huge and luminous and the perfect target for anyone looking to take this creature out.

He was not a challenge. He might even be easier to kill than the human. And *she* would be expected to follow *his* rule for the duration of this mission?

If you fail, Leader Pavul will punish you. Divak didn't fear pain, but she did fear loss of status. To never be elevated to the level of leader, to never be given the rights of harem and brood… no. She would not falter, not now. She would keep her goals firmly in mind and do the bidding of this rickety creature, and someday she would use all that she'd learned to elevate her status even further.

After all, if they someday went to war with the Glorious Hegemony, who better to lead than someone who knew all their weaknesses?

The Centauran made a squeaking sound. Divak filled her mind with the recent memory of the snakes burrowing into the cyborg's eyes, and the telepath shuddered again and looked away. *Better stay out of my head, or else.*

"Welcome on board my ship, the *Telexa,*" the Caridian said, coming over to greet her. He moved with an elusive smoothness, none of the jerking motion she'd expected from someone who appeared so insectile. "You are Protector Divak, I presume."

"I am." She inclined her head briefly. "You are Leader Ix-Nix-Six."

"Six is sufficient."

Divak snarled. "Six alone is disrespectful. I will not be entrapped into behaving with willful disrespect toward my superior. You are Leader Six."

Those huge, glittering eyes shifted somehow, even though the lobes themselves didn't move. Divak wondered how this creature saw her. "Very well. These are Drs Drexler–" he indicated first the human, then the Centauran "–and Lifhe. You have read the mission file?"

"Yes. We travel to Sik-Tar. I am your bodyguard."

"Very good. You are our second-to-last stop before we commence our journey," Six continued. "The cleansing facility is at the far end of the sleep unit, here in the front hold of the ship. Please proceed there at once to decontaminate yourself."

Divak narrowed her eyes, sensing her first chance at gathering intelligence. "Does the scent of blood offend you, Leader Six?"

"Not at all," he replied neutrally. "My olfactory receptors are quite different from your own. Many smells that others deem noxious barely register to me. But you are covered in germs, and I wish to maintain a sterile environment."

That was… reasonable. "Very well." Divak began to turn, then stopped. "You said that I am the second-to-last stop before our mission truly begins. Where is the final stop before we head to Sik-Tar?"

"We are headed to the Bor-Turia Penal Colony, to take on two more passengers."

Divak was surprised. "Prisoners?"

"Not anymore," the human – Dr Drexler – murmured.

"Specialists," Leader Six replied.

Specialists. Divak inclined her head once more and moved into the front hold, her thoughts turned inward even as her body maintained its constant vigilance. Specialists who were also prisoners. Violent offenders, perhaps?

There may yet be a threat of some interest on this voyage, to keep her from losing her mind with boredom.

CHAPTER FIVE
Grayson Bane

"Right!" The burly warden standing two feet in front of Grayson Bane spoke at the kind of volume you'd expect to hear on the bloody battlefield, not in a ten foot by ten foot cell that still somehow managed to produce an echo despite its tiny size. Grayson dodged a bit of spittle that flew at him. "Do you understand the requirements of the task ahead of you, prisoner?"

Grayson stretched his arms out over his head until he got the satisfying *crack* he was looking for from his upper back. He lowered them down, pausing to scratch at one armpit, and watched out of the corner of his eye as the warden's face got redder and redder. "S'pose I do," he said at last. "Me an' Mace have to keep the gear for a bunch of eggheads running on an alien planet, and when we're finished, it's a clean slate for us."

The warden laughed, or tried to. His throat was so padded with scar tissue it came out as more of a gurgle. Someone had nearly succeeded in garroting this gent's head right off once upon a time.

Too bad they hadn't managed it. Warden Kucinich was an asshole.

"Clean slate?" he said incredulously. "Far from it. You won't be returning to Bor-Turia, there's that, but the pair of you have a list of warrants trailing behind you like a bridal veil. The second you step one foot out of line – the second your bloody *brother* gets caught setting a toe out of line – it's back to the box with you." The warden grinned. His teeth were like stumps, worn down and flat. "I think Earth has dibs next, for that priceless painting of theirs you nicked two years ago."

"We were never convicted of stealing the *Mona Lisa*," Grayson protested lazily. "And I ain't programmed Mason's toes to move themselves around independently yet. Good idea, though. I'll tell him you were thinking of him when we meet up."

Kucinich glared at him. "You know Paris has turned its catacombs into a prison? You'll be stuck in the ground like the worms you are for the rest of your unnatural lives. Mason'll probably rust shut."

"Speaking of my brother," Grayson interjected before the warden could waste any more threats on him, "where is he? I'm not gettin' on any ship without him."

Kucinich glared. "You would if it meant freedom. No honor among thieves, is there. In fact…" He scratched his chin thoughtfully, like whatever puerile thought he was having had just occurred to him. Grayson knew better. "Reckon I could get most of those warrants on your ass taken care of permanently, if you opted to go on board this alien ship comin' to pick you up by your lonesome and explain to the folks in there that Mason had an… accident."

Grayson felt his fingertips begin to tingle. *Oh shit, oh shit, oh shit…* "And *has* he had an accident?" he asked as calmly as he could.

"Not as such, no… but we could mock one up." Kucinich continued to scratch dirty nails across his stubbly chin. "Thing is, your brother's processors have been mighty handy when it comes to keepin' the computer in this place running the way it should." The warden shrugged. "Budget cuts, eh? I'd hate to lose his efficiency, and I'm sure you could program another robot to do your dirty work for you. Some kinda genius after all, aren't you, Bane? So, leave him here with me, and–"

"My brother," Grayson said, each syllable carefully articulated so that he didn't bite down on his own tongue in his rising fury, "is not a damn robot. You hear me? He's a person. Cyborgs are people, with rights like everyone else in the Coalition, and if you've hurt him–"

"Easy, easy." The warden held up his massive trencher-like hands. "No hurting going on. We just put him to sleep, s'all. He don't even know he's being useful right now, probably dreaming of electric sheep or whatever else freaks like him dream about when their processors are bein' used elsewhere."

It was all Grayson could do to keep from reaching out and ripping the warden's nose right off his face. "That sort of treatment wasn't a part of the contract when we were brought here."

"Contract changed after your brother assimilated poor

old Mickey's bionic eye into his left arm assemblage, didn't it?" the warden snapped. "That falls under 'aggravating circumstances' as far as I'm concerned. Gave me the right to change the way we handled him. I needed to do it to make sure he wasn't a threat to other prisoners."

"I thought you meant solitary confinement!" Grayson shouted. "Not that you were going to use his brain as a way of improving the quality of your damn porn feeds!" He and his brother had been apart for three months, *three months,* and instead of solitary confinement – which was never really solitary for Mason, not the way he was these days – he'd been plugged into a goddamn prison computer? The thought made Grayson sick... and furious. He'd been looking out for Mason since he was born, and while this wasn't the first time he'd failed – not by a long shot – it never got easier.

Kucinich ground his teeth audibly. "You really want to get in my face about this, Bane? 'Cause I can come up with all sorts of excuses to keep the pair of you here. Don't know why the brass decided to hire you out for this mission anyway, but there are others who can do your job out there.

"Maybe I shouldn't stop at fakin' an accident for just your brother. Maybe I should fake *both* your deaths, huh?" He leaned in, the wash of his sour breath coating Grayson's face like acid rain. "Install you and your brother on my private ship, make you my step-and-fetch-it lad while I use him to keep my ride ship-shape. Think that sounds better?"

"You think you can hold us?" Grayson scoffed. He was as fearful as he was angry – the leeway for abuse in the prison system was a huge, and a completely ignored problem for the Coalition – but he couldn't let on. "Ain't nowhere can hold us, mate. Earth's tried, Mars's tried, hell, they even set us up on Thassia once, and didn't last more than a month. Escaping from you? Child's play."

"Oh yeah?" The warden grinned. "Why ain't you gone yet, then?"

Mason's trip to isolation had put a damper on their timetable, but now that Grayson knew what this sonuva bitch had done to his brother… he could work with that. *These Coalition assholes better be waiting for me like they said.* Otherwise, things were going to get dicey.

Grayson didn't bother to bandy more words about, just leaned in and sucker-punched the warden hard in the liver. Grayson was a short man, but almost as wide as he was tall, and he knew how to turn all of his weight into a body blow. The warden wasn't armored – more fool him – and as soon as he bent over, his face contorting as the pain reached his thalamus, Grayson followed the first strike up with a punch straight to the man's temple.

Kucinich collapsed. Grayson knelt down and ripped the rudimentary neural construct that connected the warden to all the systems in the Bor-Turia Penal Colony out of the side of his head, then placed it over his own slowly healing implant site. The feel of someone else's blood against his bare skin was *eurgh*, but Grayson didn't shy away from it, reaching out with the nanobots he'd installed in himself at the age of twelve until they attached to the construct. He bypassed the colony's password – like he said, child's play – and put every single alarm system in the entire prison on silent. Then he began to look for his brother.

Gotta hurry, gotta be fast. The longer this took, the higher the likelihood that one of the guards would interrupt them, or that the warden would get a communication from someone that required an answer Grayson couldn't give. Not that the warden was all that chatty to begin with – how many people was Kucinich hiding what he was doing with Mason from? Grayson could use that if he needed to. It would be better if they could avoid the mess that came from blackmailing, though. He needed to find Mason and get them both to the docks, where – yeah, there was the weirdo Caridian ship, strange energy signature and all. But Mason, Mason, Mason…

There. In the warden's personal office, *damn* the man. There was too much power being drawn for what he ought to have in there. Pulling up the thermal images for the room, Grayson spotted a large, warm mass directly beneath the warden's desk. *Used my brother as a footrest, did you?* He spared a moment to kick the unconscious warden while he was down. Then he began the process of waking Mason up.

He had to start with the central processor – Mason's actual, original brain. Grayson had learned the hard way that if he activated the less-complex neural plexuses first, the "mini-brains" that he'd installed in each of his brother's cybernetic limbs, that they would become prone to malfunction. Especially "Lucky Lefty", Mason's left arm, which had a disconcerting tendency to take itself for long walks without the input of the primary brain even on a good day. Quirky little shit.

Grayson took it as slow as he dared. Mason's mind never

went fully asleep, but when someone shut him down like this – and this unfortunately wasn't the first time – he went so deeply into himself that if you didn't go gently, he'd come out of it so confused he couldn't recall his own name, much less who Grayson was, and would fight to get Grayson out of his head. He'd near given Grayson a stroke the last time he'd had a hard reboot, and when he finally came back to himself, the guilt had almost killed the lad.

Not this time. Slow as we can, nice and slow... but there was already some chatter building among the other guards as to the warden's absence. Grayson gritted his teeth and pushed a little harder, removing blocks and letting the electricity that modulated his brother's brain into it. Brain stem, cerebellum, thalamus, hypothalamus, and finally the cerebrum. Watching the array of nodes light up in Mason's mind was like watching the universe turn back on. "There you go," he whispered as heart and respiratory function began to increase. "There you are."

[Hmmmm,] his brother hummed in his mind. [Um... where... we?] Mason was taking over now, activating his distal processors and stretching his cybernetic limbs. The old-fashioned wooden desk he was folded beneath cracked under the strain, sending splinters everywhere.

"You're in the warden's office, under his furniture," Grayson said, speaking out loud as he simultaneously projected his thoughts into his brother's mind. He'd never been able to separate the two actions, unfortunately, and it had gotten them nicked more than once. *Worry about it later.* "You need to get to the docking bay. We've got a ship waitin' to take us out of here."

[Ship?] Curiosity lit up the connection between them. [Steal… a ship?]

"No, we ain't stealin' it, it's here for us proper."

[OK. Walk there?]

"Sneak," Grayson corrected, already laying out a path for his brother as he accessed the station's blueprints. "Can't let on that we're makin' our way out like this. The warden's been using you to help run the station, and now he don't want to let you go."

Grayson got a strong sense of resignation from his brother's mind. [Not… again.]

"Yeah, again. We gotta stop lettin' people know what you can do." Grayson grunted as he felt someone try to forcibly restart the alarm system. The reboot effort felt like someone tapping on the surface of his brain. "If you're seen, no deaths, all right? We don't want to give these assholes any reason to rescind the contract they signed on our behalf."

[Contract? Job?]

"I'll tell you about it later. Right now, get to the docking bay and look for the Caridian ship."

[Caridian?] Excitement burbled through Mason's nodes, making their connection seem a little fizzy. [New tech?]

"Brand new tech for you to go gaga over later," Grayson chided him. "Get to the bay. Let me know if you get into trouble."

[Watch… for… yourself. Lots of people… coming… your way.]

"I can handle it," Grayson said. "Be safe, brat."

[We… will. You too.]

Grayson grinned, flexing his fingers as he delved deeper

into the prison's security system. "Oh, don't worry about me. Worry about *them*."

There were a lot of boots marching his way – ten guards coming up from the lower level via the elevator, and two different sets heading down the hall from opposite directions, each group accompanied by an ancient peacekeeper bot that had been refitted with less-deadly armaments for the close-quarters combat that was more likely to happen in a penal colony. All that meant was taking away its most penetrating weapons – no one wanted to be sucked out into space – and any automatic firing component they might have. They'd kept their military AI system, not to mention weapons like taze-rays and electro-shock batons. The first of those two groups would be here in around thirty seconds.

Plenty of time.

The first thing Grayson did was enforce an emergency stop for the elevator. He trapped it between two floors, so that even if they did manage to pry the door open with the help of their power armor – because the guards weren't as stupid as the warden and kept their gear on at all times – they'd have a devil of a time crawling out.

As for the people in the corridor outside... well, it was so kind of them to bring their bots along. Grayson dredged up the Coalition military intelligence code to override their AI that he'd memorized for a job once – hadn't been changed yet, bless their stupid little hearts for being such trusting fools – and fed it into each bot's processor, then aided them in designating new targets.

In this case, each other.

The guards were nearly to Grayson's door, less than twenty paces apart, when the bots' programming caught up with Grayson's commands. Plasma crossfire erupted in the hall, the bots hitting each other without regard for protecting themselves – prisoners rarely fought back, and never effectively. Some of the guards screamed as they were electrocuted by their own backup. Some of them began to fire at the bots. A few of the smarter ones reached out with their implants to try, fruitlessly, to get back into the computer system and put the entire prison on lockdown.

Grayson calmly listened to them fight it out for a few seconds, then headed for the warden's private bathroom.

The Bor-Turia Penal Colony was positioned in space, close but not too close to the planet of Bor-Turia itself. Being so isolated, it had to be careful with things like water usage. Toilet water was kept separate from showering water, which was kept separate from drinking water. They all had separate tubes and tunnels, and used distinct parts of the processing plant at the center of the colony before being transported back out for use again.

The largest of the transport tubes was for shower water – just wide enough to fit a person as long as they squinched up a bit. From this office to the colony's docking bay was a nearly straight shot down, just one turn here at the top and another at the bottom to get out of the main line. Gravity would help, and the program Grayson installed to open the washout valve on the other side would do the rest. It ought to open when he was within three meters, and let him out in the pump room that was just next to the bay. It would flood the place at the same time, but that was the price of speed.

Grayson calculated the time it would take to get there even as he kept a piece of his attention on the fracas outside. The guards finally got the better of their bots, going after the manual overrides on their bases. He could have reprogrammed them to shoot people as well as each other, but… lines. There were lines, still, in what he and his brother would do. Not firm ones, not clear ones, but he knew them when he ran up against them, and turning someone's killer toys on them just because they'd been stupid enough to take a job here was one of them.

Twenty seconds to reach the pump room. That was doable. More than doable, that was going to be a breeze. Grayson grinned as he got into the shower and, quickly and methodically, smashed a hole through the floor of it with the heels of his boots.

It had taken a lot of time and effort to get ferrocrete inserts for his cheap prison boots, but it was worth every penny to see the concrete foundation they'd poured for the washroom crumble. He heaved a few of the bigger pieces to the side and watched the smaller ones wash away in the swift-moving water.

Turn in one-point-two meters. Crawl it in three seconds. Down for another fifteen. Catch and crawl for another two and it's out through the pump room. Eh, tricky, but not the worst breakout he'd ever managed. That had been through a Thassian sewer, and given their traditional diet… holy Mount Mons, he still couldn't stomach the smell of fish.

Quit wasting time. The firing had completely stopped – someone was banging on the door. Grayson heard the warden groan. *No more time for dilly-dallying.* He took a deep breath and held it, then closed his eyes, bent down and crawled headfirst into the water.

It didn't feel odd to keep his eyes shut. Grayson was used to looking at the world in different ways – through the connections the implant lit up for him in his brain, or through his link to Mason and his brother's four other little detachable selves. The current was stronger than he liked, but doable. He got to the turn, changed direction, and–

Fast! The current felt a hell of a lot faster once he was going down. Hundreds of meters passed quicker than he could follow. A warning siren blared in his head, and it was only thanks to providence and a life of honing his reflexes that Grayson was able to reach out and grab the ledge that would lead him to the pump room, banging his hand against the wall hard enough that he heard the smack of it even over the water. *Shit, that hurt!*

[Big brother? You… OK?]

Grayson couldn't do more than send a general sort of sense of "managing, back off" to Mason right now. He tried to lever his body up and into the new tunnel, but the water pressure seemed to be getting harder… or was that him finally running out of air?

Up, up, up, get your bloody self up! Grayson, minding the timer in his head, waited for the moment when the pump room door burst open. He timed his push to the outlet along with it and managed to get going in the right direction at last, even though it squeezed him into a tumble end over end in the wider pipe. There! There was the exit to the pump room, now all he had to do was–

His feet emerged first, legs and hips, but his shoulders – those stuck. They were the broadest part of him, and although it wasn't a perfect seal, water still burbling past his face and out around his chest, there was no air getting in. Grayson twisted this way and that, fighting to free himself as twinkly white stars floated across his vision, but it wasn't working.

Holy Mount Mons, he was going to die in a goddamn *tunnel* in the middle of a goddamn prison right before making a brilliant escape, which meant he was going to die seriously angry because this was a *load of bullsh–*

Just before Grayson opened his mouth and inhaled his death, the crush of the exit around his shoulders lessened. He shot through, gasping, and landed in the long, metallic upper limbs of his brother, who turned him over so that he was facing downward and gently patted his back.

[There, there. There, there.]

"Quit it," Grayson said through his coughs as water gushed out around them. "Get us to the ship already."

[It's close.] Not bothering to put him down, Mason turned and loped out of the pump room and into the docking bay. A dozen different ships were settled there, but the only one that wasn't Coalition-make was the strange, skinny thing at the end of the front row. It had already extended a ramp, and standing at the top of it was the vaguely familiar outline of a Caridian, backlit by the lights within his ship. The bay itself was dark and closed, all personnel off responding to the emergency that the Bane boys had created.

"Right, put me down, brat," Grayson grunted, and

walked up the ramp to meet the alien on his own two feet. "Grayson and Mason Bane," he said, tossing his wet head back toward his brother, who stood politely – some would say unnervingly – still behind him.

"So you are," the Caridian – Ix-Nix-Six, according to the data Grayson had read – said after a moment. "I had not expected your arrival to be so…" All of a sudden the alarms came back online, filling the docking bay with noise. "Portentous."

"Look, forget that," Grayson replied, focusing on overriding the controls for the docking bay doors. "The warden was trying to short the deal you'd made to get us, an' I decided not to let him. Bastard got what he deserved, which was a nice nap on the floor while we made our escape. Nobody's been hurt so far." Except for himself – the arm he'd banged against the wall was aching something fierce, but he'd worry about it once they were out of here. "So how about we make trails and leave the explanations for the diplos, huh?"

"You – they're breaking out of prison!" another person in the ship – Centauran, had to be, with that voice and the whole "knowing things they shouldn't" deal. Filthy mind readers. "We can't take them with us! The damages they've done to this facility are monumental, they're going to be–"

"Who are you gonna listen to right now, me or that little pink pony?"

The Centauran gave an offended huff.

"If you want us for this gig, you'll never find better when it comes to keeping tech running. But you have to take us now. Otherwise, yeah, it's not going to happen." Grayson held his breath. If this Six guy decided they weren't worth the trouble, then he and his brother were going to be up to their necks in shit in just a few minutes. They were good, the best when it came to slipping out of tough situations, but everyone had their breaking point. Grayson didn't want to find his and Mason's.

[We're scared… big brother.]

"I've got you," Grayson whispered, fighting back the awful urge to beg for help. He'd tried that exactly once, back on Mars, and it hadn't gotten him squat. Never again.

Six's luminous eyes were downright spooky when they were focused right on him. Made him feel like the bug boy could read his mind as well as the Centauran could.

Finally, Six nodded. "Clear a path for us and we will be on our way, then. I will handle any negotiations about your… means of taking leave that arise." He turned and headed for the helm as the ramp began to withdraw. Grayson and his brother followed him deeper into the ship, ignoring the affronted Centauran and everyone else who stared at them right now.

Grayson looked at Mason. "Get us out of this tin cup," he said.

[We will.] Mason's eyes went distant as his body reconfigured, spreading out into a spiderlike shape that would give him more stability if a quick takeoff was required. Grayson settled into the closest flight chair nearby, strapping himself in as he looked around the forward cabin at who he was going to be dealing with for the next however-the-hell long this mission was going to take.

He'd never met any of them before, but he'd heard of one of 'em. Protector Divak and her squad had been hired for a job on Mars a few years back – wreaked so much havoc in the separatist movement there after they skinned the leader alive before taking his head that no one had tried again since. She was lookin' at him like he was something she'd scraped off her boot, so… yeah, not someone he wanted anything to do with if he could help it.

Ix-Nix-Six was a new face – new for all of them, probably, as Caridians weren't common in Coalition space. As for the Centauran, Dr Corinus Lifhe, eh – you'd met one, you'd met them all. They were clever, quiet cowards, the lot of 'em.

"Rude," Lifhe muttered from where he sat next to the only other human on this ship.

Grayson stared at the Centauran for a long moment as the ship slowly began to rise. Mason had gotten the bay open, then – good lad. The human, Dr Drexler, was one of those types that defied easy description – you could say "brown hair, brown eyes, brown skin, long and thin" and get the basics, but still know nothing. They dressed like a standard Coalition drone, but their face was damn near lit up with excitement. It made them look lively in a way Grayson had almost forgotten people *could* look – people who hadn't been beaten down by life, people who still had something, not just to live for, but to love.

Scientists. Throw 'em a problem in their field, it was like throwin' a bone to a dog – they'd gnaw all the way through to get to the meaty center, no matter how long it took. Grayson didn't know exactly what this mission was about – that part was classified both for him and the warden – but he figured it had to be pretty brainy to merit two eggheads on the trip.

Right now, one of those eggheads was staring with a little too much interest at his brother. "Problem, doc?" he asked sharply as the ship flew down the prison's departure lane. Alternating bands of yellow and white light passed over them as they headed for the exit, which surely was open now.

"Not at all!" Dr Drexler replied. "I'm just really impressed with your brother's machinery. It looks almost entirely custom-made."

"It is." Grayson had made it himself, in fact. He'd come a long way since his first fumbling attempts at fabricating cyberkinetic limbs for his brother back when he was knee high to a cockroach.

"That's incredible." They tilted their head in consideration. "Independent neural interfaces, right?"

Grayson clenched his jaw. "How'd you know that?"

"It's in the file," they said. *Oh, yeah.* "How did you get the raw material for the neural pathways?"

"Mason grew it himself," he replied.

"Like… what, cloning?"

"Like, he once had an actual, entirely meat body," Grayson said, rolling his eyes. *Cloning. What kind of rich bitches do they think we are?* "Wasn't going to waste some perfectly good nerve tissue when the time came to transition from meat to metal, was I?"

"Oh, of course, it makes total sense you'd want to use his own if you could," they said, which… actually was kind of nice. Cyborgs who kept to a standard humanoid shape were one thing, but too many people saw Mason and treated him like a thing, not the person he was. "What about–"

They all stopped speaking for a moment as the ship cleared the Bor-Turia Penal Colony, leaving behind garish neon lights for the soothing darkness of space. Six turned back to face them all. "We are receiving a number of incoming calls," he said calmly. "What a shame that we are unable to respond due to a minor computer malfunction. I believe our communications array will be back online by the time we're out of Bor-Turian space."

Grayson laughed despite himself. Perhaps this mission would be less boring than it seemed.

CHAPTER SIX
Corinus Lifhe

Corinus quickly learned a great many things about his fellow expedition members, little of it encouraging. The first, and most disappointing, discovery, was that it was going to take at *least* a week's worth of travel to get to Sik-Tar. Which…

"Why is that?" Dizzie asked, saving Corinus the trouble of doing so himself as they crowded in behind Six's chair. They were only a few hours out of Bor-Turia, and it had taken some deft handling on Six's part and a special intervention by the Martian commander before the warden of the penal colony was convinced not to send ships after them to retrieve the Banes. "Why can't you open a wormhole from here and take us to Sik-Tar like that?" They snapped their fingers for emphasis. "That's how your ships travel long distances, isn't it?"

"It is one method," Six replied, tapping his claws against the command console. A 3-D navigation map sprang up before their eyes a second later. There seemed to be pieces of it missing, at least to Corinus's eyes – something to do with the colors a Caridian could see versus a Centauran, perhaps. "Certainly, it is the most popular one for large numbers of ships. It is far easier to keep a wormhole open once you've already cut through the fabric of space than it is to make the hole in the first place. Either way, though, it is still a very fuel-intensive process, and one that is made significantly less expensive if you can find a weak spot to travel through."

"A weak spot in… what, the space-time continuum?"

"Exactly!" Six beamed at Dizzie like they were a particularly impressive toddler. Corinus didn't like feeling how Dizzie's sense of pride strengthened at the faint praise. "These can occur naturally, or in places where wormholes have been opened before."

"How do you find them?"

Six tilted his head slightly. "With a map, of course."

"But how does your map know where these weak spots are?" Dizzie pressed.

Corinus would have stopped asking after the last question – he hated to be pushy. It went against every instinct he had. But Dizzie's first impulse was always to pursue the discovery at hand without regard to propriety or social niceties.

"How are they identified?" they continued, staring avidly between the map and Six. "Is it deviations in local planetary orbits that make the wormholes harder to open? Is it chirps in gravitational waves that throw off your calculations… or maybe it's because you know the places where your people have opened them before?"

Corinus could feel interest perking in the rest of the crew.

He could read all of them to an extent, although Mason's odd, linked minds gave Corinus a terrible headache if he focused too hard on them.

Six, however, remained as opaque as a stone to Corinus's telepathy. "It's something like that," he said, his antennae waving gently. "I wouldn't really know, I'm not a propulsion engineer. My interest has generally been turned toward the long and ancient history of my people, not our more modern and very complicated machinery."

"Foolish," Divak said with a haughty sniff – it seemed to be the only way she knew how to speak. Her sense of self-importance was as elevated as a mountain peak, and Corinus disliked being aware of Divak almost as much as he disliked being *un*aware of Six. "You use this technology day in and day out; you should know how it works. What if the ship was damaged and we were stranded in the backwater galaxy around Sik-Tar with no means of returning beyond impulse power? Or what if *you* were damaged, and couldn't make the ship work?"

"Oh, you needn't worry about that," Six assured her. "I had a Coalition frigate-style jump drive specially installed as a backup for this very eventuality. I daresay with a little trial and error, the Banes could return you all to your home planets with little time wasted."

"Prob'ly," Grayson admitted from the copilot's seat. "You did a decent job settin' this thing up for someone with fingers instead of the claws you use. Just show me how to access the jump drive and the nav settings, an' I could get us anywhere in the galaxy."

Divak's eyes retracted to blood red slits. "You will show

me how to do this as well," she said to Grayson. "It is essential to our security."

"We should all know the basics of flying this ship, I think," Dizzie added, cheerfully immune to the rising tension among the others. "Just in case the worst happens."

Corinus sighed dejectedly, withdrawing as much as he could from sensing the minds of the others until his head felt like it had been thrust underwater, which was just barely better than wallowing in the mess around him. *Ugh,* less than a week out from Torus Station and he was already missing the clarity that he'd experienced back there, the ease of reading minds bent on performing rote tasks within a comforting hierarchy. Now he was stuck in the middle of a group of individualists who barely knew how to get along with themselves, much less be functional members of a group.

Corinus had been instructed to observe his fellows, Six included, and make assessments of them for Dr Yoche. But how could he make a proper threat assessment when there was so much… *possibility* inside them? When he couldn't predict what they were going to do because they themselves didn't know what they were going to do from one moment to the next? This was why he was a born theoretician – actual hands-on experimentation felt overwhelming and uncomfortable. There were too many variables to account for, too much that could go wrong.

What even *was* the worst, at this point? Was it Six being a liar and luring them into a trap of some kind? Or maybe it was Grayson Bane somehow integrating his creepy brother Mason into the ship and taking it over? Was it Divak taking a rival contract and killing them all before they even got out of this corner of Coalition space?

Was it Dizzie deciding they liked someone better than they did Corinus?

He hung his head even as he began building up the mental walls that would block out all of the input he was getting from the rest of the crew, occasionally reaching out to Dizzie like a touchstone to regulate himself before getting back to the task. It was a shameful thing to admit that he was reliant on someone else for stabilizing his mood, more shameful yet for that person to be something other than Centauran, and yet… he had worked with Dizzie for years, now. Three years of near-daily companionship, of intellectual stimulation and discovery, of personal sharing and conversation, of *friendship*. Dizzie never tried to lie to Corinus, or hide truths from him. They were readily forthright, with him and everyone else, and it was such a comfort to have them be someone he could count on being on his side.

If that comfort, that support, if that *friendship*, ended or even changed dramatically… Corinus didn't know what he would do.

"Hey."

Corinus startled, his front feet coming off the deck for a moment. "Oh!" He hadn't even felt Dizzie settle in beside him.

"You seem a little stressed," they said, keeping their voice low as they leaned closer. "Want to do a debrief?"

That was their kind way of asking, "Can we talk about feelings?" without making Corinus feel like a child again.

"Yes, please," he said morosely, and followed Dizzie back into the living quarters of the front part of the ship. It was separated into two compartments – the frontmost was where the helm was located, followed by basic flight chairs for each of them as well as a holo-compatible table. The back compartment was the very cramped living space, with tightly spaced in-wall bunks, one multi-species bathroom that had taken a lot of experimentation to figure out, and a tiny kitchenette that almost no one used for anything except making hot drinks. The back part of the ship was reserved for supplies and the massive fuel tanks that getting to Sik-Tar required.

Dizzie sat down on their bunk and patted it. Corinus sat next to them and tried not to fidget. "How are you right now?" they asked, direct as always.

"Muzzy," he said.

"Ah." They nodded. "You blocked them all out on your own?"

"As best I could. But it's still… it makes me feel a little spacesick."

"You've gone from too much sensory input to too little," Dizzie said with a frown. "Do you want a shot?"

"Yes," Corinus admitted, "but I only brought a limited number of them. Weight restrictions, you know. I don't want to get to the planet and find out I can't function without blocking my telepathy, then being unable to do so because I ran out too soon."

Dizzie patted his shoulder. "We can probably synthesize some more with the medical replicator in this thing, it's pretty advanced."

Corinus shifted uncomfortably. "That would require sharing the solution for the compound's chemical structure, which is forbidden by our hierarchs. If Dr Yoche found out…" Social shaming and subsequent isolation would be the least of Corinus's worries. Centaurans were cagey about their telepathic abilities, and for good reason. If other species could shut them down, it would be a terrible disadvantage.

"Hmm." Dizzie tapped their chin with their index finger. "OK, then that can be our last resort, but if it comes down to a choice between that and your health, you should do it. I'll help explain it to Dr Yoche if need be. You're the junior scientist here, after all – in the end you're my responsibility, and my decisions stand. Right?"

Corinus brightened as the import of Dizzie's words sank in. "That's true." If there was one thing Centaurans understood, it was the chain of command. If Dizzie took responsibility for his decisions, then Corinus was technically off the hook. "Thank you."

"You're welcome." They smiled. "Want to try to open your mind up again?"

"Yes." He was getting more nauseous by the minute. Corinus shut his eyes and focused on his own mind, revitalizing it with deep breaths and carefully conducted surges of oxygen-rich blood. Soon he could sense every mind on the ship again, if not understand them all, but the closest one was Dizzie's, and it was full of affection. He felt re-centered, reinvigorated. "Thank you," he said again.

"You know I'm here for you," Dizzie replied. "Now. We've hardly gotten a second to ourselves since this trip began. While everybody else out there is learning how to fly this tin can, how about you give me your assessment of the rest of the team?"

Corinus nodded. "Of course. I'm afraid I won't be of much help with Six, though."

"Interesting," Dizzie said. "Is that because Caridians are a psy-null species, or is it something else?"

"More like a structural barrier," Corinus said. "I can sense that something is there, that he *has* a working, complex mind, but it's incomprehensible to me." Corinus fluttered his eyelids apologetically.

Dizzie waved a dismissive hand. "It's fine. I'd be more surprised if you got a good read off him, honestly. What about the Bane brothers?"

"They're readable, but… challenging in their own ways," Corinus said as diplomatically as he could. "Their minds are frequently linked, which makes it difficult to tell whose thoughts and emotions are whose on the surface level. Beyond that, Mason Bane refers to himself in the plural, which is rather confusing."

"Oh wow!" Dizzie already knew this, thanks to Grayson's very upfront explanation of his brother and his decree that "if any of you lot go fishin' around for parts, I'll cut your hands off at the wrists." Divak had actually been impressed. "He's such a unique person, way out there compared to most military Galactic Coalition cyborgs. I guess that's the advantage of growing up on Mars."

"Or the disadvantage," Corinus felt compelled to point out. "If he had been tended to by Coalition physicians early on when he became a cyborg in the first place, he could have been better integrated into society at large. He and his brother could have used their talents for goals that benefit their entire people, rather than becoming the galaxy's most infamous thieves."

"Cor, where's your sense of adventure?" Dizzie asked with a mix of affection and exasperation.

"I... don't think I have one?" He looked at them anxiously. "Is that OK?"

Dizzie chuckled. "It's fine, ignore me. What about Divak?"

Corinus shuddered. "Her thoughts are filled with blood. Her mind is a swamp, much like her home. She thinks constantly of returning to it and beginning a brood of her own."

"Ah. Her biological clock is ticking, huh?"

"...huh?"

Dizzie shook their head. "Never mind, it's just an old human saying."

"Ah." Good. Anything identified as "old" in human terms usually meant obsolete and ignorable. "She seems determined to stick with the job," Corinus added, "but not enthusiastic about it. We are merely a means to an end to her."

"Guess we'd better try to stay on her good side just to be safe, then."

"Which side is that?" Corinus asked.

Dizzie smiled. "Whichever side is holding a weapon." They shrugged and changed the subject. "I think as long as we're on the subject of learning things, we ought to talk to the rest of the team about Xenium. Just as a safety precaution."

"None of them seem very concerned with safety," Corinus said a little mournfully. *Except for Six, but he doesn't count.* Quite frankly, Corinus didn't care how "safe" their host was, the showoff.

"We can still try," Dizzie said. "In all likelihood it won't matter, but I'd rather we did our due diligence now."

"There's so much we're not allowed to talk about, though," Corinus pointed out. "Everything with the Xenos is classified."

"We'll work around that," Dizzie said.

"How?"

Of course, Dizzie had ideas for that already. That was why the next day – or right after the next automated sleep cycle ended, in reality – they stepped firmly into their Dr Drexler persona and proceeded to give a skillfully redacted version of the events on PK-L7 and PK-L10.

"You probably all know that these planets are off limits," Dizzie said, bringing up holos of both of them with their portable emitter. "I'm sure many of you have ideas about why that is. I'm not here to confirm or deny any of those."

"I heard it was because everybody on them went crazy and turned cannibal," Grayson offered with a lazy wave of his hand.

"I was told the reason for it was an infection that gave the inhabitants incredible powers," Divak said, her eyes bright with interest. "And that the planet was quarantined in order to keep them from taking over the rest of the galaxy."

"Not confirming or denying," Dizzie repeated. "However, I will say that Xenium played a role in the... issues that arose on the Coalition colony."

"Yeah, you're a Xenium specialist, right?" Grayson pressed. "You comin' along to see if Sik-Tar is another cash cow for the Coalition? I bet the Guilds are actually mining the shit out of that place right now–" He abruptly paused and looked at his brother, who had turned his expressionless face toward him. "We *might* not hear about it on the underground channels, you don't know." There was another pause. "Of *course* we could steal it if it was out there, but we'd have to hear about it first!"

"Nonsense." Divak shook her head. "The human-run Guilds would not hesitate to lord their wealth over the rest of us if they had access to Xenium, and the Galactic Coalition would change its stance from one of peace to one of conquest in an instant. They do not, therefore they don't have it. Did the native intelligence fight back too fiercely?"

"I can't say," Dizzie reiterated with more patience than Corinus would have had. "I *can* tell you that the Xenium was not the sole source of the problems that occurred in the PK-L system, and that in all likelihood we won't encounter that combination of factors on Sik-Tar. That being said, even though the atmosphere there is breathable for all of us, I'm requiring the use of full EVA suits for everyone while we're planetside. And a mask for Mason," they added, glancing at his metal body.

"What, all the time?" Grayson demanded.

"At the very least, while we're out in the open," Dizzie confirmed. They nodded toward Six, still sitting at the helm, looking as calm as ever. "Six has allowed me to set the safety standards for this mission, and this is one I'm insisting on. Wear your masks while outside, and allow me to do a thorough check of all on-site locations before taking them off once we get to Sik-Tar."

"Typical human cowardice," Divak snapped. "You would have us be afraid of our very shadows if it gave you the chance to assert your control over the rest of us."

"Or are you afraid of us mucking up your pretty little planet?" Grayson asked with an eyeroll. "What, you think we're going to wreck the place before the Caridians take it back?"

Corinus was shaking in his boots at the feeling of Divak's and Grayson's ire, and it wasn't even directed at him. Dizzie, however, responded with aplomb. "I have no interest in asserting control over you, and I don't think there are enough of us to ruin an entire planet in the amount of time we have rations for. However, since I'm in charge of the safety of our expedition, you *will* carry out my orders when it comes to that safety, or you can stay on the ship when you get there."

Divak bristled. "I am in charge of physical security when we reach Sik-Tar. I have to be able to see you to protect you."

"Then I guess you'd better wear your mask while you do that," Dizzie said with a smile. "Or I'll complain about your conduct to Leader Pavul."

Divak turned to glare at Six, who looked back with the same blank benevolence he'd displayed for the entire duration of the trip so far. "I am in agreement with Dr Drexler," he said.

"Cowards, *all* of you are filthy cowards," Divak hissed before standing up and stalking into the living quarters, sliding the door shut with a *bang* that seemed to reverberate through the whole ship.

Grayson began to laugh. "It's like livin' in the group home again," he said through his chuckles. "They had to take the doors off the second year I was there – too many teenagers like to slam the damn things. Hormones."

Dizzie shrugged. "Hey, I'm OK with whatever makes her feel better, as long as she does what I tell her to do. Does Mason understand?"

"He does," Grayson confirmed. "Can't speak for all his body parts, but the big brain's followin' along, so I think you're good to go."

"Great!" Dizzie turned to Mason, who was staring straight forward with hazy gray eyes. "Thanks so much, Mr Bane, I appreciate your cooperation."

"He says 'you're welcome'," Grayson said after a moment.

"Great."

"And now that that's out of the way..." Grayson leaned forward. "Let's get to the good stuff, eh?" He pulled a pack of playing cards out of Mason – *literally* out of his side, popping a panel on his left lower abdomen to get at them; it made Corinus queasy just to see it – and fanned them out in his thick-fingered hands. "Poker, drinkin', and you tellin' us as much as you can about what really happened in the PK-L system. Poker's been around for a gazillion years. Everyone knows how to play."

"I can neither confirm nor–" Dizzie insisted.

"We've all seen the bloody video from PK-L10," Grayson interrupted them. "I'm not asking for, whatever-ya-call-it, phylum and class and all that bullshit. I want ghost stories."

To Corinus's shock, Dizzie laughed. "I think I can manage that."

"But… but…" Corinus started.

They looked at Corinus, then back at the Banes. "I'm not offering anything but pure speculation on my part."

"Long as it comes with a side of beating your arse at poker, I'm happy with it."

A few minutes later the game was underway, cards dealt out to Grayson, Divak – who surprisingly had come back at the promise of a "test of skill" with the playing cards – Dizzie, and Six. Mason looked like he'd been turned off, leaning up against the wall with a completely blank expression, and Corinus, of course, wasn't allowed to join in.

"Not fair to play with a Centauran," Grayson pointed out when Dizzie complained on his behalf. "It's just the way it is."

"It's fine," Corinus said primly. "I prefer not to play."

"Yes, that's certainly true. Your kind prefer to hide," Divak said, upsetting the carefully balanced mood like she seemed to enjoy doing every chance she got. "Understandable. Your people are the greatest cowards of them all."

"You're lucky Centaurans aren't warlike," Dizzie shot back, cutting the deck without missing a beat even as they glared at Divak. "Otherwise, they'd have taken over the galaxy already."

Divak's blood red eyes narrowed as her lips drew back from her rather impressive fangs. "Ridiculous."

"Logical," Dizzie countered. "No doubt Centauran philosophers have already covered this, but if the driving goal of a species is to ensure their own survival, one way of achieving that would be to take out any aliens who could conceivably threaten them in the future. Centaurans have had FTL travel for longer than any of us. They could probably have done the Thassians in while you were still little lizards swimming around your swamps."

Divak bared her sharp teeth. "They could have done the same to you!"

"Exactly," Dizzie agreed, pointing their index finger at Divak. "And yet they didn't, and here we are, all playing a nice game together as we head into the great unknown." Dizzie grinned. "Isn't that great?"

Corinus hid his satisfaction as Divak tried to find a way to be more offended and failed. As they all looked at their cards, Dizzie began to speak. "Xenium was discovered on PK-L7 over a hundred Earth years ago. The colony was set up at jump-speed, and for a while everything went pretty well. But when things went wrong… you think the footage from PK-L10 was bad?" They laid two cards down. "Two, please." Grayson handed over the new cards.

Dizzie glanced at the other players, then murmured, "Picture Xenos bursting out of the ground before the people standing on it could even move. Monsters so massive they towered twenty feet over the humans beneath them, bulging with muscles, every joint lined with spikes, mouth full of fangs, tentacles reaching out to rip people apart before stuffing them into their gullets. Firing on these creatures got their victims nothing more than a shower of ichor, but as soon as they grabbed you–" They made a slicing motion in front of their throat. "The best you could hope for was a quick death. Two, please." Transfixed, Grayson handed over another two cards.

"Imagine it," they went on. "The hopelessness of a fight like that, the futility from being outnumbered by killing machines so brutally efficient that before you could pull the trigger on your gun, you'd lost your hand. Think about how it must have felt to be face to face with your own, inevitably gory, end. Consider what would be worse – dying ripped into a dozen pieces, or being consumed by the terrible creatures you're hopelessly flailing against." They paused dramatically, then laid down their cards. "Full house."

Everyone gaped in silence for a second before Grayson exclaimed, "Piece of – you conned me out of two extra cards!"

"Not my fault you didn't pay better attention," Dizzie said with a grin. "Better luck next time, buddy. Read 'em and..."

"Four of a kind," Six said calmly as he laid down his own cards. Four Jacks stared up at them while the rest of them stared at Six. "That is a better hand, isn't it?" he asked.

Dizzie began to laugh, and the tension eased. Or at least, Divak looked a little less like she was going to kill everyone at the table when she revealed her own useless hand of cards. *Disaster averted.* Nevertheless, Corinus hoped that playing poker would only be an occasional diversion – it was far too fraught with emotion for him to deal with every cycle.

To Corinus's distaste, the poker games continued, but the

storytelling that went with them was interesting enough to make up for it. He felt Dizzie battle with themself over whether or not to talk about the mold and its potential connection to Xenium. When they decided it was safest to do so, Corinus cheered inside. It was one more secret that *he* wouldn't be responsible for keeping.

"We're not sure what created the mold," Dizzie said as they shuffled the deck of cards. "There just isn't enough data. But there *is* strong evidence that the mold is what turned the formerly peaceful Xenos violent."

"Can it infect anyone?" Divak asked. She was thinking about how to fight mold. Because of course she was. If Centaurans ever rolled their eyes, Corinus would have done so right now.

"Again, we lack the data to say this conclusively, but it seems like the mold can infect other lifeforms as well. If that's true, then it's possible it can trigger the same sort of transformations, too."

Six's antennae waved as he picked up his first three cards. "A kind way of saying the infected become bloodthirsty berserkers."

"That's me, super kind," Dizzie agreed with a smile, but behind the grin their thoughts were serious. "Given that there's such a strong correlation between Xenium and the mold, and that we're heading to a planet that has trace evidence of Xenium in its atmosphere, it's best for you all to know what the mineral looks like." They finished dealing the cards, then pulled out their data tab and turned it so everyone could see the picture. It was a still from the mines on PK-L7, highlighting the bright green rock. "Typically, it was only found deep underground, so the likelihood of us stumbling across a chunk of it is very, very low."

"That's the shite that costs more per pound than the price of feeding my entire slum for a year?" Grayson demanded. "That's ridiculous. No rock is worth that much."

"It is when it can be turned into the best fuel in the universe," Dizzie replied. "Everybody wants to get their hands on it. Even the Caridians. Right, Six?"

Six looked over at them, and even though he didn't have eyelids, he gave the impression of blinking. "We do not need it to function, but we certainly wouldn't refuse it if a source were offered to us."

"Yeah, that's why you're really going to Sik-Tar, ain't it?" Grayson discarded a card and took another from the top of the pile. "Screw hunting down a distress signal, this is about checking it out to see if you wanna fight the Coalition for it."

Corinus tensed. Grayson had just asked the question they'd all been harboring in the backs of their minds. But Six slowly shook his head.

"Truly, my primary motivation is to discover the source of the distress signal. There are few legends in my culture, but this call is one of them. Many have theorized on its origin and purpose. Is the call connected to an ancient Caridian colony ship that we lost track of long ago? Was it a beacon that was somehow stolen from a Caridian vessel? Is the distress signal truly Caridian, as it seems to be, or one of the great coincidences of the universe? We simply do not know." Six's mandibles stretched wide for a moment. "And I would very much like to know."

So would Corinus.

Exactly one standard Earth week into the trip from the Bor-Turia Penal Colony, they reached the weak spot in the fabric of space that Six had identified as their optimal launch point. Everyone strapped into their flight seats, even Mason, to watch as Six activated the one part of the ship he hadn't let anyone explore – the wormhole generator. When Mason had illicitly tried, he'd gotten a jolt that had shocked him unconscious. Grayson had almost come to blows with Six over that, despite the infiltration being his idea in the first place.

And now they would see it in use.

Corinus did his best to ignore the emotions around him and focus on his own. The tenor of the engine's vibrations changed, power being drawn in a different way, to new parts of the ship. Ahead of them, a new star sparked into existence. It swirled, mesmerizing, so many shades of blue that Corinus couldn't identify them all as the stars went from a spark to a spiraling circle of flame, then finally to a tunnel big enough to fit Six's ship through.

"Here we go," Six announced, and guided the ship into the wormhole. Suddenly frightened, Corinus closed his eyes.

What if this was it? What if he was about to die, atoms spread from one end of the galaxy to the other in a trail so thin as to be nonexistent? What if they made it in but couldn't make it out, and smashed into a wall of reality on the other side of the tunnel? What if–

"We're here!"

"Corinus." Dizzie gently shook his shoulder. He blearily opened his eyes, anxiety racing through his body standing on all four feet. "Look," they said, looking from him out the front of the ship as they smiled in pure amazement. "Look, we made it. We made it to Sik-Tar."

CHAPTER SEVEN
Dizzie Drexler

So, it turned out that Sik-Tar… really wasn't that much to look at. Once the first flush of excitement had dulled, Dizzie was able to separate "distant planet unexplored for probably millennia OMIGOSH it's the best!" back to reality. And the reality was that Sik-Tar, at least from orbit, was rather boring.

About half the size of Earth, Sik-Tar had a breathable atmosphere thanks to a vast, superheated sea that generated oxygen via thermal reactions from the massive vents that boiled up beneath the planet's crust. Its total landmass consisted of a single, unbroken continent, punctuated here and there with volcanoes both dead and alive, but apart from that there were few other geological features of note. There were no great mountain ranges, no inland lakes, no forests or tundra or life of any kind. The land was rocky and granular and perpetually misted with clouds the color of blood everywhere you looked.

The rocks themselves were interesting, though. Lots of different types, and it didn't take much investigation with the ground-penetrating radar to confirm that there was, in fact, a very significant deposit of Xenium on Sik-Tar, and most of it fairly close to the surface of the planet, vulnerable to volcanic disruption. That probably explained the microparticles in the atmosphere.

Also interesting was the fact that the Caridian distress signal that Six was homing in on as they got closer to the planet's surface was located right in the middle of that Xenium deposit. It emanated from a massive structure that, according to their imaging scans, wasn't an immediate match to any Caridian architecture. According to Six, that was a feature, not a bug.

"Ship-building records from so long ago have largely been lost, but this appears within my people's capabilities!" he declared.

The structure was so big that at first Dizzie had thought it was just another rough, pointy hillock before Six excitedly showed them that the points were, in fact, manufactured spires of some sort. "This is good," he said, mouthparts buzzing. "If there were a homing signal without a corresponding ship, I could have been in significant trouble upon my return to the Seethe."

"What? Why?" Dizzie had a hard time picturing Six being the subject of reprimand.

Six tilted his tremendous eyes their way. "I have left my people behind on a quest to find something that has no immediate value to the Glorious Hegemony. If this had merely been the result of a stolen beacon, or some other alien artifact that indicated nothing at all instead of something identifiably Caridian, I would be guilty of wasting resources. Our queens have been kind to me, but every act of kindness has its limits."

Yeesh, wasn't that the truth. At least the homing signal had a pretty good beat. Dizzie turned back to the tablet and nodded their head along to the rhythmic "beep-ba-ba-ba-beep-beep" of it as they reread the findings from the probe they and Corinus had sent down twelve hours ago. It confirmed everything they already knew – no to life signs, yes to Xenium, manageable radiation levels, atmosphere breathable if need be. It was cold down there, and damp, but not freezing. The wind was constant, but not so fierce it would knock anyone down. In short, it was looking like the on-site expedition could go ahead as planned.

Now *that* was worth celebrating.

"You appear to be in a good mood, Dr Drexler."

Dizzie glanced up from their tablet at Six, who now sat down beside them at the helm. Everyone else was catching a little more sleep before they descended – except for Mason, maybe, but it was hard to tell since his eyes never shut.

"I am," Dizzie agreed. "I've got a lot of questions about what we're going to find down there, and I'm looking forward to finding the answers. Plus, I've always wanted to study Xenium firsthand. This is really a phenomenal opportunity for that."

"I suppose it is," Six said, tilting his head again in a way that made Dizzie think uncomfortably of a praying mantis. Not that they were worried Six was going to bite their head off – that was more Divak's style – but the resemblance was uncanny.

Dizzie wasn't so uncomfortable that they weren't going to take the opportunity to poke a little fun at Six, that was for sure. "You *suppose*?" they drawled, tilting the chair back slightly so they could get the right angle for a sarcastic side-eye. "You can't expect me to believe that your people aren't just as interested in the Xenium deposits as mine are. It's a stellar source of fuel, and from everything you've said it seems like Caridians could use something like it."

"We could," Six agreed. "I can't deny that. But we have other sources of fuel available to us that are easier to get and require fewer safeguards. Finding a reliable source of Xenium is certainly of interest to the queens, but the Glorious Hegemony shall continue on its journey whether we have access to it or not."

"I guess that's why they're happy to send a historian and not a propulsion engineer out here," Dizzie said, remembering Six's admonition from earlier in the week.

"Indeed." He glanced down at the planet, just visible in the corner of the ship's front viewscreen. "There was a time when our species was bolder. We took an aggressive approach to expansion and sought to control all resources within our sphere of influence. That is the time period this distress signal originates from."

"So you think that the ancient Caridians sent a ship out here to take control of the planet?"

Six's antennae wavered slightly. "That's my current assumption. The distress signal is real. Exactly what went on down there to necessitate it… that, I don't know. Yet."

Dizzie grinned. "But you're dying to find out, aren't you?"

"Hopefully not literally," Six said. "But… I confess, the thought of seeing firsthand one of the legends of my people…" He actually shuddered, his antennae boinging back and forth like they were on springs. "It might be enough to make dying worth it."

"Well." Dizzie straightened up in the chair and clapped Six on the shoulder. "Let's not make that literal, OK?"

"Of course not." Six inclined his head. "I plan to take every reasonable precaution."

"Take the unreasonable ones, too."

Six smiled… maybe. If that was what stretching out his lower mandible until it was wider than the top of his head could be called. "As you say."

They landed the *Telexa* in the midst of a storm. It was impossible *not* to land in a storm, given the persistence of the wind, so they picked a moment when the cameras could at least get a glimpse of the ground to make their descent.

"Are you sure you can do this?" Dizzie nervously asked Six as they strapped into their flight chair. They'd already changed into their EV suit, only lacking the helmet that would complete the "personal bubble" look. Beside them, Corinus was already somewhat lilac around the edges, and they hadn't even entered the atmosphere yet. Dizzie wondered if it was space sickness or the anticipation.

"Both," Corinus murmured unhappily to Dizzie, his eyelids fluttering like butterflies in a hurricane.

"I have landed the *Telexa* in much less favorable conditions before," Six assured them all, manipulating the controls with ease as he followed the coordinates to an area a few kilometers from the distress signal. They'd chosen it for its flatness – the slick, rugged, and in some cases jagged terrain of Sik-Tar didn't make for a lot of options. They had brought along a rover that would serve to take them the rest of the way there.

Heck, they could always walk if it got really bad. A few kilometers was nothing.

"Are we all strapped in?" Six asked, leaving his body facing forward in his chair but turning his head a full one-eighty degrees backward to look at them. Everyone nodded except for Mason, who Grayson double-checked before giving Six a nod. "Excellent. This landing will probably be somewhat bumpy, so if you feel the need to expel your food, please use the bag at your feet."

Corinus went right for his. Dizzie held more tightly to the straps across their chest and tried not to look overly excited. *Be calm, be cool, you're a pro and you've got this.* Sure, they'd ridden inside the massive Guild freighters from Earth to Torus Station and back, done a field trip to the moon, and touched down on Titan before, but this… they'd never done anything quite like this.

Their entry down to Sik-Tar began smoothly enough. They were landing while it was still light out by the structure, early in the day, in fact – they should have plenty of time for their initial explorations if everything went well. The faint illumination provided by the red dwarf seemed adequate… while still in space, at least. Once they plunged down into the upper layer of the atmosphere, Dizzie's impression of it changed.

It was like having a blanket drawn over the entire ship. A wet, blood red blanket that wrapped itself around their wings and suffocated their engines. The storm buffeted them severely enough that several alarms began to blare, and a moment later the cabin suddenly lost its lights.

"Don't be alarmed!" Six shouted from his spot at the helm. "The *Telexa* is merely rerouting all available power to our stabilizers. Once we're through the stratosphere, things should calm down significantly!"

"Are we going to *make* it through the bloody stratosphere?" Grayson shouted back.

"I believe we will!" The ship rocked to the side hard enough to rattle Dizzie's head between the topmost restraints. "I am nearly positive!"

"*Nearly* positive?" Corinus whimpered. Dizzie reached out and patted his forearm consolingly, the only part of him they could reach.

"This would be a miserable, honorless way to die," Divak said. For the first time since Dizzie had met her, she sounded something other than arrogant, angry, or both. She sounded frightened. If Dizzie could have reached her, they might have tried patting her forearm too.

And probably gotten it ripped off for their troubles. Dizzie clenched down on the armrest instead and stared out into the shifting storm. If they were going to die in a storm like this – *which we aren't, Corinus, we totally aren't!* – then they wanted to see their end coming. There was something freeing about the lack of control, everything right now the exact opposite of how it was in the lab. There was nothing they could do, no structure they could impose or effort they could make that would change the outcome of this experiment. Everything was in someone else's hands now, and all Dizzie could do was see it through.

The ship shook and jolted, sometimes taking hits from debris that ought to be too big to swirl up in a storm like this but came along for the ride anyway. Always there was the red right there, coating the ship and tinting everyone inside it with its ruddy reflection. They all looked like they'd been in a massacre, even the ones who didn't have iron-based blood.

A second after they had that thought, the ship broke through the storm and all of a sudden, their violent fall became soft as the stabilizers no longer had to compensate for the force of the winds. The reddish light remained, but as the vista of the ground stretched out through the viewscreen, the feeling of claustrophobia from the entry faded.

"I will set us down momentarily," Six said, and sure enough, a few seconds later the *Telexa* touched down on the ground with a gentle groan of shocks and a final, drawn-out creak. "We may have taken some damage," he added. "It wasn't making that noise before."

"Oh, *may* we?" Grayson asked, sarcasm so heavy in his voice it was a wonder he could lift it enough to be heard. "After a passage like that, gettin' down here with all the legs of this thing still attached is a bloody miracle! You should let me have access to her brain, run a scan to make sure she's still flightworthy and doesn't need any extra repairs."

Six unstrapped from his seat and turned around to look at them this time. "I will ensure you are satisfied as to the ship's condition, but we have plenty of time to make any repairs necessary. After all, our expedition here is only just beginning."

Whatever Grayson was about to say was lost as Corinus suddenly brought the bag up to his face and was noisily sick into it. A sour smell permeated the room, and the others up and left quickly after that, putting on their helmets and grabbing their specialty gear for the first foray onto the soil of Sik-Tar.

Dizzie stayed next to Corinus. "Are you going to be OK?"

"Fine," he groaned.

"I'm sure you can feel the fact that I don't exactly believe you."

Corinus wiped his mouth on the smooth back of his hooflike hand. "Now that we're not bouncing around so much, I'm sure things will settle in a moment."

"You could stay here for the initial foray," Dizzie reminded him. "I mean, it's not going to be much more than a first glimpse at this point. You could take the time to… y'know, quiet things down up here." They tapped the side of their own head.

"I am *not* going to stay here while you go out there with them." Corinus's eyelids stopped moving, a sign of his total sincerity.

"They don't want to hurt me," Dizzie said. "We're all a team here, you know? We're in this together."

"Some of us are more 'together' than others," Corinus said darkly.

Dizzie lowered their voice. "Have you gotten something dangerous from one of them?"

"Not specifically, but neither of us know anything of them, not really." He was still piercing them with that unblinking amethyst stare. "I don't trust them," he whispered. "And I especially don't trust them with you. You're the expert on Xenium, after all – I'm just your grad student." He reached out and took their hand. "Please don't tell them about the shots. I don't want them to know that I can turn off my telepathy. I want them to have to worry about me, even if I do decide to take a break."

"I understand."

"Are you two done gabbing yet?" Grayson yelled from the back of the ship. "The axle on the rover's busted – dislodged during the storm. We're gonna have to walk for now, and the sooner we get started the better!"

"We're coming!" Dizzie yelled back, then got to their feet. They tucked their helmet under one arm hand and held the other out to Corinus. "Ready to go where no Centauran has gone before?"

"If I have to," he whined, but he got up readily enough. "I'll get the particle counter."

"Thanks." Dizzie put their own helmet on and headed for the ramp in the center of the cabin, where the rest of the crew had assembled. Six's EVA suit was a lot like the standard Coalition make, but blue, whereas Divak was still in her power armor, carrying a sniper rifle that was almost as long as she was tall.

Grayson, meanwhile, was sitting on his brother's back, while Mason was down on all fours, limbs extended out at equal length on all sides like some sort of four-legged crab. His eyes were as blank as ever beneath the helmet, but

Dizzie had been paying close enough attention for the past week that they could pick up a few of Mason's cues now. There was a faint glisten of sweat at the top of his brow. He was excited.

"I see you found a solution to not having the rover fixed yet," Dizzie said as they took up position next to the Banes.

"You try it yourself and I'll break your arm," Grayson replied just as sanguinely. "It's brotherly when he carts me around – it's damn rude when someone else tries to horn in."

"I'll be fine walking, thanks."

Grayson grinned. "That's what I like to hear."

Their suit helmets were all tuned to the same radio frequency, and specs for each individual played across the side of the screen as Dizzie looked from person to person. All suits were whole, everyone's health looked good, and they were fully kitted out for an initial expedition – thus, everyone was carrying way more than they'd probably need, but Dizzie always felt it was better to have it and not need it than the other way around.

They looked over at Six, whose hand hovered over the keypad that would open the door to the outside. "Shall we?" Dizzie asked, trying for cool and professional, but probably coming off as ridiculously excited instead.

"We shall." Six quickly typed in the code, and a second later, the door began to rise while the ramp shot out to the rocky ground six feet below them.

Moments after that, Dizzie stepped onto ground that no sentient creature had set foot on for over a millennium.

Even though their damp footprint was blown away almost instantly, *they* knew it had been there. They were the first, but not the last.

"Here we go."

CHAPTER EIGHT

Ix-Nix-Six

It was hard not to give in to the impulse to bound ahead.

Six knew he couldn't. Or rather, he knew that he shouldn't, and he was controlled enough to ensure that his body did exactly what he told it to, when he told it to. He wasn't an adolescent, after all, unable to keep a fractious molt under control. He kept himself steady, stayed near the back of the group, and watched them do their work. Surveillance was important, after all, and what he saw of how this group behaved on planet would inform the choices he made once they got to his goal – the looming, pitted structure in the distance barely visible through the winding mist.

He itched to run to it, to leave these slower beings to their steady crawl across the slippery, sinkhole-ridden ground and show them what a Caridian was truly capable of when they played to their strengths. His people, even the spies or the rare hive rogues who were banished to live among aliens, were careful about demonstrating the true extent of their abilities when others were present. He knew that everyone with him had been instructed to watch him, to make reports on what he could do and what they could glean of his technology.

Apart from his stellar ability to run and climb, they would probably be disappointed by his physical capabilities. Caridians were lightweight beings, whose bodies excelled in most environments and gravities. The hardest to get around in was open water, but that wouldn't be an issue on Sik-Tar, where the only water that accumulated inland were puddles or the occasional deep crevice where it looked as though an ancient vent had blown a hole through the crust of the soil.

As for what they could glean from the *Telexa* … well, Six rather thought he should be worrying more about what they could glean from the monolith in front of them than the modest vessel behind them.

Patience. Watchfulness. Observation. Look upon them as carefully as they look upon you, and see what you can gather from them.

Dr Drexler was the most entertaining to watch, certainly. They moved with little thought to saving their energy, flitting in one direction then the next, eyes darting from the particle reader in their hands to their ultimate destination and back, over and over again. They had to keep inputting the password to turn the reader back on – it had a very short period of use before it shut down. Perhaps it had a defective battery? Dr Lifhe, who seemed more comfortable on all fours with this much wind at his back, trotted after Dr Drexler like a shadow.

"I'm surprised," Dr Drexler said, their voice carrying

easily through the channel on their helmets. "I wasn't expecting to get such a strong reading on the Xenium from here. It's a volatile organic compound, and being exposed to this kind of atmosphere would increase the speed at which it degraded. That should mean it's underground, but I'm not seeing much of it down there, and it's not like these rocks are full of lead or schungite."

"Wait, wait," Grayson Bane interjected. "Lead and schungite shield radioactive shit. Are you saying that Xenium is radioactive?"

"I mean… yes? At least, the kinds we've studied before now have been, not that I've had a chance to see them in person. Only *mildly* radioactive," Dr Drexler added. "Enough to make it easy to detect it with our equipment, but I'm not seeing the amount I'd expect in order to produce the traces we located in the atmosphere."

"Which means what?" Protector Divak asked, sounding bored. Her gun hung down at her side, which from what Six understood about Thassians would be enough to court-martial her if her leader saw it happening. *Interesting. She does not take the rest of us seriously.* Six hoped Divak would attend to her duty regardless, even though right now her role as bodyguard looked to be entirely ceremonial.

"It means that we need to get to that structure and look inside it for me to have a clue as to what's going on here," Dr Drexler replied. They looked at Six, meeting his eyes in a way that no one else on the team, not even Protector Divak, was inclined to. "That's where we'll find all of your answers, too, I bet. You want to take point?"

"*I* will take point," Protector Divak announced as

she strode to the front of the group. The drama of her announcement was slightly offset by the way she slipped on the moist uphill slope, black droplets marring the light colors of her power armor. Nevertheless, no one laughed. Apparently, one did not mock a Thassian and expect to live a long and productive life.

Mason Bane and his rider trotted after her, the cyborg's movements slow and steady, his machinery constantly making minute adjustments to keep his brother squarely in the center of his back. Six wished, not for the first time, that he could communicate with Mason Bane directly. He had never been in such close proximity to a cyborg before – Caridians did not make cyborgs of themselves, as their society gave those with fewer limbs or neurodegeneration numerous useful occupations to choose from – and he was curious about him. Perhaps before the end, he would get the chance to satisfy that curiosity.

Last went the scientists. Dr Drexler consciously slowed down to allow Six to catch up and walk with them, welcoming him with a baring of teeth that Six knew now to be a smile. Dr Lifhe remained blank-faced; he had not spoken a word to Six that was not absolutely unavoidable. For the sake of the expedition, Six wished that they got along a bit better, but he couldn't help but be pleased for the sake of his people that Centaurans couldn't read them.

"What do you think of this place so far?" Dr Drexler asked as they trudged along, sometimes ankle-deep in water, other times striding across bare rock. The wind and the contents it carried had been rather unpredictable thus far.

"I think it is quite intriguing, despite the plainness of its appearance," Six replied.

"Plainness?" Dr Drexler raised both eyebrows. Six wasn't sure what that meant until they followed it up with, "You think a planet that looks like an abattoir is plain?"

An abattoir... a slaughterhouse. Meaning this must be a reference to color, because there were no dead things here... "Oh, is it red?"

Both doctors blinked, Dr Lifhe much more rapidly than Dr Drexler as they processed their surprise at his question. "You can't tell?" Dr Drexler asked.

"Alas, red is not a color my eyes can detect," Six said. "I am capable of seeing things in the ultraviolet spectrum, however. I see in great depth, but for me, the colors of this planet are grayscale – mostly black, in fact."

"I didn't even think of that," Dr Drexler said with a sigh.

"There is no reason you should have," Six said easily. "Caridians see in a different spectrum, and our hearing is differently attuned as well, but I assure you that none of this will affect my ability to perform as a member of the team on this mission."

"I'm sure it won't," Dr Drexler said. "Can you tell me more specifically what you mean when you say your *hearing* is attu–"

They were unexpectedly cut off by Dr Lifhe before they could continue.

"What exactly are your duties?" the Centauran asked. He managed to keep any signs of aggression out of his voice, but his posture was a deeply defensive one. "Assuming we really do find a relic of your species on this planet."

"I will investigate it and try to discover its purpose here."

"And if you cannot? What if there is nothing to be discovered other than a strange beacon and a solid chunk of rock? What will you do then?"

Six clacked his mandibles placatingly. "If that were the case, I would dedicate myself to assisting you and Dr Drexler in any way I could, of course. Xenium is of interest to everyone in the galaxy, after all, and I *am* the one funding this expedition."

"Which we're grateful for," Dr Drexler said firmly, giving their graduate student a hard look. "I've been fascinated by Xenium ever since I read about Dr Vivian Rigby and her findings on PK-L7, over a century ago."

"What is the most fascinating thing about it all?" Six asked, eager for more insight into the mind of his human colleague. Dr Drexler thought for a moment.

"I think that, for me, the search for Xenium and the events that happened in the PK-L system are most interesting because they represent real-time evolution," they said at last. "The Xenos were… well, they were *calm* when they were first detected by the Coalition. Fellow miners, not a threat, not for most of the mining colony's existence. The trigger for their change from peaceful aliens to ravenous, rapidly mutating ghouls is still unknown."

"I thought it was the mold," Six said.

"*Yes*, but what formed the mold in the first place?" they demanded passionately. "Was it always there, or was it brought there separately? If it was brought separately, who brought it in? How? Was it human miners, was it the Xenos themselves, or was it some other secret force that we don't know about yet? How much do planetary conditions contribute to mold formation? The planets in the PK-L system have next to no water. Does that mean the mold is hydrophobic, and less likely to grow here? Or if the mold is endemic in environments that contain Xenium, does it have to reach a certain threshold within the infected before it begins to initiate change? Or are a few inhaled spores enough to do the trick?

"Dr Rigby documented some evidence that the mutations only occur, at least in alien species other than the Xenos, when there's physical trauma that directly exposes the Xenium to the blood. Is that always true, or only true for when the infection caused by the mold is passed on from a previously infected individual, as opposed to something that comes about via environmental factors? How much mold does someone have to be exposed to in order to contract it in the wild, so to speak?" Their eyes looked a little wild within their EVA suit helmet. "I have so many questions."

"I do hope you can find the answers to some of them here," Six replied. "Although perhaps not the ones that pertain to the mold."

Dr Drexler laughed. "I wouldn't worry too much about that. I didn't realize how stormy it was going to be down here on the surface until we arrived, but I think it's safe to say that anything organic that might have existed has been washed into nothingness by now. That is not permission to take off your helmets!" they added for the benefit of the rest of the group. "It's a theory only! There could be plenty of microorganisms that have adapted to the wind that we simply haven't managed to detect yet, so. Just saying."

"Killjoy," Grayson Bane muttered. Then: "Beacon says this is the place. And this place is… damn. *Damn*."

"Damn what?" Dr Drexler picked up their pace, and Six and Dr Lifhe trotted along in their wake until they entered the shadow of the monolith before them. The bulk of it rose several hundred meters into the air, an enormous triangular wedge that jutted from a broad, kilometers-wide base into a tall, narrow crest, limned with long, thin spires that almost reminded Six of mammalian eyelashes. The Banes and Divak were standing to the right of the very center of it, Mason shifting his weight as his brother got to his feet. "Damn *what?*" Dr Drexler persisted.

"Come look at this." Grayson stood up on Mason's back and ran his hands along the strangely granular surface of the structure. "I didn't see it on the pictures you took from space, too blurry, but there's a seam here." He craned his neck up. "A *big* one."

"A seam… you think there might be an entrance here?" Dr Drexler asked excitedly.

"Not feelin' any rivets or seein' any weld-marks, so an entrance makes more sense than two big pieces of metal stuck together." Grayson glanced at Six. "Unless your people use methods for stickin' inanimate objects the size of small cities together that the rest of us don't know about."

"Nothing as advanced as what you're implying," Six said, reaching out and feeling for himself. The sensation was dulled through his gloves, but Grayson was right – there was clearly a seam in the surface here, created by a living being's hand. Someone, likely many someones, had made this enormity. What was it meant for, though? It was certainly grand enough to inspire, but Caridians didn't have gods, so what use was a temple? He dug his tarsal pads into the seam again. Given the height of it, perhaps it connected to a…

He walked five more meters to the right, trailing his hand at what should be the right height for a – yes, there it was. The start of the markings that every ship within the Glorious Hegemony kept outside their main bay doors, and repeated across the body of the ship to make its name and place in the fleet obvious. He stepped back and turned on his floodlamp, illuminating the wet, glistening surface before him. To most eyes, the markings he was pointing at would look like a set of random hash marks, impossible to completely read without access to the ultraviolet. For Six, though, even though most of the color was worn away by time, it was illuminating in the best of ways.

He knew his antennae were waving like flags, bumping back and forth in the confines of his helmet, but he didn't care. He was too happy to care. He had done it. He had *found it*. And more than that…

Later.

Six snapped his mandibles a few times to clear his throat. "I believe that what we are looking at is a ship."

His announcement was met with silence, for about three seconds. Then everyone started trying to speak all at once.

"That's incredible! What–"

"That's impossible, there's no–"

"Not even the Guilds are able to build ships this big, are you–"

"Please." Six lifted his claws. "I will explain, but first I think we should verify whether or not my suspicion is correct. We need to find a way into it." They all turned to look at the pitted, immense surface of the structure, stuck there determinedly in the ground like it had grown from it.

"We're not going to be able to force our way in," Protector Divak said after a moment's consideration. "Not through here, at least. We have no viable means of breaking through this door."

"We could climb?" Dr Drexler suggested, not sounding sure of themself. "Maybe make it in through one of those spires? If this is a ship, then those might have been used as exhaust stacks or something like that, so there could be a way in at the top."

"Which is great if you want to end up sitting on top of this thing's engine," Grayson Bane said. "Then you'd have to climb right back out again. Bad idea."

"What is your suggestion, Grayson?" Six asked before the tenor of the discussion could turn acrid, as it had so often in the time they had all been together.

He patted the back of his brother's head. "Let Mason here do the looking."

Dr Drexler frowned. "You just said we shouldn't climb it."

"Yeah, 'cause *we* would suck at it," Grayson Bane said. "Mason's built for this kind of thing, though. Literally. If he can't find a way in, then there isn't one. Besides, who knows what's in there? He can protect himself better than the rest of us can."

Protector Divak looked insulted. "Protecting us is *my* job."

"Sure." Grayson Bane smirked at her even as he tapped a few spots on his brother's back. Mason moved into a sitting position, crossing his legs in a way that made him seem very human. "When we're all on the ground together. Not when one of us is five hundred feet up in the air. That's around a hundred and fifty meters for you metric plebs," he added.

Protector Divak opened her mouth to say something else – probably something that would turn this argument into a genuine fight – then closed it again as both of Mason Bane's arms dropped off his body.

"Fascinating," Six said. Even Dr Lifhe stopped blinking, staring with awe and perhaps some horror at the sight. For a species that alternated at will between two and four legs, the prospect of losing two of them had to be disturbing.

"But how will he – oh!" Dr Drexler cut themself off as they all watched the arms crawl over to the wall. Additional digits extended from hidden compartments, their tiny hooks and grapplers searching for any spot big enough to serve as a grip. Once found, the limbs began to hoist themselves up the wall, occasionally collaborating and assisting as one got a better purchase than the other. It wasn't long before the elaborate contraptions were nothing but tiny black specks high above them before finally disappearing from Six's sight.

"That," Dr Drexler said, finally breaking the silence that had settled over them all, "is the coolest thing I've ever seen."

To Six's surprise, both of the Banes turned their heads in unison toward the doctor, Grayson with appreciation in his face, Mason with his usual blankness. It answered a question for Six. *It's more than Mason and his many parts up there. When these two want to connect themselves together, they can.*

He wondered what they were seeing up there right now. It had to be awe-inspiring; Caridian ships, after all, were designed for both function *and* form, and this one was one of the most impressive he'd ever seen.

Yes. It had to be an absolutely extraordinary experience for them.

CHAPTER NINE
Mason Bane

Mason was used to living with multiple voices inside his head – that was what happened when you linked your central mind to four different mini-brains. But it was a special kind of commotion whenever Grayson started speaking in here. Especially annoying, for the most part.

"Screw this bloody damn slick piece of – watch it!"

[It would be easier for us to climb if you were a little quieter.]

"Screw you, little brother. You try staying quiet when you're worrying your head off that the priceless tech you spent decades refining might fall hundreds of feet to the ground because of a random gust of wind. I'd be yelling my head off if it wouldn't make the rest of these assholes look at me funny."

Right-arm Mason reached a tendril up another few inches, searching for a divot in the surface that would provide sufficient grip to move on. [We're surprised they're not looking at you funny already.]

"Turned my helmet comm off. As long as I mutter, they won't notice shit. Don't head straight up that spire, are you mad?"

Right-arm Mason got lucky. A few more feet and they would be onto a flatter part on top of the ship, and able to move more quickly. [We'll move more easily along the base of them. We won't actually go up it except as a last resort. Although…] Left-arm Mason made it to the base of the spire and tapped it consideringly with his middle finger. [We think it's more than an exhaust port. It could really be a viable way into the ship.]

"Well, start with something less dangerous. There's got to be some other ingress up there, for refueling or removing waste or as a – Lefty, what the *hell* are you doing?"

[Lefty!]

Left-arm Mason, as he was wont to do, suddenly made the unilateral decision to climb that stack.

[Lefty, stop that! Get back here!]

Mason wasn't capable of blushing with embarrassment, which was good because he would have been red enough to match Sik-Tar's dim, distant sun's light right now otherwise. [He isn't listening to us.]

"Shit."

Left-arm Mason was, in fact, heading up the stack at a good rate of speed. There were ridges every foot or so that made getting up it much easier than climbing the surface of the ship had been, and there was no way Right-arm Mason was going to be able to catch up in time to pull his brother-in-arm back down to the safer section of the ship. [None of our transmissions are making it through to Lefty right now. We'll continue looking for a way in down here.]

"That bloody arm of yours better not get lost or crushed or damaged, or so help me..."

[You threaten because you care.]

Right-arm Mason crawled along the base of the stacks, searching for another entrance to the ship. Mason split his internal sight between his arms, following both of them at once.

Back when he was nine years old, shortly after the fire that had raged through the Martian slums and taken his limbs, Grayson had built the first version of Mason's new body. Freshly placed in his rough mechanical shell, with no therapies to help him along and trying to integrate a huge amount of new technology into his central nervous system, he'd gotten the worst headaches trying to maintain split images in his mind, bad to the point of needing to shut down to keep from having a seizure. Now the process was as simple as breathing – more simple, since breathing wasn't something he really did anymore. All the oxygen Mason needed was siphoned through gill-like structures along the sides of his "neck" and filtered into the broth that encased his brain. The limbs had their own, smaller versions of the gills to feed their own neural cores.

[Nothing so far from either of them.] Mason's minds wandered along with his bodies. [Do you think there's actual Xenium here? The kind we might be able to find and take back with us?]

"Maybe. Would be nice, wouldn't it? We'd be able to sell it for enough credits to set us up for life, anywhere you want to go."

[That would be nice.] A chance to let all of his brains rest for a while, to not be overworked for a job or forced into hibernation like they had been back at Bor-Turia. He'd fought it, Mason remembered. Fought it because he didn't like the idea of leaving his brother alone without his help. Grayson liked to think he didn't need help, but Mason knew better.

"It's not our first priority, but it's definitely a priority," his brother prattled on. "Wouldn't want to let a chance like this go to waste. You've got enough space in your core to stash, what, about ten pounds of the stuff?"

[About that, we think.]

"Reckon we could get a hell of a good deal for it on the black market. We could – don't you dare, you little shit!"

Left-arm Mason, far from being cowed by Grayson's shout, tapped around the edges of the top of the spire he had reached, then casually tipped himself over the edge and down it. Mason felt the surge of momentum rush through their brains, making his grounded body sway for a moment. [Turn on your light! Lights, Lefty, lights!]

Left-arm Mason finally remembered to turn his lights on. For a moment they showed nothing but smooth-sided metal, much cleaner than the dust-exposed surface he'd just climbed up. Then there was a *clang,* and all of a sudden the arm was in freefall.

"Get your extensions out! Grab onto something, you pillock, don't–"

Clang! The reverberations Left-arm Mason made as he hit the bottom of the spire were enough to numb all the Masons, graying out their collective vision for a moment.

"Oh, hell," Grayson muttered.

"Oh damn, is he OK?"

That was ... was that ... that was the other human, the ... Drexler, Dr Drexler. They must have noticed him acting off. He couldn't reassure them, so he left it to his brother and focused on Left-arm Mason.

[Up and at 'em, Lefty.] Two of Left-arm Mason's fingers twitched. [There we go, get those connections working again. Rough fall, huh, luv? But we're all right, we're all right now. We've got this. Good, now try the other ones. Very good!]

All of his fingers were functioning again. The extensions took a bit longer to reel in – one of them wouldn't retract at all, something inside of its servo motor was broken now, but it could have been a lot worse.

Mason looked around. His arm was in a vast chamber, so big that the little light he was equipped with couldn't illuminate the ceiling in any detail. What the hell was this place? [Activate your positioning system, Lefty. See if you can detect the rest of us, then start looking for a way out.]

Right-arm Mason was already on his way back to the main body – because *he* was an obedient body part who understood the importance of not gallivanting off on adventures whenever he wanted to.

"Don't even bother tryin' to teach that bastard arm a lesson, brat. Lefty's hopeless."

[None of us are hopeless, don't be rude.] Mason watched as Left-arm Mason's position alert finally lit up, a small constellation of dots representing his rogue body part flaring to life not a hundred feet away. [Good, we're close! Come toward us and try to find a way through. We know you can do this, Lefty.] His left arm brightened a bit at the praise, picking up his pace until he'd reached the exterior wall.

[Look for a control panel.] It probably wouldn't function, but it might be able to tell them other things. Left-arm Mason crawled along, extensions feeling the wall for any sign of another entrance or exit or–

[Door! That looks like a door!] A much smaller door than the massive one that had stymied them so far. [Perfect. Do you see any sort of handle? Anything that could help us open it?] There was definitely *something* up there.

Left-arm Mason climbed the wall until it reached what looked like a control panel next to the door. There was no power going to it, but there was a teardrop-shaped handle marked with bright yellow and gray lines in the *up* position. It seemed like it was specifically shaped for a Caridian claw.

[Good, Lefty, really good. Do you think you can pull it?] Mason watched as Left-arm Mason reshaped his hand into a clawlike shape, maximizing the force he'd be able to exert on it. Then he pressed his extenders hard into the wall just below the handle, braced, and pulled for all he was worth.

One arm, no matter how specialized, couldn't exert as much force as a complete body. Mason watched Lefty's battery levels diminish with concern as the arm pulled again and again. The handle seemed stuck. He'd have to direct himself to disengage soon, go try to find another door, or maybe send Right-arm Mason up and inside to join–

The handle moved. Not much, but enough to sense a corresponding chance in the door's seal. [That's it, Lefty! You're doing great!]

"Pull, you little shit, pull!"

[No need for insults when we're doing such a good job,] Mason chided his brother.

"Don't tell me how to speak to your arm! I programmed that son of a bitch, and he'd better–"

The handle dropped another inch, then another, finally settling into a smooth slide all the way down to the bottom of its arc. The door it was next to released its tight grip on the wall, ancient seals opening with a puff of dust and sand. Mason sensed the others in their party running over to where the fresh hole appeared in the surface in front of them, but didn't follow. He needed to be whole first. Right-arm Mason had already returned to him, rejoining the main body. Lefty, a little low on power but still feeling spunky, crawled out the door's gap, through the forest of crewmembers' feet obscuring his path back to Mason, and finally reconnected to their body with the metallic sigh of a job well done.

[We're so proud of you,] Mason told Lefty. All the other body parts agreed. [But you really ought to listen better next time.]

Lefty sent the equivalent of a virtual shrug. Mason would have laughed if he was capable of it.

"Get over here, Mason! You're gonna want to take a look inside."

[Yeah? Is it cool?] Mason asked, reconfiguring himself into a standing position and walking over to the door, which was pulled completely out of the way now. It was tall enough for a Caridian to walk through without having to bend, which meant that all of them, except Divak, could get through with ease.

"Yeah, mate. I'd say it's pretty goddamn cool."

CHAPTER TEN
Protector Divak

Beyond the dust, inside this vast structure, there was nothing but darkness. Not a sound existed other than the breathing of the rest of the crew, a noise that Divak would have preferred to go without hearing. Making sure these fools *kept* breathing was part of her job, though. As little as she liked being here, she would like shaming herself even less.

Divak stepped deeper into the cavernous opening around them, relying on both her power armor's readings and her own eyes, well suited to the dark, to illuminate things for her.

The acoustics of the place were strange, seemingly never-ending in some directions, close and dull in others. Her armor's sensors were able to pick out the dimensions of distant objects, their laser-guided readings precise, but they couldn't analyze them with any success.

Item not found in database. Because it was ancient Caridian, of course.

"We need light," she declared, and turned to Grayson. "Send your brother off to see if he can access some sort of internal power for this place. To walk around it as it is right now is to invite danger."

"Yeah, and him walkin' around in it by *himself* is inviting its *own* kind of danger," Grayson snapped. "To *him*."

"You didn't mind so much when you sent his arm off on its own."

"That was a fact-finding mission! And an arm is a lot easier to duplicate than the rest of his central nervous system, ya bint, and I'm not–" He paused and turned to look at his brother. "What, really? You sure?"

"Sure of what?" Dr Drexler asked.

"He thinks he might have seen something when he was falling from up there the first time – a switch that could get this place running," Grayson replied.

"If this ship is what I think it is," Ix-Nix-Six said, his voice reverent, "then there ought to be a series of such switches on the back wall. They are manual backups to ensure that operations can be shut down to prevent catastrophe in case the automatic systems fail."

"Catastrophe?" Dr Lifhe – the simpering piece of pond scum – whimpered from where he was half hiding behind Dr Drexler. "What… what kind of catastrophe?"

"What kind of ship do you think it is?" Dr Drexler asked, bright and obnoxious as ever.

"I'm sure it doesn't apply to our situation," Ix-Nix-Six said to the Centauran in what he probably meant to be soothing tones.

It was time to take control of this ridiculous situation.

"What *exactly* do you think is going on here?" Divak pressed, stepping closer to the Caridian as Mason Bane slunk off into the darkness, his brother's eyes following his every move. "Why do you seem to understand this place? I thought it was ancient! You said the distress signal has been going off for over a thousand years, and now all of a sudden you know what's going on here?" Her talons itched to bring the gun up to bear, but that would only alarm the rest of the simpletons.

Besides, she was quite sure she could kill the Caridian with her own hands if necessary.

"I have a thought, a thought only," Ix-Nix-Six assured her, either oblivious to the threat she posed him or dismissive of it. *How dare you dismiss me?* "I promise, if I'm right, I will tell you in–"

THOOM!

A brief flare of greenish light in the distance was followed almost immediately by a cascade of softer, whitish lights coming to life along the walls. They rose up from the ground like a waterfall in reverse, filling clear tubes that culminated in a single point of illumination at the very top of the space. It was incredibly bright, after the darkness Divak had become accustomed to, and she blinked furiously even as her helmet darkened, protecting her vision somewhat.

Well. Whatever that Martian cyborg had been up to, at least he'd found the–

"Mason!"

The cyborg flew through the air, blown back from whatever switch he'd flipped or panel he'd been poking at. He hit the ground headfirst and lay in an unmoving heap.

His brother took off running toward him, and the rest of the party followed suit.

Divak did not. Cleaning up after accidents wasn't her job. She was here to handle threats, not coddle human brains in jars. She looked around at what the lights had revealed, and found herself unexpectedly spellbound.

The chamber was immense. She had known it would be, judging from the outside of the monolithic ship, but seeing it laid out as it was – seeing the tall, sharp-edged machines that appeared to penetrate directly into the floor beneath them; seeing the rows and rows of neatly packaged containers extending into the distance as far as her unaided eyes could make out; seeing the ships to the left and along the back walls... wait... the ships...

Ships. There were ships here! Small ones, perhaps a third the size of the one Ix-Nix-Six had transported them all in, but the design was faintly reminiscent of it. Not nearly as sleek, but the materials, dusty as they were, seemed almost modern in design and flow. The ships themselves were oddly shaped – hexagonal boxes with oversized eternal thrusters and the most basic of visual amenities, but clearly something that was meant to be flown through space. They wouldn't do well in a planet with any sort of atmosphere, which Sik-Tar had thanks to the constant swirling moisture.

Purely exploratory vessels? Then why did they show up in such numbers – she counted three, four, more in a long line marching around the periphery of the room... and they appeared to be stacked along the walls as well, held in place with some sort of ratcheting system. Perhaps...

"... have to get it off him!" Grayson shouted loud enough to draw Divak's attention.

"We can't risk it! He'll be exposed to the atmosphere if we do!"

"So bloody what? It's breathable, isn't it?"

"There's no telling what kind of substance he could be exposed to if we–"

"His life support system's disconnected from his lungs," Grayson snarled at Dr Drexler, menacing them with some sort of tool ... what did they call those things ... wrenches? Screwdrivers? Something for nest guardians who didn't know how to wield a sword. "If we don't take his helmet off, he'll be exposed to *death* without air running over his skin, so sod you, but I'm not gonna let that happen to my brother on my watch." He reached down and undid the clasps at the top of Mason Bane's helmet, twisted it to release the seal, and then pulled it off over his head.

There was no subsequent gasp for air or similarly dramatic indicator that the cyborg was functioning again. That was something Divak liked about them, actually – they didn't embarrass themselves with protestations of pain or discomfort the way so many other, lesser types did. As Divak finally strolled over, she saw the cyborg slowly open his closed eyes. His pupils were blown wide, but it didn't take long for them to normalize. His skin, which had gone a bit gray, regained its boring beige tinge. Then all at once, every limb on his body convulsed, like his brain was running a systems check, making sure the rest of him was still functioning.

"He says he's all right," Grayson reported after a moment,

his face losing some of its stress lines. "He feels fine. No permanent damage from the fall, although that was a helluva kick from the batteries that run this place coming back online."

"I am sorry for that," Ix-Nix-Six said, yet again apologizing for things that were out of his control. What a useless habit. "I believe this structure uses nuclear energy. It makes sense that it would still be functional, even after so long untended, but clearly the conduits he touched were not in their best condition."

"Don't blame you for it," Grayson said, pulling his brother into a sitting position. "This asshole shoulda taken more care." As soon as he saw that Mason was stable, he reached up to his own helmet and, in a few short seconds, had it off and on the ground next to him.

The human scientist squawked like a molting swamp owl. "No! Don't take your helmet off too! There could be all sorts of issues with silica and radiation and infectious agents and–"

"Eh, stuff it," Grayson snapped. "I'm not gonna let you make my brother into your 'control variable' or whatever the hell you eggheads like to call it. You scanned the place and didn't find anything livin', right? And the silica's all outside, where the water's tampin' it down, and none of us knew this place was nuclear powered before Six told us that because it's shielded so bloody well, so *stop* frettin', and relax, would you?"

There was a moment of silence, and then: "Your logic seems very sound," Six said, something oddly satisfied in his voice. He then took off his own helmet.

"No!"

Divak didn't need to be told again. She retracted the face shield for her power armor and breathed in deep, tasting the old, musty air. It smelled like ozone, and emptiness, and… something else. Something new, a scent she'd never smelled before. It was sharp at the edge of her senses, almost like… like someone had captured lightning and held it nearby. What was that? She moved closer to the source of it.

"I think the chances of harm coming to us from in here are very low," the Centauran told his colleague. Divak rolled her eyes – if even a coward like that was willing to risk going without a helmet, then surely they were safe. "We did a very thorough scan of the planet before disembarking, after all."

"What if we missed something?" Dr Drexler insisted. "What if we couldn't detect it because we didn't know how to scan for it? Take yours off if you want, but I'm leaving mine on until I make sure none of you come down with strange tumors or fevers or respiratory distress."

Dr Lifhe bowed his head in acknowledgment of his superior's will and left his own helmet on.

"Think it's clear what they were doing here," Grayson called out from where he'd ambled over to the closest wall, where a series of those black, fifty-meter-high machines was set up. Each of them had a hole in the front of it, where debris – rocks, perhaps, what else could you get on this boring planet?– could go. Those led onto conveyor belts that most likely led to a mill or a furnace of some kind – the first step in what was probably a lengthy smelting process, given the size of these machines and the fact that they stretched from close to the entrance all the way to the back wall.

"This is definitely a mining setup," Grayson went on as he pointed up at distant holes in the ceiling, where some of the machines were connected via long, slender metal pipes. "An' those probably lead out to some of the spires we saw outside. Don't know what they were originally, but they'd been converted to smokestacks."

"Mining." Dr Drexler, their tiff over the helmets already forgotten, moved over to the nearest machine with a gleaming eye. "Mining for what, I wonder. The Xenium in the atmosphere was in such trace amounts…"

Divak didn't really care what they were mining for; she was more interested in the ships. It might be ancient Caridian technology, but there was almost certainly a modern analogue to it, and everything she could glean from her surroundings was information her people could use against the Glorious Hegemony someday. That they would eventually go to war, she didn't doubt, and if she was still around by then, then by tooth and tail, she was going to be on the winning side.

The ships were all sectioned off neatly except for the one at the very end, closest to the massive door they hadn't opened. This one had been shifted slightly, almost like it had been *pushed*. Even as small as it was, it still had to weigh several tons. That was more than she could shift even in her power armor. What had pushed it? Another vehicle of some kind?

There appeared to be something in the space between it and the ship beside it… Divak crouched down to take a look.

Oh. *Interesting.* "We have bodies," she announced.

That got everybody's attention. Divak backed out of the way to make room for Dr Drexler and Ix-Nix-Six, who were the first to reach her.

"Those are… remains, certainly," Dr Drexler said after a moment. "Very ossified. No sign of clothing or armor, but after so long it's not impossible that they deteriorated, even out of the weather. Two individuals, I think."

"Yes," Ix-Nix-Six confirmed. "There are two skull carapaces. Two of my people died here many, many years ago." He tilted his head for a moment, the light refracting in a way that made his eyes gleam extra bright. "I believe I know what this place is now."

"Great," Grayson said as he joined them, Mason and Dr Lifhe trailing after him. "Want to share with the rest of us?'

"Indeed. This is a legendary ship called *Nexeri* that was lost one thousand, three hundred and fifty-eight of your Coalition years ago to a malfunction during wormhole travel."

Dr Drexler held up a hand. "Wait. Your people could travel by wormholes back then?"

"No," the Caridian said, shaking his head. "We could not. Not with any reliability – the technology was in its infancy. This ship was a grand fool's errand, the result of one hive's desires for autonomy. They planned to transport themselves into the middle of what has become Coalition space – well before most of the species living there achieved space travel. Then they would set up mining colonies on various planets and pave the way for the Glorious Hegemony's eventual arrival. Instead… the wormhole sent them here."

Ix-Nix-Six looked around. "I assume that their landing on this planet was the result of a crash. However, it's clear they tried to carry out their mission."

"And your people thought they had simply been destroyed?" Dr Lifhe asked.

"Indeed. That is the most likely outcome of wormhole malfunctions, especially back before we had developed any safeguards to keep the space-time continuum from ripping us to shreds, but there was always the barest chance that they had survived somehow. And now we know that they did, at least for a time." He seemed excessively pleased by the discovery.

"Great." Dr Lifhe didn't sound anywhere near as happy. "Now we have to worry about what *did* kill them. Wonderful. I wish I could go back to my bunk," he said with a sigh.

Dr Drexler patted him on the front shoulder. "Leave worrying about their deaths to me. You try to figure out what they were mining."

"What they died of is irrelevant."

Everyone turned to look at Divak with varying degrees of disbelief. "It *is*," she insisted. "Such a long period of time has passed that it is impossible that whatever killed them will be a bother to us."

"Killed them?" Ix-Nix-Six's antennae perked up a bit. "What makes you sure that they were killed, rather than simply dying on their own?"

Divak scoffed. Did he think her a fool? "Look at where they are, tucked between two of these ships like they were trying to hide… or perhaps to burrow, knowing your insect roots," she added snidely. "I cannot be sure, but either way, this is neither a case of accidental death, nor is it a proper burial. Unless Caridians are even stranger than I've imagined."

"We are quite strange at times," Ix-Nix-Six said, not taking offense. Curse him. Divak was raring for an argument. "But not so strange we wouldn't inter our people properly." He looked around the massive room. "In fact… I wonder where we *did* inter them. A ship of this size, with this many pods – the crew must have numbered well over a hundred. If they did not all die at once, then the ones who lived the longest would have made a point of burying their comrades."

"Maybe they did so in another room, or underground," Dr Drexler suggested. "We can look as we explore the rest of the ship."

Grayson Bane had already moved on from the corpses, heading back to the refineries. "What were they mining?" he asked, looking the equipment over before moving on to the stacks and stacks of crates to the left of them, piled up in the space between the machines and the little pod ships. "What was so good about bein' here that they figured they might as well stay and mine instead of tryin' to get out of here with their ships? I mean, look around." He gestured vaguely toward the massive door that would open to the outside. "Not much here really, right? Pretty dull place, all things considered. Their little ships might not have been able to go beyond impulse, but they could get to a better system with a few years of steady travel. So why not make the trek there?"

"Xenium," whispered Dr Drexler. "It's got to be…" They unslung the particle detector from over their shoulder and turned it on, typed in a quick password to modify its operations, then pointed it around the room. "Ha. A*ha*!" Their smile was triumphant. "The concentration of Xenium particles in this room is more than a hundred times what it was outside!" They stepped toward the refineries, then the crates. "The concentration is particularly high inside there. Mason, would you mind opening one up?"

Grayson Bane muttered something, and a moment later Mason plodded forward, still on two feet, still looking at nothing in particular. For all that he moved slower than a tortol, though, he was able to rip through the outer covering of the crate with no hint of strain whatsoever. Divak respected that strength – reluctantly, but she did respect it. She would have to kill him first, if it came down to such a thing.

Within the crates were a set of eight large metal bottles, around one meter high and half a meter wide. Divak sniffed, flaring her nostrils – the strange scent she'd caught a hint of when they first entered was stronger now.

"Those," Dr Drexler said rapturously, their eyes wide and their mouth stretched in a smile so broad that if they had been Thassian, Divak would have considered it an offer to duel. The device in their hands was practically buzzing, working overtime to share whatever it was in the process of discovering. Despite herself, Divak drew closer to Dr Drexler. Their enthusiasm was catching. "Those are full of Xenium."

"What? Nah," Grayson Bane said, leaning in and pushing

one a little. There was a distinct sloshing sound from inside. "Can't be Xenium, then, that's a rock." He glanced at Dr Drexler. "Unless you're holdin' out on us, doc?"

"Not holding out, just not prepared for this!" The two Coalition scientists exchanged excited glances before Dr Drexler continued, "I've never heard of Xenium like this before, but it seems clear to me that the Caridians who landed here located the Xenium, then managed to refine it into a liquid state. This is the purest form of Xenium imaginable! One bottle of that could probably power the jump drive for a ship like ours for dozens of journeys within Coalition space." Their eyes were as bright as stars, and burned almost as intensely.

Oh, really?

Perhaps Divak was going to get more out of this trip to Sik-Tar than she'd originally planned.

CHAPTER ELEVEN
Dizzie Drexler

For all that it was tempting to break open one of those tall metal bottles and get a closer read on the Xenium within it, Dizzie wasn't entirely sure what exposing liquid Xenium directly to the air would do to the mineral… or to the air and everyone standing in it, for that matter. It was a powerful but also highly combustible compound, and they didn't want to tempt fate, especially without any precautionary measures. So, despite their desires, Dizzie left the bottles alone.

Just for now, though. Later, they had every intention of cracking one of these open – all safety protocols followed, of course – and getting a firsthand look at the mineral they'd dedicated their entire career to, in an entirely novel form. Just the thought of it was enough to make their head spin.

To safely open one of these bottles up, they'd need the right environment. When Six suggested all of them split up to examine the *Nexeri,* Dizzie was the first to agree. It was risky, exploring a new place with less backup, but also it would give Dizzie a chance to look for what they were really interested in without having to deal with Grayson's bitching or Divak's irritated huffs – the labs. There *had* to be labs on a ship this big, didn't there?

Corinus volunteered to come along with Dizzie, which they appreciated. Six walked with them for a way as well, which Dizzie knew that Corinus *didn't* appreciate, but wasn't going to speak up against.

"Does it distress you?" they asked as they left behind the immense hangar-slash-storage space-slash-refinery, entering a narrow hallway located in the far north end of it that had a series of tall oval doors on each side, all spaced about six meters apart. Meeting rooms? Crew quarters? Kitchens?

"Does what distress me?" Six asked as they peeked into one of them. Hmm, lots of chairs and tables – perhaps a mess hall.

"Finding out the fate of your legendary ship. Discovering that they all… well, died."

"Not at all," Six said with equanimity. "Everything dies eventually. It's the only constant in the universe, and the most comforting one as well."

"Comforting how?" Corinus asked as they all glanced inside the next door. This room was small, and there were individual stalls and holes in the ground and – ah, toilets. This was a bathroom. They let it be and moved on.

"Because it means that no matter what one's life amounts to, whether it is full of joy or full of sorrows, in the end everyone you've ever loved or quarreled with will be exactly like you. Entropy is an equalizing force, and I appreciate equality. Self-direction is largely frowned upon among Caridians," he added, tracing his clawed fingers against the wall. There was some sort of imprint there, a slight change in texture, but Dizzie couldn't make out enough of it to be sure of the shape, much less know if it said anything. "That said, I've always found value in making my own path. That impulse is one of the things I admire most about humans.

"There are many things to admire about Centaurans, too," he added for Corinus's benefit. "Your homogeneity and commitment to the greatest good for your people before all else is very admirable." Corinus just blinked at him.

The next room was full of what looked like dusty, archaic palm fronds jutting down from the ceiling and curling to the floor. Dizzie had no idea what they were, but Six seemed instantly charmed. "A library! Oh, how delightful!"

"This is a library?" Dizzie and Corinus exchanged a look. "Caridians don't believe in digital media?" Dizzie asked.

"Reading for us is best experienced as a tactile thing," Six said, wandering over to one of the twisted fronds and picking it up in his claws. "It is as much about the feel of the words as it is about apprehension of their intent. Our stories are meant to be read from bottom to top, with new lessons gleaned along the way in accordance with the individual's age and height. These ones at the bottom would be appropriate for our youngest nymphs."

"Oh." That was… kind of cool, actually. And a perfect place to ditch Six in search of the laboratories. "Well, I think Dr Lifhe and I are going to keep exploring, but have fun here. Remember to keep your helmet close," they added, still supremely irritated that they and Corinus were the only ones still wearing them. "So you can hear the comm if anyone needs to get in contact with you."

"Absolutely. Enjoy your discoveries, Dr Drexler."

"Oh, I will." They resumed walking down the hallway, and once they were out of earshot Corinus said, "He's so creepy."

"Corinus."

"He is! He never gets upset about anything, that's weird! Wouldn't you be upset if you'd found the skeletal remains of humans from centuries ago just shuffled off to the side like that? Wouldn't it make you curious? But not him." Corinus inhaled sharply, his equivalent of a derisive sniff. "He doesn't have that kind of heart."

"I think you might be projecting a little," Dizzie said, looking into another room. This one went on for a long way, and had a slender center hallway and triple rows of familiarly narrow, oblong bunks set into the walls on either side. Living quarters, such as they were. Caridians certainly didn't value privacy the way that humans did.

"I'm not, though! It's clear he doesn't feel things the way *we* do. I don't know that he feels them at all."

"You don't think you're being unduly influenced by the fact that you can't read his mind?" Dizzie asked. There was just one door left in this hallway. "After all, I know you're used to – aha!"

"Aha what? Oh, it's a laboratory?" Corinus said, answering his own question by sensing Dizzie's emotions as he, too, stopped in the door.

"I think so," Dizzie said. It, like all the other rooms, was lit with ambient, yellowish light from the waterfall walls. There were three long tables making a U shape against one wall, covered with the remnants of what seemed to be experiments in situ – devices clearly meant for precise measurement, for holding samples, for… honestly, it looked rather reminiscent of their lab back on the station, minus the computer interfaces. Instead, there were more of the frond-like data storage devices drooping down over the tables from the ceiling, much skinnier than the ones in the library had been. *Fascinating.*

They stepped inside, hand automatically going to the left of the doorframe to adjust the controls for the lights, which was ridiculous – this wasn't their lab. It wasn't like there was going to be any sort of correlation, and yet…

The room went from low-level lighting on the floor to shockingly bright in an instant, darkening Dizzie's faceplate for a moment. Dizzie's questing fingers had come into direct contact with a control panel of some kind. There was also a low hum in the room, and a quick look over in the near corner by the door revealed a blocky piece of machinery that, judging from the way it pulsed with energy, was probably a battery of some kind. Separate power for the lab, maybe? "Oh cool, that's convenient," they said with a grin, then looked down at Corinus. "Want to check out the testing chamber?"

"How do you know it's a testing chamber?" Corinus asked as he obediently followed Dizzie over to the far wall, where a recessed, pen-like area was set just off from the main laboratory.

"What else could it be?" they asked. "It's clearly not used

for storage – they wouldn't have left access to it open like this if it was. I doubt these ancient Caridians set spaces aside just for convenient naps, either. Look along the edges of the wall, here." They ran their fingers along the entrance to the chamber. "See the bumps? These could be part of an energy projector, to put up some kind of force field between the scientists out here, and whatever the experiment they'd designed was doing in there."

"It doesn't seem very secure for the type of experiment I imagine they were doing," Corinus ventured, sticking his head through the hole to look more closely at the chamber. "With Xenium, one would think it was about analyzing the energy content of the crystals – or liquid, in this case."

"Maybe they found other things to do experiments on while they were here." Dizzie started to get excited. "Maybe," they said, lowering their voice and leaning in toward Corinus, "they found *mold* here."

Corinus turned a startled look to her, his eyelids fluttering wildly. "Don't even say it!" he hissed, looking around like a mold-infested Xeno was going to jump out at him from behind a corner any second. "That's not funny!"

"It's something we have to consider! Especially given the lack of bodies we've found so far." Dizzie tapped their helmet. "No one has reported anything like a graveyard or corpse interment so far in any of the other sections of the ship. Six didn't say anything about Caridians following cremation or liquification practices. Maybe–"

"No!" Corinus shook his head hard, turned around and stalked over to the entrance to the lab. He stopped there, haunches quivering as though he was barely restraining himself from running out of here, away from the person who was causing him so much pain.

Dizzie felt a little guilty despite knowing that they were right about this. Honestly, despite their insistence on keeping their helmet on, the likelihood of any biological contaminant being the cause of death here, and as a potential killer for them and the rest of the expedition, was incredibly low. Everything had a finite lifespan – hadn't Six just mused about the beauty of death a little while ago? Everything died, and in an inhospitable climate like this place had, they died faster than normal.

"I'm sorry," Dizzie said, projecting the emotion as genuinely as possible with their thoughts. "It's probably not mold. I just want to make sure we're being thorough."

"I know." He wasn't coming back over, though. Clearly, he was still miffed by their lack of concern over his anxieties. Corinus didn't get into moods like this often, but when he did it could take a while to get back into his good graces.

"How about this?" Dizzie asked with a coaxing smile. "We go find Six and get him to help us figure out how to decipher things in here. If we can get access to a computer, maybe get the power up and running to the machinery in this room, he can show us some of the basics of how to work this equipment. Maybe he's got a translation device we can use, too. It would be cool to power up some of this stuff, wouldn't it?"

Corinus looked back over his sloping shoulder. "It would," he agreed, softening the way Dizzie had been hoping for. Science for the sake of science was all very well and good to Corinus, but at his heart he was an engineering nerd. He'd never told his mentor that – probably he hadn't had to; Dizzie was willing to bet that Dr Yoche knew. But while his personal preferences wouldn't get him out of doing what needed to be done for the Centauran species on the whole, Dizzie had long since learned that the easiest way to get Corinus excited about something was to point out its technicalities.

"Maybe the type of containment field itself will give us details about the experiments they performed in it," Dizzie went on, sidling over to their friend and shutting off the light as they led the way back down the hall. "You'd do things very differently for biological experiments than you would for concussive ones, I'm betting."

"I wonder what the environmental controls are like for the lab," Corinus said, finally getting into the spirit of things. "Whether the testing area has its own separate ventilation system. Maybe they even hooked it up to the refineries, to add an additional element of cleansing to their byproducts rather than simply venting them out into the atmosphere or burying them underground."

"Good point, we'll try to find out. In fact…" It had been a while since they'd all separated. "Let's call a meeting, huh? Get everyone together and see what they've all come up with."

Dizzie did so, and fifteen minutes later the group came back together in the same spot where they'd parted. Divak and Mason both looked slightly dusty, and Six looked like he was in some sort of Caridian rapture state, if the wavering of his antennae was any indicator. They also all looked significantly cooler than Dizzie was feeling right now, thanks to chucking all their helmets back in the main bay.

Dizzie reported their findings, and it didn't take more than the vaguest of suggestions for Six to agree to come back with them and try to figure out how to get the lab into a working, if basic, state once more. Divak, who had been examining the hallway that was this one's mirror on the far side of the main bay, reported finding nothing more intriguing than another dormitory, a mess hall, what might have been a machine shop – her description was pretty lacking – but not the one thing *she* was most interested in finding, which was an armory. Even the small ships along the walls carried no weapons.

"Which is foolish, and also atypical for Caridians," she said with a suspicious look at Six. "Your people are not pacifists. They arm their ships. Even your own small ship has a weapons station."

"That's true," Six said, "but remember, this ship was designed in the spirit of scientific exploration. It was being sent to a part of the universe where it was unlikely to face any serious threat from an indigenous population. I have no doubt that many of the Caridians on board were armed, and that they were prepared to manufacture more weapons at will, but I'm not surprised that you haven't found a cache of them. Once they began their mining operation here, I believe the *Nexeri* was reconfigured to make that its primary function, and all lesser concerns were dismissed in favor of supporting this new goal."

"Makes sense," Grayson said. "We managed to send Lefty a ways down into one of the refineries in here – if these people were mining Xenium, they were going *deep.* Got lots of it in storage, tons of the stuff, but it had to be costing a premium in labor and time to get it out of the ground."

"They must have been running all kinds of tests on it, too," Dizzie muttered. "We found a lab," they clarified when Grayson and Divak gave them a strange look. "I think with Six's help, we could get it running well enough to figure out some of what the last inhabitants here were doing with it. Nobody knows much about Xenium, myself included, and nobody *at all* knows anything about liquid Xenium. We don't have a measure of how much energy is released when it's activated, we don't know its volatility, we have no clue of its–"

"Eh, easy enough to find out." Grayson grinned. "Let's set some on fire and see what it does."

"That's a terrible idea!" Corinus objected immediately. "You could blow us all up!"

"It's a rash idea, but maybe not the worst one," Dizzie said. Corinus looked like he'd just been stabbed in the first of his two hearts. "I'm just saying, until we get a read on their experiments, we won't know much about Xenium other than what we find out for ourselves," they went on, setting a hand on Corinus's shoulder. "I actually think it might be worthwhile to do a small ballistics test to see how reactive this stuff is. From the little I've read before, solid-state Xenium appears to be inert and safe to handle as long as you're wearing a radiation monitor." *Except for the mold problem, but that was more of a Xeno issue,* they added silently.

"That's what I like to hear!" Grayson grinned broadly, his

wide, flat teeth looking too big to be contained by his thin lips. "Mason can go in for a sample, we can set it up outside somewhere, attach a little popper nearby or something, and–"

"I will shoot it," Divak announced.

"You'll shoot it? Something so far away you might not even be able to see it in all this mist?" Grayson challenged her. Divak visibly bristled and leaned in closer to him – not just leaned, *loomed*.

"I could shoot the hairs off your ugly head from over a kilometer away and leave your pitiful brain untouched," she hissed. "You procure it, I will shoot it, the rest of you will take measurements and samples and whatever else it is useless, soft creatures like you do."

"Well." Six, when he spoke, sounded almost the same as he usually did. *Almost.* There was an undercurrent of excitement there that not even his natural imperturbability could hide. Dizzie noticed Corinus's eyes widening slightly. Was he finally getting a read on their least readable member? "This sounds like a lovely plan. By all means, let's blow something up."

They decided to start with a very small amount of liquid Xenium – a single milliliter of it, to be precise. Divak scoffed, and Grayson looked disappointed, but Dizzie insisted that they needed to prioritize their safety over the fun of a big boom. "Besides," they added to Divak, "eagle eye or no, it's got to be big enough for you to hit from a kilometer away."

"It could be half the size of your little test tube and I would still hit it," Divak snapped. "And I do not have *eagle* eyes. My eyes are as sharp as the fiercest of predators, not some ancient Earth dog breed that sniffed out overgrown rats."

"No, that's beagles, not–" Oh, whatever.

Getting the Xenium from a storage bottle into a test tube had been the first trial, solved when Mason carted one of the large, incredibly heavy containers out onto the plain, then came back and used his arms at a distance to make the transfer into two different shatterproof tubes safely – one for the test, and one in case something happened to the first one. Then he'd wedged a test tube between two distant rocks, carefully hoisted the larger container of Xenium onto his back again, and returned, giving the spare tube over to his brother before anyone could make a fuss about it.

Dizzie and Corinus both had their multitools out, switched over from particle detection to energy measurement. It wasn't going to be a perfect calculation, given everything they still didn't know about liquid Xenium, but it would give them a starting point.

The problems didn't start until Divak took her first shot. With all the rest of them standing behind her, their backs pressed to the ship while she stood a few meters ahead, she swung her rifle up to her shoulder, aimed, and fired in under five seconds. It was a masterful display of control, over her weaponry and her own reflexes.

Or it would have been, if she'd hit the test tube.

She didn't. Or at least, it didn't provoke the explosion that every one of them was expecting.

"Ha!" Grayson was the first one to say something, and he chose probably the worst thing to say. "So much for your sharpshooting skills, eh? You sure you don't need to move a bit closer, lass? Maybe put a big neon sign over it with an arrow that points right to it?"

"Shut your mouth," Divak snapped. "I neglected to appropriately account for the wind, that's all." She raised her rifle again, sighted more carefully, and fired off another shot.

Again… nothing.

Grayson snorted. "Forget an arrow, you need a laser targeting system."

Divak whirled around to glare at him. "That one should have hit! It must have ricocheted off one of the rocks the tube is being held in."

"Right, 'cause those rocks can definitely stand up to the ammunition you're packing." Grayson shook his head. "Admit it, you can't do it. Either move closer or – *herkk*!"

Before any of them could react, Divak had closed the distance between them and wrapped her hand around his throat, exposed since he wasn't wearing his helmet. "I would rather move closer to you," Divak snarled, ignoring everyone else's shouts, "and remove you like the pathetic little worm that you–"

Divak suddenly dropped Grayson. She had to – each joint of her power armor had just been rapidly infiltrated by Mason Bane's extensors. They projected from every limb and latched onto Divak's spine, bending her backward until her armor creaked with warning. In under two seconds, Mason had her off the ground, in his octopus-like grip, completely immobile. Even her mouth was silenced, an extensor shoved so far down her throat Dizzie could see the bulge of it in the side of her neck. Only her eyes were still free to move, and they darted this way and that, ruby-red and getting redder by the second in the darkening gray pallor of her face.

"Let her go!" Dizzie shouted. Mason didn't react. Dizzie turned to his brother. "Grayson, get him to let her go before he kills her."

He didn't seem very concerned. "Weren't she goin' to kill me?" he asked, staring at the scene with satisfaction. "Some protector she is. Looks like she's getting a taste of her own medicine, eh?"

"Grayson!" Desperately, Dizzie looked over at Corinus. "Can you stop Mason with your telepathy?" He'd never done it before as far as Dizzie knew, but they also knew that in desperate times, Centauran telepathy was good for a lot more than reading minds.

"We're not allowed to use it that way with other species!" Corinus protested with a shrill voice. "I can't – I just, it would be wrong, I *can't–*"

Corinus's ethical dilemma was forestalled by Six, who stepped forward to look squarely at Grayson. "Release her, or your contract with me will be voided, and I will return you to the authorities at the Bor-Turia Penal Colony the moment we return to the center of Coalition space," Six said, his voice as calm and composed as ever.

A second later, Mason's extensors retracted, and he dropped Divak on the ground. The Thassian lay there for a long moment, catching her breath, before she surged to her feet and drew her chainsword off the back of her power armor. "I'll destroy you," she screamed, her voice rough and garbled from its recent invasion. "I'll kill both of you and hang your heads from my belt!"

Six stepped forward. "Do so, and I will inform Leader Pavul that you acted without honor and control in your time with me, and that you should be demoted back to trooper."

Divak hissed at him. "You wouldn't dare!"

"You have no idea what I would dare, I think," Six said, cocking his head slightly to the side. His antennae were perfectly still. "It is best that you don't find out. Now. Fulfill your task and shoot the Xenium so that we might learn something about its volatility, or keep showing us evidence of your *own* volatility and ruin your future. It's entirely your choice."

Dizzie held their breath as Divak actually seemed to think these options over. It took ten full seconds for her to straighten up and put her blades away.

"Very well." She sounded back in control of herself, for whatever that was worth. "You are the leader of this expedition, and I will obey your judgment." Her discontent with that judgment was obvious, but when she bent down to grab her rifle, she didn't spare either of the Banes a single glance. Divak turned back to the distant target, shouldered her rifle, took a long, slow moment to center herself, and then–

BOOM! The sound of the explosion was bad enough, but Dizzie had just enough time to see the backdraft from it come at them, accompanied by a literal wall of displaced water, before it hit them. They put their hands up over their face instinctively, even though their helmet was protecting their head, and waited for the impacts from the localized storm to die down before they opened their eyes again.

Everyone else – except for Corinus and Mason – was coughing, retching up dirty water and spitting it out onto the ground. Rocky fragments dislodged by the explosion littered the ground all around them – they were lucky no one's suit had been penetrated. It had to be bad enough to have a bunch of wet gravel smack you in the face like that.

Dizzie and Corinus shared a rightfully smug expression before they turned their attention back to their readings. "Well," Dizzie said brightly, "judging by what I was able to detect with the energy readout, the joules released by that milliliter sample of Xenium come out to about the equivalent of a kiloton thermobaric bomb. Pretty impressive, if I do say so myself."

"Holy Mount Mons," Grayson said between coughs. "Tell me we're done with testing this stuff, because I ain't in this to get my head blown off."

"I don't think we need any more ballistic tests," Dizzie assured him. "Figuring out how to take it from its current form and use it as fuel will take a lot more work – actually, Six."

They turned and looked at the Caridian, who had just finished wiping down – ugh, wiping down his *eyeballs* with the fuzzy ends of his own antennae. How did that not hurt? Did his eyes not have pain receptors? "Maybe you can make that your research priority? I know you can't let us look at the *Telexa*'s inner workings, but maybe you can do some comparisons between your engine and what they'd built here and see if they'd already modified these ships to use Xenium as fuel."

"Certainly," Six replied. "Once we get you and Dr Lifhe well situated in your lab, of course."

Aw, how nice of him to remember that. "Of course," Dizzie agreed. They were excited at the prospect of really getting down to work on the mystery that was Xenium. The discoveries on the verge of being made! This was following in Dr Rigby's footsteps in the purest way possible.

Well, except for the Xeno problems Dr Rigby had had to deal with, but given the volatility of this climate, it seemed less and less likely that mold would be a problem here. Dizzie was both relieved and a little disappointed by that. After all, when would a chance like this ever come around again?

CHAPTER TWELVE
Corinus Lifhe

The moment the fight between Grayson and Divak broke out, Corinus got a headache. It wasn't merely the fact that the Martian and Thassian were thinking vile thoughts and having vile feelings toward each other – even among Centaurans, there were rivalries that sometimes erupted into violence. Corinus understood that, had dealt with that in his youth, just like all of them learned how to. It was more the fact that these thoughts were coming from two *separate* species, all while Corinus was trying to deal with the stubborn blank spot that was Six living rent-free in his mind, along with surges of near euphoria from Dizzie that should have buoyed him up, but instead made him feel like he'd eaten something that disagreed with him.

It was too much. It was just too much, and he couldn't handle it anymore, but he couldn't turn it off either. All his usual tricks for filtering out others' thoughts and feelings weren't working right now. Mason Bane's five bickering brains, all of them very active now whereas on the ship they'd been largely passive, didn't help. Four of those minds had the vocabularies of precocious human toddlers, but that just made them more annoying.

Corinus waited until Dizzie and Six were ensconced in the far corner of the lab trying to get power to the tables that held the equipment before reaching into the bag at his waist and pulling out the drug that would turn off his telepathy for a while. Now, to inject it right into his third eye and–

Oh, wait. He'd have to take off his helmet for that.

What does it matter? Almost everyone else in the expedition has done the same. You can put it right back on. You'll be fine. You don't want to wait until you get back to the other ship for this, do you? You'll be useless for the rest of the day.

With a sigh, Corinus unsnapped his helmet and gently set it aside. Then he reached up and, very carefully, inserted the needle into his skin and pressed the micro-syringe to the soft, painful pulse-point of his third eye. Within seconds, it was like a cloud had been pulled across his mind's vision, blocking his view of everyone else's too-bright, repugnant thoughts.

The relief it gave him was so visceral he slumped down onto the floor, his back legs collapsing completely and his front only barely holding his head and torso upright. He hoped Dizzie and Six were too busy to come looking for him now. For the first time in their partnership, he hoped that Dizzie had forgotten about him, just for a while.

The blankness stayed with him through the rest of their work that day, making the setup of the lab into a slightly clumsy process. Dizzie and Corinus had only brought the barest bones of their own equipment along with them from the ship on this initial foray, but what they had they found places for, as well as planning where the rest of their equipment would go. In the end, as tempted as Dizzie was to further investigate the ancient Caridian tech that had been left here, they'd come to the conclusion that it didn't make sense to spend time on it when they already had what they needed to do most of the experiments they could think of.

The only thing they got to work conclusively that had already been here, other than the lights, was the energy field in front of the testing chamber. Six had managed it somehow, and shown them how it could be cycled through different settings to block concussive force, radioactivity, light, specific particulate matter – definitely useful if they were studying a fungus or a … or a …

There's no mold here. There were a few bodies, and plenty of mysteries surrounding where the *rest* of the bodies had to be, but there was no mold. And with his telepathy spread wide and not dampened by the drug, Corinus would be the first one to know if something risky went down. He would be able to get to safety, if it came down to it. Keeping himself safe was his first, and most important, duty to his people.

Don't forget Dizzie. He didn't think it was possible for him to forget Dizzie, but he knew the importance of prioritization as well as any Centauran. He and his own kind always had to come first. Once their interests were secured, then he could worry about people who were unconnected to the wellbeing of his species.

Corinus tried not to dwell on how Dizzie would feel if they knew he considered them disposable. The practice didn't go both ways – Dizzie would risk death to save him.

He knew that like he knew the shape of their thoughts, the gentle push of their mind. He knew that what they felt for him wasn't reciprocal. He wished it was, though, for his own sake more than theirs. He knew he had to stand firm, like Dr Yoche said, but he didn't like the way the inequality made him feel like less, instead of more.

The whole point of the injection was to avoid being tormented with thoughts! Stop moping and get back to work.

Only there was little work left to be done on site. It was getting late, the distant red sun slowly wending its way toward Sik-Tar's rocky horizon. The mist had finally cleared, and the brilliant brightness of the sunset reminded Corinus of the light shows he used to go see with his rearers when he was very small – so vast to such a little person back then, it had terrified more than tantalized him. This was also vast, and even more terrifying.

Finally, it was time to head back to the ship for the night. Everyone was exhausted, but a lot of good work had been done. The Bane brothers had mapped out the ship's ventilation system, sending one of Mason's arms in through the ducts above the mining machines and along over a kilometer's worth of piping. The batteries powering the ship were set into the walls and fed by geological reactions churning deep below the surface of the planet, the same reactions that made the ocean so inhospitable. Now that those batteries had been turned back on, there was little fear of the lights shorting out any time soon.

Divak had looked around one more time and, to her great disgust, failed to discover any hidden caches of weapons or an interment area for bodies. The only thing of note she mentioned was, while sitting outside at the base of one of the stacks – which she'd freeclimbed up to like a fool, did none of these people have any survival instincts? – she'd noticed that the deep gouges in the landscape around the monolith were surprisingly regular. "It looks like they were cut there deliberately," she said.

"Perhaps it has something to do with the mining operation," Six suggested, moving without any suggestion of exertion despite the steepness of the last hill they had to climb before getting back to his ship. "Boreholes or spots for more equipment to dig down or something."

"I'm not so sure," Dizzie said, panting a little inside their EVA suit. Corinus leaned in and offered them a shoulder to hold onto for stability, and they smiled gratefully at him. "Initial scans show no signs of Xenium on the surface of the planet except what's already been mined and the particulate matter in the air, and no indications of more for half a kilometer down. I'll break out the ground-penetrating radar tomorrow; that should get us a read as far as two kilometers underground. Still, I'm thinking the Xenium might be even farther down than that. The gouges Divak shared footage of don't look conducive to reaching that kind of depth."

"They might have been mining something else," Grayson put in. "Reckon there's precious metals on this planet? Lanthanum? Neodymium?"

"I'll check for those tomorrow, too," Dizzie promised.

Conversation dropped off as soon as they were back at the ship. People split up – some to change and shower, some to prepare food, some to check their equipment and get ready for tomorrow. Corinus took advantage of everyone else's distraction to slip out of his EVA suit and lie down on his bunk for a moment. He shut his eyes and tucked his knees in close to his chest, perfectly composed in his own cocoon, still alone in his mind and finally, for once, alone in every other way, too. It was bliss, to lie there in solitude and just *be.*

He didn't know how much time had passed before Dizzie touched him on the shoulder, drawing him out of his reverie. "Shower's free," they said, toweling off their fluffy brown hair. They sat down on their own bunk, right across from Corinus's, and asked, "Do you feel better since shutting all the extra noise out?"

Corinus's eyelids fluttered guiltily. "How did you know?"

"I can always tell when you're on your meds," Dizzie replied. "Your face gets dreamier, and your movements become less… careful, I guess. When you're aware of everyone, you never, ever bump into people. You bumped me twice in the lab today."

"Oh. I'm sorry, I–"

"It's not a problem," Dizzie assured him. "I just want to make sure *you're* not having a problem, and if you are, I want to be able to do something about it."

"I'm fine," Corinus said. It felt good to be able to tell them the truth. "I just needed a bit of distance today. There were many… fraught emotions."

"*Fraught.* Yeah, that's one way of putting it," Dizzie agreed with a grimace. "If I never see that many tentacles coming out of one person again, it'll be too soon."

Corinus blinked. "I believe they're called extensors."

"Eh, close enough." Dizzie rolled their shoulders out and

sighed. "Never mind. Listen, it'll be better tomorrow. We'll all have our tasks ready to go, we'll split up almost as soon as we get there, and we won't have to see each other again until it's time to come back here."

"Can we take our helmets off tomorrow?" Corinus asked meekly. "It's just, it got so stuffy after a while, and I hate the nutrient paste that those things feed you."

"I hear you." Dizzie turned their head to the side until their neck made a faint cracking sound. "But I also don't want a lungful of this weather if I can help it."

"Just inside, then?"

Dizzie grinned. "Fine. Just inside. Preferably where the rest of the group can't see us being hypocrites."

"All right." They sat in silence for a moment before Dizzie got up.

"I'm going to go make us some dinner and pack up the equipment we need to take along for the lab. Grayson is working on the rover now. He says he thinks we'll be able to use it tomorrow."

"That's good."

"Yeah." Dizzie smiled. "Go get a shower, then come out and join me when you're ready and we can talk through some of the experiments I want to set up." They left the sleeping cabin, and Corinus felt a warm pang in his heart as he watched them go. They were always looking out for him.

Silently, he promised himself that he was going to do all he could to look out for Dizzie as well.

CHAPTER THIRTEEN
Grayson Bane

There was value in being able to do things that others couldn't. For Grayson, that had meant making himself and his brother into the most amazing, unstoppable team of thieves the galaxy had ever seen. To do that, he'd had to become proficient in everything from neurosurgery to electrical engineering to computer programming, in both human *and* alien languages. There was no shortage of artifacts out there that others were happy to pay the Banes to steal for them.

Doing so meant prestige for the new owners, a growing reputation for them, and Coalition credits or the currency of choice for wherever they were based out of at the time. The harder the job, the more of everything everyone got. It hadn't been an easy life, but it had been a satisfying one.

Then had come their first tour in prison when a client turned on them, then them breaking out and going on the run, then being recaptured and doing *another* stint in prison. It became a pattern that Grayson didn't fight too hard because they ended up getting as big a reputation for breaking out of places as they did for thieving. Plenty of people were willing to pay top credit to learn the ins and outs of the various Guild and Coalition penitentiaries, and the Bane brothers were more than happy to pass on what they'd learned for a price. What did they care about "compromising galactic security" and all the other loads of shit the prosecutors piled onto their cases against 'em? The galaxy had never done much for the two of them, after all.

Then came the job that landed them in the Bor-Turia Penal Colony, an escapade that went bad thanks to a group of Water Guild bastards installing new security just a day before the heist Grayson and Mason had been paid for. And now… hell. Here they were. Living in close quarters with a crazy Thassian and a bunch of wet-behind-the-ears scientists, on this moist bunghole of a planet, trying to figure out ancient tech that might blow you up as soon as work the way you expected.

Well, all right, that part was actually pretty neat. Not that Grayson would ever admit it.

[Aww, but it's cute!]

"Shut it," he muttered, tightening the last few parts on the newly reinforced axle of the rover. Fixing that had taken the longest, much of it spent waiting around for compounds to meld and stick together, so Grayson had redone the tread on the wheels in the meantime.

[No, really. We love your hobbies. We would never have thought to model the tread after the Martian dune-rollers you and us used to play around with as kids.]

"If you don't shut your head up, I'll beat you about it until you do."

[You wouldn't do that to us,] Mason crooned. [Especially not after we saved you from the bloodthirsty Thassian.]

He was right, of course, but it didn't do to let him get a big head about it. "Saved me?" Grayson scoffed. "You were about to get us thrown back into the clink, and this next time might be our last! What do you want to bet they'd throw me into a hole so deep I forget what light looks like, and you'd get stuck as a footrest under the warden's desk permanently?" Not that Grayson wouldn't do everything in his power to keep that from happening. From the feel of his brother's amusement across their connection, he knew it.

[So overprotective,] Mason laughed. [You know we could always have escaped once we got back to the home system. You worry too much.]

"Maybe you don't worry enough," Grayson muttered. Maybe none of them did – except for the Centauran, who seemed to do enough worrying for the lot of them. "How long do you reckon we'll be out here anyway, eh?"

[The original contract said one standard Earth lunar month. More for travel, of course.]

"God, I hate having to measure everything in *Earth* standard."

[Yes, you've complained about it before, shut up now. That leaves us with twenty-nine more days of exploration here.]

"Ugh." Twenty-nine more days mucking about this red-tinged hell with this lot? It couldn't get much worse.

[You're so dramatic.]

"Shut up and get in so I can test whether the new welds will hold." If the rover could carry Mason's weight, it could carry the rest of the group with no problem.

Grayson watched as his brother shuffled over and clumsily pulled himself into the center of the rover. *Gotta work on smoothing out his movements next.* The rover's shocks whined a bit, but nothing broke. "Good enough. I'll tell 'em to load up." Grayson opened the door between the rearmost storage compartment of the ship, where the rover was stored next to the ramp it would drive down, and shouted, "Hey! Get your arses back here, we're ready to go!"

[So classy.]

"Shut *up*." Did Mason have to have an opinion on everything? "You'd be getting us into ten times the trouble I ever have if your mouth survived the fire, you know that?"

[Yeah, yeah.]

Shortly thereafter, the rest of the crew filed into the storage compartment and took their places on the rover. Six took the driver's seat for himself, then activated the exit and deployment of the ramp. As soon as it was stable, he drove the rover down it and took off for the distant refinery – ship – *whatever* it really was to a bunch of ancient Caridians.

Grayson might have mused on it more if he wasn't being jostled around so hard he almost fell over the edge of the bloody rover. "Holy Mount Mons, slow the hell down!" he shouted.

"I merely wish to be as efficient as possible!" Six said over the noise of the motor, clacking his mandibles cheerily. *Too* cheerily – this lunatic was enjoying driving like a maniac. Grayson was about to tell him off again, when the next bump hit hard enough that Dr Drexler – who hadn't had time to fasten their seatbelt – flew into the air.

Mason caught them before they could fall off. "Nice catch," Grayson muttered as his brother resettled the flustered doctor in their seat.

[We're a gentleman, ask anyone.]

Grayson spent the rest of the trip to the *Nexeri* focusing on not losing his rations before they got to the bloody monolith. Once they finally slowed down and came to a stop outside of it, he – and probably everyone else – breathed a sigh of relief.

"OK, tasks for today," Dr Drexler said, hopping off the rover and pointing to Divak. "We've got the capacity to load two tons of liquid Xenium onto the ship in storage compartment B, so that's your job. Check to ensure the bottles that you choose are firmly sealed – we don't want to risk any leaks when we get back up into space.

"You two–" they pointed at Grayson and Mason "–keep trying to figure out the refinery system. I want to know how deep those tunnels go. I'll scan for the Xenium myself later and we can compare our results.

"Meanwhile, Six and Dr Lifhe and I will continue to work in the library and the laboratory, respectively. Sound good to everyone?"

There was a ragged chorus of "yeah" and a few nods, which seemed to satisfy them. "Great! Let's get to work, then." They led the way inside the ancient ship, and Grayson was gratified to see both the scientists take their helmets off the moment the door was shut behind them all.

Decided it's not so dangerous after all, did you? Knew you delicate flowers were all buzzed up about nothing. Their group dispersed, and Grayson headed for the nearest refinery stack a few hundred feet away. "We're gonna send Right-arm down again this morning," he said. "Best we can do without proper probes, and from what you checked of the machinery down there, there should be plenty of rungs for you to cling to as you head down. Battery all good?"

Mason didn't say anything. Grayson turned around and saw his brother standing exactly where he'd come in, motionless. "Mason? *Mason,* what the hell are you–"

[Lefty says he saw something.]

Grayson groaned and marched back over to his brother. "Lefty is a reactionary piece of shit; he spends half his time daydreaming and the other half disobeying orders. Ignore him and let's get to work."

[But Grayson, he's right. The rest of us looked, too.] Sure enough, Mason's eyes were turned to the side, where the tiny pod-like ships were arrayed in their neat rows... except for the last two.

"What about it, then?" Grayson asked. "What do you see?"

[It's what we *don't* see that's the problem.]

"If you don't stop speaking in bloody damn riddles, I'm going to–"

[The bodies are missing.]

"The..." Grayson abruptly ran out of ire. He turned to the spot where the ancient Caridian corpses had lain yesterday, little more than dried out husks. Dried out husk or not, though, there was nothing in this place that should have been able to move them. They hadn't let in the wind, and there were no living creatures other than themselves around who could have shifted them.

Well, that settled that.

"Betcha it's Divak, that bitch. Tryin' to spook us. You go take a look, see if she shoved the poor sods farther back, an' I'll call in the rest of 'em." He activated the collar comm unit. "Right, you bastards, who was it moved the bodies, huh? Because apart from bein' disrespectful, that's just nasty."

"What?" Dr Drexler's voice sounded first – of course it did, they seemed to welcome any invitation to start babbling. "What are you talking about?"

"I'm talkin' about the *bloody* corpses of the *bloody* Caridians," Grayson snapped. "They're gone. Divak, get your ass over here and tell us where you stashed 'em!"

The Thassian had moved deeper into the crates of Xenium since they'd arrived, but she popped her head up at this. "You dare accuse me? I haven't touched them."

"The hell you haven't! You're the one keeps complaining of being bored, right? Decide to make a little of your own fun, eh?"

"Certainly not. Dead meat is of no interest to me," Divak said, coming closer and theatrically licking her lips. "I prefer it live."

"Yeah, yeah, you're a bad bitch and we all know it. That's why you're the one who moved the bodies, isn't it?" Grayson sneered. "What, thought you'd give us a scare? It takes more than that to get a rise out of me."

"I don't think I *care* to know what gets a 'rise' out of you, you filthy human."

"No need to get your tail in a knot about it, you Thassian piece of–"

"Whoa-kay!" Dr Drexler ran into the room, hands held up in the universal sign for calm down. "There's no need to get personal about people's species. We can't help how we're born, right? Let's focus on the issue at hand." They looked toward where Mason was disappearing into the crack between the pods. "The bodies are gone? You're sure?"

"Would I have caused this hullabaloo if I wasn't sure?" Grayson asked. "Think I don't have better things to do with my time? Yeah, I'm sure."

"Very well." Six took over, looking at each of them. "And did anyone here move them, for any reason at all?"

"You doubt my word?" Divak was nearly hissing with anger. "I already told you, I have no interest in the dead. I–"

"I happen to know that Thassians are actually disturbed by the bodies of the dead," Six said calmly. "Perhaps because of the smell, perhaps because of the reminder of your own mortality. There are plenty of instances of Thassians destroying bodies on battlegrounds."

"That's completely different."

"Perhaps it is. You, of course, would know better than me, but don't test me by lying to me about it."

Divak bristled for a moment, then said, "These corpses were ancient. Uninteresting. Useless. I didn't touch them."

"Thank you." Six turned his gaze to Grayson. "What about you and your brother?"

"Hey, I don't give a shit about a few old ass corpses lyin' around as long as they're not in my way," Grayson said. "Besides, Dr Drexler already scanned 'em for biological contaminants and found nothin'. So what do I have to worry about?"

"I did scan them," Dr Drexler confirmed. "And I…" They suddenly blanched and reached for the portable multitool lying against their hip. "It's nothing," they muttered as they punched in a password and adjusted the settings rapidly. "We're fine, just let me confirm… oh, shit." They looked frantically at Grayson. "I'm detecting biologicals here."

"Be calm," Six said, clearly taking his own advice given the way his antennae waved slowly. "We ourselves were in here yesterday, most of us without our helmets. It's entirely likely that the biologicals you're detecting right now belong to us."

"No, they don't!" Dr Drexler was starting to sound panicked. Grayson was more worried about the Centauran, though – his eyelids fluttered so quickly they looked like they were about to fly right off his face. "I entered all our genetic profiles into the scanner when we first got together on the ship; it knows to discount us! It even knows to discount all species modifications based on common diseases, so it's not about to ping like this if one of us is coming down with a cold. This is…" They lifted their head and stared into the spot where Mason had shimmied in between the little ships a minute ago. "This is something different, an entirely new biological signature. It wasn't here yesterday."

[Grayson…]

Grayson diverted all of his attention to his brother. "What is it?" he said.

[We can see something back here.]

"Get the hell away from it," he barked, turning in a panic toward the pods. He couldn't see where Mason had ended up, which meant he was too far away. "Get back out here, *now*."

[It's not one of the bodies. It's… I'm not really sure, but it's covering the wall back here.]

"Get out here!"

"What does he see?" Dr Drexler asked anxiously.

[It looks like – well, here. Look.] Mason opened his mind up and shared his vision with Grayson, and a moment later he saw it for himself, zoomed in and focused on even though he could feel Mason backing away. It looked… odd. Definitely organic, but glowy, like something you'd see in a cave.

"The hell is that?" he asked.

"Describe it," Dr Drexler said tightly.

"Green and clingin' to the walls in the back. Seems to be glowin', or – what's the word – phosphorescent, like a–"

He was cut off by a shrill squeal from Dr Lifhe, who was moving from all fours onto his hind legs as he began to pace with agitation. "We have to get out of here!" he shrilled. "We have to get out of here now! We need to get back to the ship before we're infected!"

Infected? What the *hell*, infected? "Mason, get back here *right now*."

"The mold didn't utilize an airborne vector of infection before," Dr Drexler said, managing to make their voice soothing for the sake of their hysterical friend. "There's no reason to think it will now. Nobody's touched it, and Mason is incapable of inhaling the spores – right?" They verified with Grayson, who was beginning to think this could be a big damn deal.

"Right. His lungs don't work that way."

"There. See? It's going to be fine, we just have to–"

Crash! One of the pod ships in the back row next to the wall had suddenly flown straight up in the air, landing with a metallic bounce a few seconds later. It happened so abruptly, and with such violence, that they were all stunned into silence for a moment.

Grayson was the first one to recover his voice. "What the *hell*?" he snapped. "Mason, quit screwing around and–"

[It's not us! We're not strong enough to lift one of these things.] Sure enough, a second later his brother reappeared at the edge of the unsettled pod and scuttled back over to them, spider-style.

Divak brought her gun up to bear. "The Centauran coward is right, for once," she said. "We need to return to the ship and leave this planet immediately."

"We can't get back into the home system without an extensive quarantine first," Dr Drexler said. Dr Lifhe whimpered, but Grayson could barely hear it over the sudden rush of blood through his head. Quarantine?

"You just said we weren't infected!" he shouted.

"I said it was *probably* fine, but I don't know that for sure! Do you want to be responsible for bringing–"

Another pod flew into the air, rolling across the tops of its brethren before falling off and coming to a stop just a few meters away from them. Corinus screamed shrilly, and Divak's hands tightened on her rifle.

"We will return the ship to orbit and wait out our quarantine there," Six said. "Let's get back to the rover now." He turned and began to head for the small door they'd come in.

"Wait." Dr Drexler grabbed his sleeve. "Look."

"What's there to see?" Grayson demanded. Another pod flew into the air, this one a row forward from the last. Whatever had been percolatin' back there before they arrived, it was well on the boil now. "There's nothing in front of us and somethin' *nobody* wants to see behind us! Let's get the hell out of here!"

"We shut the door after we came in!" Dr Drexler insisted. Their face was unusually gray. "I *know* we shut it all the way. I wouldn't have taken off my helmet otherwise! It shouldn't be open. So how did it get cracked open?"

Their nascent question was answered as the door, open only a few inches, suddenly jerked back a few more. Into the space crept a… hell, Grayson wasn't sure what to call it. At first glance it looked like a dead tree branch, spotty with age and eaten through here and there by insects. Only there were no trees or insects on Sik-Tar. It worked its way farther into the space, and now he could see the mottled gray surface of it was touched with bright green up by the joint, and–

Oh shit. That was a *joint*. That thing was a *leg*. It bent and sidled, maneuvering deeper into the crack, and soon it was joined by another limb – an arm this time, creeping in over the top of the door. It got a grip on the heavy metal oval, jerked it backward, and ripped the entire thing right out of the wall. A second later a series of long, skinny limbs compressed themselves and slipped in through the relatively small opening, unfolding into a–

"Bloody hell," Grayson whispered. "That's more than one body." It was… shit, he couldn't even guess – at least two heads, he could see them overlapping each other on top. Four arms, five – no, six legs. There hadn't been this many Caridian bodies in this entire ancient ship – where had it gotten the other bits from?

"Xenos," Dr Drexler whispered, their eyes bright with fear and… excitement? *Freak.* "It's a completely new type of Xeno. I didn't know the mold could resurrect tissues that had been dead for so long, but it's taken the Caridians and turned them into… into revenants."

The once-dead revenant's lower head had six scythelike mandibles attached to the bottom of its jaw around a center point, like petals on the universe's most hideous flower. It clacked them menacingly, shifting more of its weight onto its longer, thicker front legs, then charged.

Dr Lifhe broke. He turned and ran away from the rest of them on all fours just as Divak opened fire, focusing on the revenant's bottom head. Bits of carapace shattered, but there was nothing beneath that shell for the rounds to destroy – no brain to speak of, or if it had one, it wasn't in the bloody thing's head. It ignored the shots completely and went after Dr Lifhe, closing the distance with terrifying speed as it ambled forward on its six malformed, overlapping legs. They ought to be gettin' in the way of each other, ought to be makin' it clumsy, but it moved as gracefully as any predator closing in for the kill.

"No!" That came from Dr Drexler, who'd surged forward while the rest of them were standing there stunned. They had their scanner up between them and the revenant. With a twist of a knob here and a push of a button there, they shot a bolt of literal lightning at the creature, enveloping it in bright, sizzling blue. The revenant stiffened, every one of its limbs sticking straight out before it collapsed in a heap, the moldy spots on its carapace smoking.

"Oh wow!" Dr Drexler looked at their multitool with a pleased expression. "First time trying to reverse the lightning rod function on this thing. It worked better than I–"

The closest leg of the revenant lashed out, hitting them squarely in the side. The scanner tumbled to the floor as Dr Drexler flew backward, hitting the ground and rolling until they collided with the nearest of the refinery machines. They groaned and tried to sit up, one arm crossed over their midsection, before falling down again.

The revenant was jerkily getting back on its feet. "Screw this," Grayson muttered, looking at his brother. "We're gettin' out of here."

[Let's go.] They sprinted for the door, clear now that the enormous Caridian bug-zombie was out of the way.

They were almost there when another pod flew into the air, this one sailing right over their heads and impacting the wall ahead of them – right where they were about to exit through the ruined oval door. Mason reeled backward, hooking extensors into Grayson's collar and hauling him back as well. There was a gap there now, big enough for Grayson to get through, but Mason wouldn't make it unless he took himself to pieces first. They didn't have that kind of time. "Shit!" Grayson turned around and saw another shape slink out of the shadows.

This one wasn't like the first revenant. It was smaller, more like the normal Caridian it had started out as, just…

thickened. Thickened by mold, which clung to it like a layer of armor, hard and dense along its limbs and still in a state of ooze around its joints, lending them both strength and flexibility. Unlike the other revenant, which had eyes about the size of Six's, this one's were huge, easily three times bigger.

Grayson knew he was gawping, but he couldn't stop, boggled by what he was seeing. It was crazy, like something out of a nightmare… that's what this had to be, a nightmare. He'd fallen asleep on this boring-arse mission, and this was just his mind playing tricks on him, right? It was as good an explanation as any, until he saw the smaller rev reach for another pod and pick… it… up, like there wasn't any such thing as leverage and weight differentials and goddamn *physics*.

[Grayson!] Mason jerked him off his feet and backward, and a second later the pod landed right where he'd been standing before ricocheting in their direction. Mason jumped them over it, jarring Grayson's back something fierce in the process.

"Ow, shit!"

[Sorry, but there's no time to be gentle! Come on!] Mason slung him onto his back and spider-ran for the crates.

"Don't lead them in there!" Six called out, one of his unfortunately revenant-reminiscent pincers extended. "If they manage to break open one of the bottles of Xenium, everything could explode!"

"He's right," Grayson grunted around the pain. "Take us up instead."

[Got it.] Mason changed his run into a great leap, landing them on the side of the wall. Grayson wrapped an arm around his brother's neck and held on for dear life as Mason began to climb. He glanced down to see how the others fared.

Divak had taken cover behind one of the pods, and was firing at the larger revenant with startling accuracy, given how shit she'd been at it yesterday. She'd already destroyed the uppermost head and was working on the lower one now, but the reanimated Caridian, which up until now had seemed like nothing but a set of basic impulses and urges, seemed to have learned a measure of wariness. As Mason watched, it reached up and broke off the stalks of its newly grown eyes off with a sickening *crunch* and pressed them against its abdomen. Globs of virid green mold coagulated around them, attaching the eyes to their new location. A moment later the revenant charged again – not toward Divak, but toward Dr Lifhe, who was helping Dr Drexler to their feet.

Welp, they're goners.

Except they weren't, not quite. The Centauran picked Dr Drexler up and threw them past the belt of the refinery they'd wound up against after firing their lightning bolt, hurling them straight back into the belly of the refinery. He jumped in after them just as the revenant got close enough to lash out with one of its thorny, secondary sets of arms.

Huh, no screams and no blood. Lucky bastards must have made it in there. Not that it would do them much good – they were cornered, and until someone else got the revenant out of there, they wouldn't be able to–

[Hold on!]

Mason's steady climb turned into a flying leap from the light-filled column he was climbing to the smooth wall half a dozen feet to the left. Where they had been a moment ago, a light sizzled and died as the smaller revenant's claw punctured right through its hard casing. The revenant turned its vast, dull eyes toward them, then reached out with its other claw and began to climb in their direction.

"Go, go, go!" Grayson screamed. Mason let all of his extensors loose, scrambling across the wall like a spider with an ungainly egg sac on its back. He was fast, but not fast enough. Whether the revenant was going through a rapid learning process or reviving ancient instincts embedded in its DNA, it was clear they weren't going to be able to outpace it for long.

"Gonna have to put me down," Grayson panted. His arms were on the verge of giving out. "Get low enough so's I don't break my legs and I'll drop, and you can act as a distraction while I–"

[No.]

"Mason! Stop being a brat and listen to me! You need to–"

[No! We're not going to let you sacrifice yourself to save us! That's stupid, we *need* you! We're in this together or not at all!]

"You *idiot*, you–"

Grayson lost his train of thought completely when Mason abruptly let go of the wall, twisting in midair so that he fell on his hands and feet as they hit the ground. Grayson grunted again – his back was killing him, but at least he was alive – and stared grimly ahead as Mason maneuvered his way around the crates of Xenium, heading for the hallway across the hangar that led to the labs and whatnot the scientists and Six had all been so enamored with lately. Somewhere to hide and lick their wounds, somewhere to–

Crash! The revenant landed close behind them, only it hadn't been careful about where it put its feet. It fell right into one of the crates of Xenium, sending barrels of it rolling in all directions.

A sharp smell filled the air – the smell of the most powerful fuel source in the galaxy, maybe the universe. It was liquid death for everybody on this side of the planet if someone set it off, though.

"Don't fire on this one!" Grayson shouted to Divak, who had already pulled her rifle back with a sour expression on her face. "We've got to get the bastard outside!"

"How?" she shouted back. "If you haven't noticed, it's fixated on you! It won't stop until it takes you as its rightful prey!"

Hell, maybe she was right. Maybe it was fixated on them...

Maybe it could be fixated on just a *part* of them.

"Send Lefty over to get its attention," Grayson muttered to Mason. "Then you can–"

[We've got it, we've got it.] In a flash, Left-arm Mason detached from the central rig. He scuttled on his extensors straight back toward the revenant, which stepped right over him on its inexorable path toward them.

Come the hell on! "Be a bigger arsehole to it, Lefty! Holy Mount Mons, the one time I *want* you to be a nuisance and you can't manage it."

[Oh yeah? Watch *this*.]

In a flash, Lefty slid between the revenant's legs, crawled straight up its body, and used its main hand to rip one of its enormous eyes right off its head. The revenant hissed, its ossified mandibles clacking, and reached for Lefty.

Who was already booking it for the door.

Mason took cover behind one of the battered pods just a little way down from Divak, but it was hardly necessary at this point. The revenant followed Lefty straight to the ruined oval doorframe. The creature then shifted the lopsided pod out of its way, able to slip through much easier than the huge, composite revenant had. It left a thin trail of liquid Xenium behind on the floor.

Grayson turned to glare at Divak. "Well? What are you waiting for? Shoot the bloody thing!"

[Not this close,] Mason warned.

"I can't yet, it's too close," Divak replied in an annoying echo of his brother. "Keep it from catching up to that arm and perhaps shooting it is not out of the question."

Grayson looked at Mason. "You got–"

[Yeah, yeah, we heard you. We'll keep it moving. Lefty's going as fast as he can, but it's a lot harder to handle the big stuff when you're only a few feet long.]

Grayson closed his eyes and focused on the connection between himself and his brother's mind, watching through Lefty's vision as it scurried as fast as its extensors would carry it across the wet, rock-covered plain outside.

"One hundred meters…" Grayson said.

"Keep it moving," Divak replied, heading over toward the ruined door. She took a firing stance there, raising the gun to her shoulder with fresh purpose. "I can't fire until it's farther away."

"Two hundred meters." Grayson felt ill as his vision slipped from distant to close, one second aware of everything around his own body, the next clouded with the glistening red landscape of Sik-Tar. Lefty was moving as fast as he could, but they could all feel the way he had to dodge and jump to avoid the beast behind him. His mind was going crazy trying to track his pursuer, find the best route forward, and process the sensory data from over a dozen extensors.

"Three hundred meters."

Lefty's battery was getting hot, hot enough to make his micro-brain feel feverish. It made staying properly oriented even harder, and before the Banes knew it Lefty was slip-sliding down a steep crevice, unable to catch himself. The revenant slid down after him.

"Get him up again!" Divak ordered. "Get him up, or I won't be able to hit the creature until it's coming back at us!"

Lefty managed to climb back out of the ravine, but not without a casualty – one of the revenant's claws sliced three of the extensors right off his back. He kept going, though, doggedly racing across the inhospitable ground, and the revenant followed.

"Four hundred meters."

Something loud was happening on the other side of the room, sounds of screaming and crunching and crashing, but Grayson couldn't focus on that right now. He was caught in Lefty's plight, caught up in this bitter chase and the end he knew was coming. The feelings he got from Mason were of both pride and horrified nausea.

"Five hundred meters."

"Finally," Divak snarled, and at last she fired her gun. In the distance, the sky blossomed in a huge, fiery tower.

In the Bane brothers' heads, a distant piece of them stuttered, briefly overwhelmed with sizzling heat, then went dark.

Two seconds later, a compression wave from the explosion hit the *Nexeri*. Divak had already leapt out of the way of the gaping hole where the door had been, but Mason, still stunned from losing a piece of himself, was too slow. The heat cooked his exposed forehead, making blisters pop up immediately.

"Shut your lids, damn it!" Grayson reached around and threw his hand over his brother's eyes, but the damage was done. Mason's sight went from clear to filmy, then wavered with the wateriness of lymph and blood.

Then Mason, like Lefty, went dark.

CHAPTER FOURTEEN
Lefty

Lefty had tumbled down a steep hill ahead of the revenant chasing him just before Divak fired. That was all that kept him from being atomized by the explosion. The force of the blast still hit Lefty like a tremendous hammer, turning him end over end like a tumbleweed. He lost pieces of himself along the way to fire and impact before he finally came to a stop against an enormous boulder. He lay still, mind like static, wondering if he should be getting up.

[Mason, Mason, Mason help, Mason, Mason, help me, help me.]

But Mason wasn't replying. Something was wrong with their connection. Lefty needed to rejoin the mainframe.

Lefty tried to pull himself up, but he didn't have enough extensors left to manage it. No matter. The boulder, precariously balanced on a slurry of smaller rocks, solved that conundrum for him when it tipped over and crushed him into the ground.

[Mason? Grayson?]

[I'm scared… I'm scaaarredd… Iii'mm sccaaarrrreeeee…]

CHAPTER FIFTEEN
Corinus Lifhe

He had known not to run, was the thing.

In their distant past, Centaurans had been a prey species, four-legged herbivores grazing on the never-ending plains of their planet of origin. Their planet was home to a great number of predator species as well – enough to make their fossil record dizzyingly complex, and largely filled with evolutionary wins for the predators. Centauran anthropologists theorized that the reason their particular species had risen to the top of the food chain, so to speak, was entirely due to the development of their telepathic abilities – the ultimate defense for any prey. They had gone from the hunted to the hunter, and were able to confound and, eventually, destroy all their natural predators because of it.

The old instincts were still there, though, and still had to be fought against. The greatest of these was the urge to flee in the face of danger. All Centauran children had to take classes that walked them through interactions with aliens who demonstrated predator characteristics, in order not to run from them if they interacted in the future. They also learned to use their telepathy, their powerful hind legs, and their strong, flat foreheads as tools for self-defense. Fleeing… that was the act of a frightened child.

That was how Corinus had felt when he ran. Like a child, or a fool, out of control and forgetting everything and everyone around him as he ran for a place where the revenant – with a mind so hollow he couldn't influence it, his thoughts bouncing against nothing but each other – couldn't reach him.

Fleeing failed him. It only served to make him the choicest target, the focus of the hideous creature's wrath. He had known even as he ran that there would be no escape for him. The distant part of his mind still capable of thought had calculated the moment of intersection, the instant he would feel the first sharp pain of death come upon him.

Dr Yoche, I have failed our people. I have failed myself.

And then… a miraculous reprieve.

The crackle of lightning filled the air, along with the scents of ozone and burning dust. Corinus turned, panting, and watched Dizzie blast the revenant with the weapon they had made out of their scanner. Of course they came to his rescue – they always looked out for him. And they were so clever, and so brave. Corinus felt his twin hearts begin to slow their furious racing as the revenant collapsed in a heap.

"Wow," Dizzie said, sounding as pleased as they felt. "That worked better than I–"

Relief turned to dismay, and the brief hope Corinus felt shattered as the revenant's legs straightened with terrifying speed. One of them caught Dizzie square in the chest, hurling them back until they hit the closest refinery with a muted *clang*. Corinus felt their pain and disorientation like it was his own.

This is your chance. Get into the smaller hallway, head to the lab, lock yourself inside the testing chamber. The revenants won't be able to get you in there. You'll be safe. You have to be safe. It's your number one priority.

Only…

Only it wasn't. Not right now. For the first time in his life, Corinus felt with complete clarity the absolute rightness of setting someone else's safety ahead of his own. The revenant wasn't back on its monstrous spiky legs yet, twitching from residual electrical impulses and the impact of Divak's rounds blasting into its heads and chest. Corinus set his jaw, lowered his shoulders, and sprinted across the room to Dizzie.

"Cor'nus?" They recognized him, at least. Hopefully that meant they weren't wounded too badly. "You… what hap'nd?"

"The lightning didn't keep it down for long," Corinus said, wrapping one arm around Dizzie's shoulders and pulling them to their feet. "We've got to get to the lab. We can–"

It was Divak's mind that alerted him to the danger – he felt her go from focused to furious, which always meant something wasn't going her way. If her shots weren't stopping the revenant…

"Get in!" Corinus shouted, but he didn't wait for Dizzie to remember how to coordinate their limbs, just threw them straight in through the narrow inlet of the refinery they'd wound up against and then jumped in after them. The revenant was so close to catching them that Corinus could practically feel the wind whistling past his hind legs before he escaped into the narrow compartment – too narrow for the revenant to come in after them.

That didn't mean it wasn't going to try. Claws scrabbled against the front of the refinery's open-ended pipe, mindless and wild for a few moments before they pulled back out of view. Corinus shifted against the uneven wall at his back, molded together centuries ago out of parts scavenged from the *Nexeri*'s original components, most likely. This ship hadn't been intended to be a refinery, but its owners had done a thorough job of repurposing it.

Too bad they hadn't included the weapons that Divak was so fervently wishing for right now.

"What's it doing?" Dizzie whispered. Corinus wasn't sure whispering was necessary – the revenant knew where they were, after all – but he responded in kind.

"I can't tell. I can't get a clear read on its mind." He shrugged helplessly. "I'm not even sure it *has* a mind, to be honest. More like…"

He concentrated on the hollowness he'd felt before. There was a structure there, a boundary holding this thing's killing instincts together, perhaps even granting them. He'd never felt anything quite like it, but he had come close once before, when he was learning about the M'noth, an intelligent race of trees that lived both individually and as a single organism on their home planet.

"More like a collective, very rudimentary consciousness,"

he finished. "This revenant doesn't feel like a Caridian at all."

"The mold," Dizzie said, staring at him with wide eyes. "Could it be the mold? Can mold even have a consciousness?"

"Before now I would have said no, but this… we know it's capable of creating change, both mental and physical, in its victims," Corinus replied. Half-remembered images from Dizzie's holos swirled before his eyes – hideous, tentacled beasts attacking and devouring humans as they desperately fought for survival.

"That's amazing! If that's true, it's a – *aah!*" Dizzie jerked Corinus's head down just in time to get him out of the way of a long, spear-like appendage that… hadn't existed a moment ago. It was crusted all over with mold, and looked like it had been pieced together out of a random assortment of Caridian limbs. "Shit! We need to get farther back!"

"But the slag hole is back there!"

"There's a grate covering it, come on!"

They crawled backward until they reached the edge of the grate that led into a chamber. No, a furnace. Even a thousand years after the liquid Xenium had been produced here, the air still smelled faintly of its sharp, chemical tang. In another lifetime, Corinus would have been worried about the minute traces of radiation he was exposing himself to by being inside one of these things.

In this lifetime, he had more than enough to worry about right in front of him. The revenant's new limb followed them down the tunnel, smashing back and forth against the walls as it sought them out. Its edges were sharp and serrated, like the blades of an ancient saw, and the point at the tip would probably skewer straight through one of their EVA suits if they got in the way. They ducked down low, pressing their bodies up against the back wall and keeping their heads on the floor as the revenant swept the space less than half a meter over their heads.

"Maybe if we stay quiet we can make it think we escaped," Dizzie whispered. "Or it'll…" Their next, unspoken thought filled them with shame, but Corinus quite agreed with it – it would be far better for the revenant to fixate on one of the others than to keep harassing them. The lives of the rest of the party weren't Corinus's concern. Only his and Dizzie's were.

A faint buzz sounded in the back of Corinus's mind – a manifestation of his stress, most likely. He was certain he'd never been so adrenalized in his entire life.

The limb retracted a moment later. Cautiously, Dizzie sat up and looked down the refinery tunnel. "I think it's still there." In the distance they heard Divak firing, and the crash and bang of numerous impacts. "Shit, if anybody sets any of the Xenium on fire we're all toast."

Worse than that. More like toasted molecules. The buzz got louder, stronger.

"I wonder where Six is?" they went on. "Perhaps he's–"

The buzz suddenly coalesced into a single, powerful voice inside Corinus's head. *GGGEEEETTT DDDOOOOOWWWWNNNN!*

He tackled Dizzie again, and a second later *two* long, spiky revenant limbs came shooting down the tunnel, scraping horribly against each other as they searched for prey. One of them scratched a line across Dizzie's shoulder – not quite deep enough to break through the EVA suit, but the ease with which it penetrated it was just as awful as Corinus had feared.

The second, newer limb was more mobile than the first, able to get some play vertically, not just horizontally. They huddled in a pile as far back on the creaky old grate as they could, but it was only a matter of time before one of them was fatally skewered.

That same new, buzzing mental voice started Corinus out of his horror.

CCOOOVVERRRR YYOOUUURRR EEAAAARRRSS!

It was Six! Corinus, almost out of his mind with fear, nevertheless managed to clap his hands over his earholes. Dizzie followed his lead, and a moment later–

The sound began as a low growl, rising to a metallic gnashing of teeth that made Corinus feel like he'd been swallowed by some ancient, benthic beast. The chamber they were in rumbled alarmingly, and then the rock crushers that lined the tunnel came on. The noise then was a physical blow, like being punched in the head over and over again. Carapace cracked and crunched, and a second later they were both showered with shards of it as the activated belt fed the pieces of the revenant forward into the furnace they were sitting in.

A furnace whose grate was getting hotter and hotter.

"Tell him to shut it down!" Dizzie screamed, but it was so loud in here already that Corinus only heard them in his mind. "Shut it down before it burns us up!"

It was worth a try. Corinus mustered all his faltering

mental capacity and focused on Six's odd hum-buzzing mind. *Shut it down!* he projected.

A second later, the crushers stopped. The machine went back into a resting state, and the rising heat dissipated. It took a while for Corinus's head to stop ringing, but once he recovered enough to make sense of what he was seeing, he gulped.

The tunnel was filled with bits and pieces of the revenant. At the far end of it, the lower half of the body still twitched and twisted a bit, but there was far less mold down on those pieces, and no sensory organs. They were aimless now – but probably not for long.

"Let's... let's get out of here," Dizzie said breathlessly. "We need to get the rest of the revenant's legs in before the mold transforms them again."

Corinus agreed. "You go first," he said, pointing at the tunnel.

Dizzie smiled. "Whatever you want." They led the way, and Corinus watched them go with a sense of satisfaction.

Dizzie was alive. He had done it; he had saved his best friend. He had fought against his instincts and won. Him! A Centauran, putting someone else first! He felt deeply relieved, sure that for the first time in his life, he was the emotional equal to an alien he admired. They'd been colleagues for so long... now they were *truly* friends. He felt almost overwhelmed with emotion, reeling with glee.

Goodness, he was *really* reeling right now. Too much exposure to others' minds and hearts. Corinus stumbled as he slid out of the refinery tunnel. Dizzie was already picking up the nearest leg, which seemed surprisingly light – their

EVA suit gave them a decent increase to strength, but nothing like power armor.

"Good thinking with turning the crushers on!" they called out to Six, who was standing by a glowing screen on the refinery's wall. His expression was as imperturbable as ever, his mind thankfully closed off to Corinus once more, but his antennae were waving in an excited manner.

"I was merely in the right place at the right time," he demurred. "I could not have guaranteed your safety without Dr Lifhe's help."

"Oh, of course!" Dizzie looked at Corinus with admiration in their eyes. "You finally made that mental connection with him, huh? Good work!"

"Thank you," Corinus said faintly. His legs were starting to tremble. *Exhaustion, the aftereffects of adrenaline, low blood sugar. Your brain needs food, now.* "I think I should… maybe I should sit down for a moment." He slid – more like slumped – to the ground, hind legs out in front, and that's when he saw it.

The split in his EVA suit.

No, not just a split. A *rend*. And beneath it was the stain of his pale blood, oozing out of two puncture marks.

"Oh no…" Corinus breathed. He met Dizzie's confused eyes, his own eyelids blinking so fast he could barely see them. "It bit me."

CHAPTER SIXTEEN
Dizzie Drexler

Reconnecting with Divak and the Bane brothers should have felt triumphant. After all, they were still alive – they had survived the first attack of a hideously vicious, dangerously evolving predator that no one had seen coming.

They should have, though. *Dizzie* should have; they were the expert on Xenium here, the one who knew the most about both the mineral *and* the mold. Not that what they knew could fill more than a thimble – they didn't even have a way to properly scan for the mold, not like they did with the Xenium, since no one had a complete record of its molecular structure – but still. They should have enforced more precautions, made everyone take more care. They should have been more careful back when careful could have helped, before it was too late.

Now Mason Bane was recumbent on a table in the ancient ship's lab while his brother fussed over the severe burns that had destroyed his eyes, and Corinus was locked up in the testing bay along with a sample of mold while Dizzie pored over the data they'd collected over the past few days, trying to answer the question everyone was asking – how in the hell did this happen?

"Yelling at me isn't going to make my work go any faster," they said for the fifth time to Grayson, who was using a roundtable approach to shout at anyone and everyone about his brother.

"What are you even doing? You should be figuring out a way to fix your friend, not staring down a microscope!"

"I'm examining a sample of the mold." They'd already taken a DNA sample of it, gingerly scraping Corinus's festering, darkened wound with a swab without meeting his eyes. Their particle analyzer was processing it right now. Dizzie had a theory about why the mold had reconstituted, but they weren't about to broach it with the rest of them before they'd proven they were on the right track. "It's incredibly responsive. It changes to protect itself in the presence of heat and pressure and pH variation… and does so quickly." They pulled their face off the scope and looked over at Divak. "It's a good thing you burned up the other one when you shot it. That probably reduced the speed with which its mold will spread to the other body pieces."

Divak lifted her chin. "Reduced it? I would say I demolished all chance of it. The explosion was bad enough to do this sort of damage to flesh from half a kilometer away." She indicated Mason, who gave no indication that he was aware of anything going on around him. Dizzie wondered if he was in shock.

How do you treat a cyborg for shock? Put his feet up?

"I wish I could confirm that you did enough," Dizzie replied grimly, "but this mold is one of the most tenacious materials I've ever encountered. I'm not sure *what* would be enough to completely eradicate it once it's infected a host."

"It's a simple enough problem to investigate." Divak gestured to the testing chamber, where Corinus was lying on his side with his knees pulled up to his chest, muttering to himself in his native language. "Kill this one and see what happens."

"Screw you!" Dizzie snapped as Corinus simultaneously leapt to his feet and shouted, "No!"

He shouted it on more than one level – both out loud and psychically. Everyone in the room was driven into a pained crouch with the reverberations of his telepathy – except for Six, who didn't even seem to hear it, and Mason, who was already prone.

"Sorry, I'm sorry," Corinus said shamefacedly as Dizzie straightened up with a grimace, "but please, please, don't kill me. I can't die, I'm not supposed to die here. I'm not! I need to live, Dizzie, for my people! They need me back! I promised Dr Yoche that I would come back!"

"I know," they soothed him. "I know, I'm working on it. First, we need to figure out why *you* were infected, and not the rest of us."

"He was bitten," Grayson said slowly, like he was talking to a child. "Got the mold into his bloodstream."

"Look at the rest of us!" Dizzie snapped. "We're all covered with cuts and bruises and – hell, even open wounds, look at Mason! There's mold on all of us, and half of you haven't put on a helmet since the first day! But the only one obviously affected by it so far is Corinus, so why?"

"Perhaps it is a matter of concentration," Six suggested. "Small amounts of mold over a large surface area can be fought off by the immune system, while a larger amount deposited directly into the bloodstream results in an infection that can't be cured."

"We don't know that yet," Dizzie insisted. "It might still be curable." Corinus curled back up into a ball and began to whimper inside the chamber. His skin had darkened with fever from milky white to a sickly grayish shade, and his inhalations sounded painful. "I'm not giving up," Dizzie insisted. "But I need to know more. Like–"

The particle analyzer beeped, indicating the results were ready. Dizzie downloaded them to their pad and opened it up, half eager and half afraid to see what they would find there.

Well, shit.

"I think I know how this happened," they said, forcing the words out past stiff lips.

"How?" Grayson demanded.

"The mold… it's carrying DNA markers that link it to the original Caridians, the carapaces we found here, but there are also DNA markers linking it to *us*."

Six walked over, his mandibles clacking in distress. "What does that mean?"

"It probably means that the mold was here when we arrived," Dizzie said numbly, trying to cope with the magnitude of how greatly they had underestimated this organism. "It was ancient, though, dried out and completely inert, but not *dead*. This stuff… I already pointed out how adaptable it is. It was affected by our secretions, our bioshedding, our live cells. As soon as we took our helmets off, we started giving the mold what it needed to revitalize itself. Think of it like… like a living glue that's using these skeletons as a framework."

Grayson's face went dark. "Are you blaming my brother for this? Because he couldn't help that his mask broke when that goddamn bolt of lightning threw him halfway across the hangar out there."

"No," Dizzie said tiredly. They leaned one hip against the table, suddenly exhausted by the inevitability of it all. "No, I'm saying that… that probably *anything* would have been too much. Every time we exited and entered the ship, air that was permeated with our cells entered the atmosphere. And Six, you programmed the ship to deposit loads of waste straight into a hole you cut into the ground beneath the ship, right?"

Six's antennae waved so hard his head wobbled. "I did."

"So, there's more biomatter right there. Harder to get at, but in a concentrated quantity. Losing our masks didn't help, but without going back in time and converting this expedition to follow strict hazmat protocols, I don't think we could have avoided this."

Corinus's whimpering grew louder. Dizzie shook their head, bringing one hand up to wipe away a traitorous tear. "I don't know how to fix this," they confessed. "I don't know how to cure Corinus or how to make sure that we won't become infected ourselves. The longer we stay on Sik-Tar, the greater the likelihood that we're all going to become infected with the mold eventually. Our immune systems will only be able to fight the airborne particles off for so long."

"We must return to wearing masks immediately," Six said.

"That will help," Dizzie agreed. "What we really need to do, though, is get back up into space and go into lockdown protocol. That's the next step for the four of you. I'm going to stay here in the lab with Corinus and keep working on a way to–"

"Don't be an idiot!" Grayson snapped. "He's as good as gone, and you know it. You need to get your head out of the stars and resign yourself to the fact that the only person who's gonna be stayin' on bloody Sik-Tar from here on out is Dr Lifhe, and – the *hell* are you doing, Divak?" Grayson sounded horrified.

Dizzie turned just in time to see Divak touch the panel beside the testing chamber that was keeping it enclosed, turning the force field off. "He asked to come out," she said in a monotone voice.

"He's using his telepathy on her – Corinus, no!" Dizzie shouted. They leapt toward the testing chamber as Divak stepped forward, but collapsed at his front feet a moment later, the victim of an aggressive telepathic attack. Grayson and Dizzie followed suit.

Dizzie had never been the subject of a Centauran telepathic attack before. They'd known it could be deadly – there were several instances in Coalition history of dozens, even hundreds of people dying as a result of Centauran self-defense. They had imagined it to be like cutting a wire – one second the brain worked fine, the next it was blank, the equivalent of a computer in sleep mode.

This was nothing like sleep. This felt like their brain

was on fire, burning up inside their skull, all their ability to think and move and feel reduced to a singular sensation of pain. Was this what Corinus felt right now? Was he simply sharing his pain with them, or did he even *feel* pain anymore?

"Dizzie," Corinus murmured, grabbing them by the upper arms and lifting them up. Their brain burn cleared slightly as they focused on their former friend. "Dizzie. This happened to me because of you." His eyelids were steady, completely unblinking. This wasn't the Corinus that Dizzie knew.

"Corinus," they said weakly, trying without luck to pull away. "Let go of me."

"I can't. You're all that fills my mind." Tiny bumps began to appear beneath his skin, bleeding through to turn the smooth white into mottled grayish green. "I see you. Stay with me. Join me."

"Join you in what?" Dizzie asked, fumbling a hand toward their pocket. Corinus had a tight grip on their upper arms, but if there was enough wiggle room to reach their pocket...

"In a new existence." As Dizzie watched, his right eyeball began to pulse, the violet center of it protruding farther and farther from his eye socket with every push. "A new way of being. Living out a discovery like this is the ultimate goal of every scientist, isn't it?"

"Oh, Cor."

Green pus seeped around the edges of his eyeball, and a second later the liquid expanded into a circle of tiny spore-like protrusions, a mockery of his own eyelashes. He didn't even flinch.

"You're not living out anything," Dizzie whispered. "You're already gone."

Gripping the syringe tight in their right hand, they brought it up the center line between their bodies and stabbed it into the soft flesh of Corinus's third eye.

His telepathic attack instantly eased. As the others got back to their feet, Corinus kept staring at Dizzie, holding them even closer than before.

"Interesting," he said. "What else can we learn from you?"

A second later, Divak brought her chainsword down with a shout, severing both of Corinus's arms at the elbows and freeing Dizzie. She kicked Corinus back into the testing chamber and reset the force field before he could even stand up again. The arms fell to the floor.

Dizzie stared at him with guilty fascination. He wasn't bleeding from his horrific new wounds. By the time he was back on his hind legs, it was mold that oozed from the fresh cuts instead. He stared straight at them, then prodded the spot where Dizzie had injected him. "*Very* interesting."

Divak snarled at him, then turned to face the rest of them. "I'm not staying in the same room as that filthy creature," she hissed, all her usual haughty disdain replaced by quivering anger… and maybe fear. "I'll prepare the rover for our return to the ship instead." She stalked out the door before anyone could so much as take a breath, much less argue.

Dizzie felt like the world had slipped out from under their feet, taking all of their surety along with it. "I never meant for this to happen," they whispered. "Please, I never – I would never have brought you if I'd known this was possible."

"He is gone," Six said, probably trying for comforting but failing. "And there is no sense in apologizing for something that isn't your fault. The expedition was my idea, after all. In the end, all responsibility lies with me."

"Best thing you can do now is torch the body before it has a chance to spread," Grayson opined. When Dizzie glanced back, they saw that Mason had righted himself. His face was still a mess, but with the number of cameras built into his body he probably still had five times the vision that anyone else did.

"Whatever you just did to stop his brain from makin' us let him out, there's no way of knowing that the mold won't find a workaround," Grayson finished.

"But…" Dizzie couldn't deny the practicality of that suggestion, but not only would it mean losing the body of their friend, it would mean losing the chance to *study* him.

Have you lost your mind? What is wrong with you? How can you pivot from best friend to lab rat so quickly?

Dizzie tried to justify it to themselves – they were both scientists first and foremost, and keeping Corinus around for study was honoring him in the only way they still could. He would do the same to them if he got the opportunity, too. Dizzie knew full well that Centaurans were trained from birth to prioritize first themselves, then their people, then their own research before things like the lives of other species.

But he saved you. He risked his life for you, and this is how you'd repay him?

The fact that Corinus had saved them was a testament to their friendship, but Dizzie had to face facts. The odds of figuring out a treatment that could actually save Corinus was now nonexistent, while the knowledge that could be gained from studying him was… compelling.

"I know we need to leave," they said, forging ahead after their moment of uncomfortable introspection, "but this is probably the only chance I'm ever going to get to study the effects of the mold in person. There are still so many unanswered questions about it! How similar is it to the molecular structure of the mold found in the PK-L system? Is it the same species? It seems like the effects on the infected here might come on even more rapidly than the original strain did – does that make this strain more advanced? Maybe *this* one is the site of origin!"

Now that they'd started thinking about it, they couldn't stop. "Speaking of origins, is it native to this planet, or did someone else bring it here? Is mold possibly a natural byproduct of Xenium, or perhaps the other way around? If it *is* a natural byproduct of Xenium, how long did it take for the ancient Caridians to find that out? It seems like they came to Sik-Tar with the purpose of mining Xenium – would they have dedicated an entire ship to this process if they knew the risks were so incredibly high? Did they–"

"That's bloody damn enough, already!" Grayson's shout startled Dizzie out of their monologue. "Whatever questions you got, this ain't the time or the place to answer 'em, not if we want to survive! You said we need to be wearin' helmets – well, mine's back on the ship, and so's Mason's. You said the chance of infection goes up if the mold gets into a wound – look at his face, mate!" Grayson pointed to his brother's ruined skin and lymph-coated, unseeing eyes. "He's got a helluva wound right now! An' I'm not taking any chances that he could become like that *thing* in the chamber over there, so we're packin' up our shit and gettin' out of here now. Got it?"

"Got it," Dizzie said in a small voice. He was right. Of course he was right. Scientific curiosity or not, the focus now had to be on survival. And Dizzie had the feeling their own chances of survival would plummet if they didn't go along with Grayson's plan. It was such a terrible waste, but… Corinus had already proven himself a very risky experimental subject. Their time with him was over. "I've got plenty of readings to work with," they said with a deep sigh of regret. They activated their communicator. "Divak, is the rover ready to go?"

There was no answer. The three people in the room with working eyes and no mold infection exchanged fearful glances. "Divak, come in," Dizzie said. "Divak, come in!"

"Do y'think another revenant got her?" Grayson asked quietly, glancing back at Corinus like he was thinking of running despite the barrier between them.

"If I may," Six said after a moment of consideration. "I'd like to put forward another theory." He picked up his tablet from the nearby tabletop and tapped it a few times. "The rover has a positioning system relative to both my ship and myself, as well as a camera. In a moment, we will be able to see whether Divak made it there."

They all held their breath as they waited to see what the camera showed them.

A second after the image lit up the screen, Grayson let out a litany of swearwords so long that Dizzie wondered how he was breathing around them. "She's takin' the rover and running!" Sure enough, the camera was on the move, bouncing up and down as the rover made its way over the wet ground. "We've got to get out there, now!"

"It's worse than that," Six said, adjusting the camera so it was pointing backward toward where Divak had just abandoned them. "Look at the ground. Do you see it?"

Dizzie squinted for a second, then felt a fresh chill course through their body.

The ground behind the rover – ground that was mold-exposed after the rev that Lefty had lured away had exploded – was moving. And it had taken the shape of an entire army of undead, bright green revenants.

Well. It looked like they knew where the bodies of most of the dead Caridians had been kept before now – outside, perhaps buried in a mass grave, perhaps abandoned wherever the mold left them and blown into rocky crevasses over time.

Now they were awake once more, and on the hunt.

CHAPTER SEVENTEEN
Protector Divak

The moment she was released from the infected Centauran's psychic bondage, Divak knew she had to flee. This enemy had already shown itself to be incredibly adaptable, and its skills would only increase the longer they fought against it. Whatever was happening here was so far beyond the bounds of her original contract that she felt absolutely no guilt in severing it.

This was not her fight. These were not her people. If Divak was to live to create her own nest someday, she had to get out of here now. The odds of escaping and seeing Thassia again increased dramatically if she left the rest of these useless creatures here, so that was what she would do.

She didn't feel a hint of remorse as she ran down the corridor that led to the expansive hangar. The air stank of charred bone and ash, with the faint tang of the liquid Xenium beneath it all. It was a smell that Divak was looking forward to leaving behind her for good, except... Just as Divak reached the door, she slowed.

There was no good reason for her to walk away from

this empty-handed. She had already come up with half a dozen reasons why leaving her companions behind was a necessity, up to and including outright lying about their survival, but the fact that Divak was ranked a protector made using them challenging. After all, she had been hired to *protect* – if she were the only one to survive, it would invite censure from her superiors. Her future might be over anyway in that case, despite surviving this mess.

But if she came back with a store of liquid Xenium to soften the blow of the others' deaths… that would surely allow her to borrow enough glory to overcome a dishonorable fate. Or, if she didn't want to risk it with Leader Pavul, she could simply take Ix-Nix-Six's ship as her own and vanish into the underbelly of the galaxy, selling liquid Xenium at a premium price and making a new life for herself that way. It wasn't ideal, but it might be the best she could get.

Think later. Work now.

Divak strode over to the nearest broken-apart crate of liquid Xenium and hoisted two of the containers over her shoulders. Alarms registered in her power armor – this stuff was *dense,* heavier by far than most liquids. Two bottles of it would have to be enough. Any more and the rover might have trouble climbing the hills between here and the ship.

Divak stepped out into the blowing, blood red mist with a sense of satisfaction. She crunched across the gravelly paste she'd sent flying with her first shot at the Xenium – it felt so long ago now, even though it was only yesterday evening – and made her way to the rover, which waited for her like a prize of war. She set first one, then the second container of liquid Xenium in the storage area in the rear of the rover, strapping them down firmly so they wouldn't bounce around on the trip back. Then she got into the driver's seat, strapped herself in, and turned on the motor.

"Divak, is the rover ready to go?"

Divak allowed herself a chuckle as she pulled slowly away from the *Nexeri*. Sure enough, the Xenium was going to slow her down, but not so much she wouldn't make it to the ship ahead of her former comrades in plenty of time.

Perhaps she would fire on the *Nexeri* from the ship – *her* ship – once she was in orbit. Set the rest of the Xenium ablaze and spare her former crewmates the horrible deaths that awaited them all. It would be the charitable thing to do.

"Divak, come in."

They could talk at her all they wanted, but she wasn't going back for them. Her future was set, and as long as she decontaminated in time to avoid infection, it was very bright.

"Divak, come in!"

Divak was tempted to say something in reply, if only to enjoy her status as the top… what was the human phrase, hog? Top hog of the group, yes. But something pulled her out of her enjoyable thoughts of listening to their cries of dismay. It was a faint rumble – so faint that probably none of those lesser species would have heard it had they been here. A new storm rolling in? The mist behind seemed to be parting, somehow, settling down and pulling back like cobwebs floating away on a breeze. Some sort of geological incident?

In the name of every god those fools worshipped, if

they'd gone and set fire to the Xenium in the great ship just to take her out along with them, Divak would be… well, impressed. Furious, but reluctantly impressed.

Divak glanced over her shoulder at the ship. She blinked. Could it be… but the scientist, Dr Drexler, they had hypothesized that it was due to their party's concentrated bioshedding *inside* the *Nexeri* that had led to the resurrection of the new type of Xeno within it. They'd said nothing of leaving enough biomatter *outside* to resurrect more of the mold!

You blew up an enormous revenant not an hour ago. You really think you incinerated every single piece of it? That none of it might have infected more organic matter if it found it lying around? That it couldn't have turned into… that?

"That" was, at first glance, a living carpet, like waterbugs spread so thickly over the surface of a pond you couldn't see the fish beneath them except then they came up for the kill. It seemed to shimmer in a line between the great ship and the spot where Divak had blasted the last revenant to bits. She enhanced her vision with her power suit's pop-up display.

Waterbugs were not an apt comparison. These looked more like tiny versions of Ix-Nix-Six, stripped of his upright posture and intellect and given twice the length in leg- and arm-blades. They were not particularly large, but they were numerous, and their numbers were swelling by the moment as more bits and pieces of ancient, long-dead carapace, guided by the mold in some sinister alien fashion, shepherded them through their reconstruction into a new phase of life – a dark resurrection.

There were too many of them for Divak to successfully fend off. However, as long as she stayed her course and maintained her vigilance, she would make it to the ship before the vast majority of *them* made it to her. It would not be easy, but she didn't like easy.

Her blood sang through her body as she switched the rover to AI controls, then turned around and stood up tall, swinging her rifle into firing position at the same time. Some of these new revenants were truly fast, the wind whistling a deadly lullaby through the gaps in their clacking limbs as they sprinted toward her. Divak bared her teeth in a grin as she began to shoot them down.

Blam! Blam! Blam! Her gun had a much more significant effect on the little ones, shattering them into pieces and scattering them across the ground. Those broken carcasses probably meant more fodder for the mold, more bones for it to seek out and infest now that it had so thoroughly come back from the dead, but Divak didn't care. All she was interested in was the hunt, and right now, she had the upper hand.

Five, six, seven – two at once that time, yes, line yourselves up for me and make it even easier for me to dismember you. Ten, eleven, twelve… beautiful. Just beautiful.

As fun as target shooting like this was, it wasn't easy – the AI did what it could to keep the ride smooth, but the ground was uncooperative and the load was extreme. The bounces, Divak could endure – she had shot down tougher enemies from worse situations. This was nothing compared to free-falling through a hurricane in the hopes of firing off her jetpack in time to land her on the target's remote island hideout with no one the wiser. But the first true swerve almost sent her tumbling right off the rover.

"What in the…" Divak turned back to look at the controls and saw that the AI, after calculating the odds of getting up the last hill between them and the ship – the most direct route by far – had decided to reroute itself around instead, taking a hard left at the last second and sending them on a path that would add an extra three minutes to the time it took to get to the ship. *Murky mudspawn of a machine!* That was three minutes that Divak didn't have to spare.

Setting down her rifle with a grunt, she ran a quick program to see how much time she would save by getting back on the fast course. Almost a minute… but the odds the rover gave itself of making it over the hill in the first place were only seventy-two percent.

It will be worth it if it means I manage to–

Her lack of attention to her surroundings almost cost Divak her life when a revenant leapt out from behind a dark red boulder she'd just driven by and onto the rover. Its oversized mandibles clacked menacingly as it bore down on her, preparing to bite her – or perhaps to simply slice her head off with its overly sharp front legs.

Not this Thassian. Divak had her chainsword out in less than a second and cut the revenant's legs out from under it, sending it crashing down on top of the Xenium. It clutched at the nearest barrel, the tips of its remaining clawlike appendages scraping at the metal in a worrying way. If it punctured it–

There was no if. It had punctured it. *Useless dung beetle!* Twisting around so she could reach the straps, Divak cut through the ones holding the compromised bottle of Xenium. One more bump sent it rolling off the back of the rover, taking the revenant with it and leaving a smear of mold behind.

What a waste. But it was better to get rid of the punctured container than try to save it – it was too risky to slosh such a volatile liquid around, and the one she had left still carried enough Xenium to set her up in style once she returned to Thassia.

The rover was working better now, too. Divak's dark thoughts brightened as she continued pressing on to the ship. Her estimated time to arrival was one minute, thirty-two seconds now – that ought to be good enough. She turned the AI on again and settled back in to shoot off the interlopers who dared to come after her like some simple-minded prey species.

The smaller ones were coming faster and more numerously now, but her sniper rifle had enough ammunition to last her through a siege – it would certainly do to get her to the ship. More of the creatures emerged from behind boulders, and she shot them down like the irritations they were. Boulders to the right, boulders to the left… good thing she hadn't considered using them for cover, given how many revenants they hid.

As the rover finally turned onto the open plain between it and the ship, Divak was tempted to turn and focus on what was coming toward her, not what she was leaving behind. A sixth sense kept her looking back, though, and her diligence was rewarded a second later by gifting her with a moment of true terror, a moment that stood out in

Divak's mind as the worst experience of her life, because it rendered her still and dumb, as passive and helpless as any prey.

The boulder, or rather the giant *revenant*, unfurled itself like a pill bug waking up from a nap – its hard exoskeleton revealed an internal arachnidity, a form both like and unlike Ix-Nix-Six's own. Could this be one of the original revenants, one whose new infusion of intelligent life had decided it liked what it saw? It didn't look like any of the others – this was a broad creature, with shorter, stubbier legs and far more of them. This was a cockroach, seven meters long and three meters tall. A cockroach with jaws that could consume half the rover in a single crushing bite.

The dark spots wavering in front of her eyes finally reminded Divak that she needed to breathe. Shuddering, she hoisted her rifle up again and aimed it at the monster coming to try to end her life. *Blam! Blam!* The shots had no effect. Divak turned up the intensity of the blasts and tried again. Still nothing – it was like watching a blood bat peck away at the shell of a black-backed armorfish.

The new revenant was slow, though. That was her only chance. A monster this big could seriously damage the ship, but it would have to reach it first. What was it following? Her bioshedding? The energy of the rover? Heat signatures from both of them? It was time to change tactics, then. She could deploy the rover as a decoy.

Divak programmed in a new course, then leapt into the back and cut the ties holding the remaining container of liquid Xenium down and hoisted it onto her shoulder. A second later she jumped, hitting the ground at such an intense speed that her power armor was barely able to keep her on her feet. The rover veered to the left, buzzing off at a merry pace. Divak crouched down, keeping the Xenium container in front of her just in case it helped mask whatever had made her a target, and watched as the forefront of the smaller revenants turned to chase after the rover. A moment later, the lumbering beast turned with them.

Just as I suspected. Now all she had to do was make it another few hundred meters to the ship and take off before it came back. She knew she could do it. Ix-Nix-Six, praises be upon his fool head, had taught her well.

She stood, hoisted the container up again, and began to run for the ship. She no longer noticed her tiredness, no longer felt any sense of fatigue. Everything had narrowed down to one crystalline goal, and that was just how Divak liked it.

Three hundred meters to go. The first fifty was easy, but then Divak heard the telltale *scratch-scratch* of claws across gritty, wet rock, coming up behind her. No! They were supposed to be following the rover! Still running, she raised her rifle, twisted around, and fired at the first thing she saw moving.

Blam! The revenant burst into pieces. Two more of them ran past its remains, while a third stopped in the midst of the fresh carnage and…

Was it adding the pieces of the dismembered one to itself? It was – a few seconds later Divak had three revenants coming up fast, two of them small like the one she'd just blasted apart, and the third twice their size but just as fast. The clicking of their mandibles was nearly audible.

Divak gritted her teeth with frustration. She had two hundred meters left to cover and no other means of stopping these creatures. She would have to do the best she could with her sniper rifle. Even though the first one had re-formed, the firing slowed it down somewhat.

Blam! Blam! Blam! All three revenants shattered, but Divak didn't stop to watch them re-form. She was running at top speed for the ship, lengthening her strides and ignoring the brutal ache developing in her shoulder. Her power armor was maxed out. Her only advantage now was speed.

Out of the corner of her eye, she saw another small, four-legged revenant running toward her. *Blam!* It burst.

Another. *Blam!* The wind picked up, carrying mist into her sweating face. She inhaled some of it, had to fight with her lungs to keep working instead of stopping to cough. She had less than a hundred meters to go. She could do this.

Crunch-crunch. This sound was heavier than the light-footed ones she'd heard before, and it was getting closer.

Seventy meters. The crunching was still there. *Sixty meters.* She didn't look back. *Fifty–*

A sharp whistling sound filled the air, and a second later Divak stumbled and fell to the ground on one knee. She dropped the container of Xenium and panted, hacking up the murk in her lungs as she tried to get back to her feet, but she couldn't. Why? Why were her feet so – oh, *shit.*

She had no feet. She had *foot,* just her left foot. The right one was gone. Her power armor had sealed the wound off already, protecting her as best it could and injecting her with a powerful compound of painkillers, but now she could *feel* it – the thud of blood leaking from her open wound into the space around it, the hideous, mind-shattering pain of losing a limb that adrenaline was trying to keep at bay.

Divak rolled over into a sitting position, raised her rifle, and fired at the enormous revenant who had done this to her, this ugly admixture of too many of its own kind who had taken her leg, and screamed loud enough to make it stop its mad charge.

"You think you can simply *take* a piece of *me?*" she shrieked, firing until the undead beast's multiple sets of mandibles were blasted into parts so fine it would never be able to reconstruct them. "You think you get to have *me?* The Nightmare of Thassia? *Never!*" She fired until her rifle was so hot it refused to respond, so she threw it into the corpse of this ancient Caridian, a foolish revenant reborn to dare think they could hunt her down like an eel in a bucket.

She'd killed them all. Or, at least, she destroyed them so thoroughly that none of the ones close to her were even quivering yet, despite the bright green mold on their bodies already multiplying, expanding to create a newer, better monster. She watched with fury as the mold consumed her severed limb as well. It thought it could use *her* to make itself stronger?

No one used Divak and lived.

She didn't bother to look over her shoulder at the ship – she knew how far away it was. Fifty meters might as well be fifty miles; there was no way she would get there in time to escape the wave of revenants she could see coming for her in the distance, stirring up the crimson mist with the bulk of their lumbering bodies. Would she slink along the ground like a coward, trying to preserve her life at the cost of everything that made her Thassian? Would she be stabbed from behind again, taken apart piece by piece and turned into a far superior host than these ancient Caridians for the mold?

No, she absolutely would not.

Divak reached for the container of liquid Xenium. It was harder to haul over to her side than she'd anticipated. *Blood loss, you're suffering from severe blood loss. Shock will set in soon.*

Not too soon, though. Not soon enough to stop what she had planned.

Using her sword, Divak punctured the top of the container. The sharp smell of liquid Xenium filled the air, enough to make her eyes leak in reaction. Divak tipped it onto its side and watched as its contents flooded across her lower half, the dry ground beneath it, and the pieces of the revenants before her that were just now beginning to stir. She drenched herself with Xenium and took a brief moment to revel in the fact that her death was, from one perspective, the most expensive homage to greatness any Thassian had ever experienced. Who else could say their pyre had consumed an incalculably valuable amount of fuel?

No one else. You are legend. Even if only in her own mind, even if only for a moment.

The mist was getting closer. It was time. Divak, breathing

heavily, held her sword aloft. "Come and meet me in battle!" she shouted to the horde of revenants bearing down on her. "Come and join me in death!"

She powered up the chainsword, more exhortations of bloodlust and glory fighting to free themselves from her lips, then dug it into the rock she was sitting on and sent up a shower of bright yellow sparks.

Then she, and everything else in a half-kilometer radius, was vaporized.

Including Six's ship.

CHAPTER EIGHTEEN
Lefty

While the latest explosion buried some things, other things it uncovered.

Left-arm Mason, half-crushed by a boulder a dozen yards from where his revenant pursuer was blown up, found himself freed with the advent of the second blast. His mind was fuzzy with separation from his main brain and something else, something slowly unfurling through his synapses like seafloss caught in a Martian tide, strove to focus.

Lefty's battery was broken, leaking, barely functioning anymore. Most of his extensors were gone as well, and two of his fingers were broken.

Good thing he could use these other scattered body parts to help himself go. They just clicked right in, too, like they were made for him!

Lurching like a half-crushed sand crab, Lefty headed out across the rocky field, feeling his way back home.

Mason would be so happy to see him again.

CHAPTER NINETEEN
Dizzie Drexler

The impact from Divak's explosion knocked Dizzie off their feet. Divak had already knocked them off their feet figuratively when they saw her abandon the rover through the camera and run off toward Six's ship – *she's leaving us, she's really leaving us, oh shit oh shit oh shit* – but this time it was literal. One moment they were standing there jury-rigging a power source for the welding tools Grayson had come up with to reseal the small door that closed off the hangar from the outside world, the next Dizzie and everyone else was on the ground, thrown off balance by the intensity of the earthquake shuddering through the *Nexeri*.

It did more than knock them all to the ground – it killed the power to the hangar, leaving them in total darkness except for the sliver of light showing through the last crack in the door.

"Well… bollocks," Grayson said after a minute. "Guess the Thassian went out on a high note after all." He snorted, trying to seem unaffected, but his hands shook. "Drama queen."

"Holy shit." Dizzie pressed up to their knees, activating the built-in lights in their EVA suit so that they could see at least a little way around them. Lights on their collar, wrists, and ankles glowed, illuminating their surroundings with a cool blue sheen. "That was… I mean, I know these containers are pretty big, but that seems like a lot of explosion for just one of them!"

"It was two," Six said from where he was already on his feet – of course. Nothing ever seemed to keep him down for long. "You recall? We saw the footage of the first one falling from the back of the rover before the revs tore it apart. Once Divak blew up the first container, the fire from that blast undoubtedly set off the second one."

"Ah." Yeah, that made sense. "That's… not good."

It felt a bit awful to hope that Divak had been killed before she made it to Six's ship, but only a *little* bit awful. After all, she was pretty awful herself, trying to abandon them here on Sik-Tar while they escaped on their own. And now… "I'm sure she took the ship out too." Now they were stranded here, just the five of them – well, four in all honesty – against the revenants in a fight for survival.

Surrounded by mold and revenants and people you barely know and can't trust, look what Divak did to us, and now we're stuck here and Corinus is gone and you'll never get out of here, you're going to die here and no one will ever find your body and– Dizzie was spiraling. They pinched their leg, hard, the brief flash of pain knocking them out of their spin into hysteria.

What did they know, for sure? That staying alive under these circumstances wasn't a fight they could hope to win in the long run. Dizzie knew that, but they weren't ready to give up yet either. "That blast probably bought us a reprieve from the revenants," they said, brushing dust off their knees and the seat of their suit. "We need to figure out the power situation, then shut this place down as fully as we possibly can. We might–"

"The hell are you on about?" Grayson demanded. In the dim light of Dizzie's suit and the glow of the streams of tiny lights set into his brother's limbs, he looked somewhere between furious and distraught. He was dusty, sweaty, and clenching his hands into fists so hard Dizzie knew it had to be hurting him. "We're done! Toast! Reached the end of the line! Divak destroyed the *ship,* you mad thing – there's no other way for us off this planet! We're done here!"

Dizzie held out placating hands. "I know it looks bad, but we haven't explored all our options yet. We haven't even explored all of this ship yet! It's possible we'll run across something that will let us–"

"Let us what?" Grayson demanded, closing the distance between them. "Let us find another store of Xenium all ready to be blown up? Let us discover a fresher load of moldering corpses all set to be turned into revenants? Let us activate a little *more* mold so's it gets into our bloodstreams that much faster and turns *us* into more of *them*? Do you want to end up like your buddy Dr Lifhe, hey? Because I don't!"

"What, so you just want to do nothing at all?" Dizzie asked, losing their own carefully managed sense of calm. "You want to just sit down here in the dark and give up?

Or maybe, oh, maybe we should blow this place sky-high! With this much Xenium in it we might actually reach the sky with an explosion. Is that the best course of action to you right now?"

"Better than sitting around waiting for death to take us!"

"What is, running toward it with open arms? To hell with that!"

"To hell with you! Who died and made you the boss of us all?"

"Nobody had to make me the boss of you!" Dizzie poked their finger at Grayson. "I started this expedition as the boss of you, I am *still* the boss of you, and I am telling you right now, we're not giving up!"

Grayson sneered, giving them both of his middle fingers. "And how's bein' the boss worked out for you, eh?"

"Please." Six held up a claw. "The last thing we need right now is to fight among ourselves. I believe we ought to finish sealing this outer door, then return to the laboratory and ensure that Dr Lifhe is still being held securely."

"Oh." *Oh shit.* Dizzie hadn't even thought of that yet. "You don't think–"

"Recall that the power in the laboratory is run off its own battery," Six said, and Dizzie felt a wave of relief that evaporated as he continued, "However, given the damage that the structure has sustained, there is no telling how well that battery survived, if at all. We had best check."

Yeah, we'd better.

There was only a sliver of light still coming into the main hangar of the *Nexeri,* only a few inches of door to close. It should have taken almost no time at all – objectively, it *was* very fast. But fast felt pretty damn slow when you could literally hear a bunch of alien zombies pulling their dismembered bodies back together in the distance, the rattle of carapace and crunch of pointy Caridian feet impacting rock as they came closer and closer. By the time the door was sealed, the first of the revenants had arrived, and was pounding hard on their fragile fix-it.

"That's all the time we got. Let's head back," Grayson muttered, backing away from the door with an apprehensive look on his craggy face.

With their suit lights to guide their way, Dizzie ran on shaky legs across the hangar and into the corridor. They slowed down right outside the lab, though. If the power was off… if the containment field was gone…

There was nothing to do but look. Dizzie took a deep breath, set their multitool to the stunner function they'd used on the big revenant earlier just in case, and opened the door.

They exhaled a huge sigh of relief when they saw the warm glow of yellow lights within the room, and the light indicating that the containment field was up and running at the far end. Corinus was awake and turned to stare at them with eyes that somehow seemed *bigger* than they had before. More Caridian.

The mold was evolving him right before their eyes. Dizzie hoped the camera they'd put in place was still recording – this would make for absolutely invaluable data for… well, whatever came next, once Dizzie could bring themself to look at it all the way through.

Or *who*ever came next and found their notes, if Dizzie

was already dead. Which seemed likely at this point, but they weren't going to dwell on that right now.

Six and Grayson followed them in, Mason bringing up the rear, moving slowly. His movements had a hint of a lurch to them now that he had no eyes *or* left arm, but Grayson didn't seem overly concerned, so Dizzie wouldn't be either. "We still have power," Dizzie said.

"Do you think this battery extends solely into the lab?" Six asked. "Or does it reach farther into the rest of the ship?"

"What're you asking them for?" Grayson said, sounding slightly less grumpy than he'd been out in the hangar. "We'll get a read on it. Mason, c'mere."

An extensor protruded from the cavity where Mason's throat would have been, a special one with attachments that let it glom onto the ancient control pad.

"Easier than I thought it would be," Grayson muttered, his own eyes going vague. "Let's see… feels like it can be extended to cover this whole section of the ship. The other bunkhouse we looked in earlier and the hangar each have their own power sources."

"Hmm. Do they also have their own security measures?" Dizzie asked.

Grayson raised a caterpillar-like eyebrow. "What, you mean like weapons? I told you, this place ain't equipped for that kinda stuff. It's not gonna give us the–"

"No, I mean like…" What exactly did they mean? Dizzie had to stop and think about it for a second. "Hang on." Their head was absolutely aching, their legs quivering with fatigue, their stomach was growling… they needed to eat. First, though, they all needed to do what they could to secure themselves against the violence that was coming their way.

"I'm talking about turning on more of these force fields, like the one we've got in here. I doubt the components are unique. If we could get some in place over doors and run power to them, then we could keep the revs outside from breaking through, and be able to block out the mold, too. It would give us breathing space and a chance to take stock of what we've got and see what makes the most sense for us to tackle next."

They looked at Six. "You've got access to the library. See if you can find a manifest of the ship's parts in there. This force field is pretty specialized, but also pretty important – I can't believe they wouldn't just have the pieces around for one, in case some part of it broke."

"Your thought is good," Six said. "I'll go at once."

"An' Mason and I'll go finish the work on the door," Grayson said. "Better than sticking around here lookin' at that freak," he added contemptuously as he turned and walked out into the hall. Mason followed him. With them gone, that left Dizzie and Corinus alone.

He watched as they got a nutrient-dense meal bar out of their pack and munched at it mechanically. Dizzie had always disliked the crumbly, waxy taste but managed to get every morsel down before washing the remnants away with half of their remaining pure water. Their EVA suit had a store of water in its internal reservoirs, but Dizzie wanted to save that for an emergency.

Well, a bigger emergency.

We should have brought more supplies with us from Six's ship. The thought of everything they'd had in there, all the equipment and food and water that had gone to waste made Dizzie's head hurt even more.

Not just wasted supplies – a wasted chance. This had been the opportunity of their lifetime, and they unequivocally blew it. They should have been stricter about the suits, should have gotten everyone out of there as soon as Mason found the bodies, should have looked more carefully for evidence of the mold in the atmosphere. Dizzie had been so focused on looking for traces of Xenium that they hadn't even thought about trying to find evidence of the mold beyond generally searching for organic molecules. After all, Sik-Tar was so different from the planets in the PK-L system. They should have figured a mold variant existed as well. If they'd just tried a little bit harder, maybe…

"You look sad."

They jerked out of their reverie and stared over at Corinus, whose enlarged eyes now protruded from the sides of his head, giving him more of the three-hundred-sixty-degree vision that Caridians had.

Don't talk to him – it – don't talk to it, don't talk to it…

They couldn't help it. There was just too much to be learned about the mold from the creature who used to be their best friend. "How do you know?"

"How do I know what?"

"What sadness looks like?"

Corinus tilted his head. It was a startlingly alien gesture, from him. When he was all Centauran, he'd evoked almost all his emotion through his eyelids, and now… now he didn't have eyelids. "What do you mean? I have seen sadness many times."

"*Corinus* has seen sadness many times. You're not him."

"I am him," the revenant said calmly. As Dizzie watched, a tiny tentacle slid out of his right-side nostril and up, swiping over one of his big new eyes like it was cleaning it. "I am more, as well."

There was no denying that last part, at least. "I've never seen anything like you before."

"I know."

"What else do you know?" Dizzie asked, despite their brain screaming *do not engage, do not engage!*

"Very much. I carry the lives and deaths of billions of beings over countless years. I carry their knowledge, their experiences. What one knows, all learn."

Dizzie shook their head. "No. You're nothing but a pile of instincts – you fight, you kill, you consume. There's no higher knowledge within you."

"Then how am I able to speak to you?"

Dizzie shrugged sadly. "I have no clue. Maybe it has something to do with Centauran brain structure, maybe it's something about their telepathy, maybe it's just that you want to consume him in a different way. But what I'm hearing right now isn't either of you – it's just a predator's lure. You're saying whatever you think will work to make me open the door to you. You don't mean any of it."

He tilted his head again. "Can a pile of instincts lie?"

Dizzie snorted. "If it can revitalize itself off nothing more than spit and a few skin cells, then I'd say it's tenacious enough to do almost anything."

Corinus nodded. "Like evolve sentience. Like carry on a conversation with a fellow thinking, feeling being."

"Like evolve a mechanism by which you can get your prey."

"Is there really a difference?"

Dizzie sighed. "I think there is. Maybe I'm wrong, but… I can't risk it." They reached over and adjusted the force field to block sound. "Now how about you keep your poison to yourself for a while?"

Dizzie looked down, distracted by what their mold-infested friend had said. The question of what kind of creature the mold actually was – whether "mold" was a truly accurate term for it or not, given the rapid evolution it was capable of causing – was the sort of question that Dizzie was dying to answer. And its ability to use Corinus's telepathy so quickly… was that because the mold itself was telepathic, or just wildly efficient? Either way, it was worrying.

The urge to turn around and keep up the discussion with Corinus was incredibly strong, but they had to be stronger. They couldn't give into it. Not when they knew, without a shadow of a doubt *knew*, that no matter what the mold actually was, it didn't mean any of them well. They were nothing more than things to be devoured.

"You seem pensive."

Dizzie startled at the sound of another voice in the room. They realized their throat was dry again, and their hands cramped from being in the same position for an extended period of time. "Oh… how long have you been gone?"

"About an hour," Six said. "Not so long. Are you unwell?"

"No. Just…" How did one explain an existential crisis to a Caridian? Did they even think that way?

This, at least, was a question that Dizzie could get an answer to. "I'm not physically unwell, but I feel very... upset about what's happened here. And responsible. I feel like I could have been a better leader, and a better friend."

Six's antennae waved gently. "The first incident of bioshedding was beyond anyone's control, when the faceplate in Mason's helmet cracked. And you rightly pointed out that I was irresponsible with my dissemination of ship waste. Neither of these incidents can be blamed on you."

"But they should be. I'm the one in charge, the one making the plans!" Dizzie insisted. "I'm the one who should know better, aren't I?"

"Are you?" Six challenged. "You have been on how many field expeditions before this one?"

"Two."

"And were either of them to distant, potentially dangerous planets? Or expeditions that you yourself were responsible for planning?"

"No," Dizzie muttered reluctantly, "but just because I lack the practical fieldcraft doesn't mean I wouldn't have fought tooth and nail to get a spot on this expedition anyway. This place – the answers we could find here, the new questions we could discover if we had the resources... it's incredible."

"True, but you didn't know that ahead of time," Six said. "And neither did your superiors, who made the final decision concerning your addition to this team. Truly, I'm surprised my efforts to put together an expedition were taken as seriously as they were. I half expected the Coalition military ships that found me to lock me up in a lab where they could do experiments on *me*. Instead, I was given a chance, and so were you. And that chance," he added gently, "is not yet lost."

"It is for him." Dizzie jerked their head in the direction of the testing chamber but resolutely didn't look into it. They didn't care to keep looking at what Corinus had become.

"And for Protector Divak, but it is impossible to control every action of every person. We all have our own beliefs and impulses, our own sense of what is right and what is not. It's one reason my people tend to keep to themselves – the wider universe makes so little sense, otherwise." Six patted their shoulder with a claw. "But I'm glad I made the effort to go beyond my comfort level, Dr Drexler, even if it has not turned out quite the way I had hoped."

Dizzie gave him a half smile. "I think we're past the formalities at this point. You should call me Dizzie."

"I would be honored to. I would also be honored to share with you the good news that this ship is, in fact, prepared to seal off this corridor from the central hangar."

They brightened. "You found the right parts to put in the doors?"

"No. I discovered that the technology to lay force fields over these places is already embedded in the ship itself."

"Really?" Dizzie was impressed. "That's very forward-thinking of your ancestors. Have you had a lot of experience with contagions in the past? Plagues, infestations, that kind of thing?"

"Fortunately for my species, we have not." Six clacked his mandibles. "I believe, in this case, we must simply count ourselves lucky."

Dizzie was about to reply, but got cut off by the sudden crackle of the radio. "The two of you need to get out here," Grayson said. He sounded excited. "I think we might have a way to get off this hell-damned rock after all."

A surge of excitement rolled through Dizzie. They exchanged a glance with Six, whose antennae waved with more force now.

"We're on our way."

CHAPTER TWENTY
Mason Bane

It was good, Mason reflected as he listened to his brother in his minds, chattering about this and that, that he had developed an ability to shield Grayson from truth. Not *lie,* he was never interested in outright lying to him, but it was important to Mason that he be able to keep the worst of the things about his existence as a cyborg out of Grayson's head. None of it was his brother's fault or problem, and he had done the best he could by Mason.

As far as Grayson knew, Mason didn't experience pain. Why would he? The original receptors in the brain that would have generated the pain response had been reprogrammed – there was nothing to feed them, after all. Mason's body was five separate minds all feeding into one consciousness, not a bunch of messy limbs flailing about getting bumps and bruises.

The truth was, though, that Mason's original body had been lost to an act so memorably painful that his mind wasn't able to get past it. The pain lived in his brain, a part of his past and, in its own way, always there in his present. Certain stimuli sent spikes of ancient agony through his head – the crackle of fire, the sound of metal rasping against itself, and high-pitched screams were some of the worst. The tension of the fresh burns on his face was another one of those stimuli – fairly lowkey by comparison, but the receptors in the cells knew what had happened, and transmitted a series of signals to the brain that he couldn't help but interpret as "Ow, ow, ow." It made his remaining limbs stiffen and spasm from time to time, a tell he hoped Grayson was too busy to notice.

That, and not being able to see out of his largest brain's eyes sucked balls, too.

The pain was slightly soothed by the sheer exuberance in his brother's voice as he explained their observations to Dr Drexler and Six.

"Look around you," Grayson said expansively. Mason could sense him spinning in a circle. "What do you see?"

"Um … a mess?" Dr Drexler offered.

"A refinery," Six said.

"A *hangar*," Grayson clarified. "It's a bloody hangar for these pod-things. That's what it was originally, right? These were a bunch of escape pods for the Caridians who flew this big-ass ship here in the first place. Sure, it seems like most've 'em have been turned into Xenium storage or hollowed out for parts and glommed onto the refineries, but I think some of 'em could be turned back to their original use. We just have to get enough of the right pieces together to make it happen, and make sure the one we pick is already in one of the launch tubes." Most of those had been converted to smoke stacks, but a few that were farther from the refineries had been happily ignored.

"That's… huh." Mason tilted his right hand so the sensor in it could see Dr Drexler. It could only see them in UV light, unfortunately – he really needed some work – but it was better than nothing. "That's a great idea."

"I'm a goddamn genius, yeah."

"*If* we can find a likely pod," they went on, "and *if* we can get the ship to launch it, and *if* we can make it accept liquid Xenium as fuel, and *if* we–"

"Y'need to stop being such a killjoy," Grayson huffed. "You think we haven't thought of that already? Mason's been all over the ones that are left in the launch tubes, and one of them looks real good."

"Oh? Which one?"

"Go show 'em," Grayson said.

Mason wended his way between the crates to the pod at the very back of the hangar, the others following him. This one had been the clear choice for him when it came to narrowing down a pod to use for their potential escape. It had a different feel from the others – he didn't quite know how to explain it, but it just seemed like it was built with more of a personal touch. The seats inside were in a wider configuration, the controls seemed more inherently understandable, and even the self-care facilities in the back of it were different from the ones in the other pods. Like they covered more functions than a Caridian's basic act of cleansing and "expulsion".

It felt like it had been designed with another species in mind, in fact.

[Do you think it's possible the Caridians were accompanied here by other aliens?]

"Maybe. Do you actually care?" Grayson muttered.

[We're just curious.] Mason let his right hand and its extensors spread out over the control panel until he found the power switch he'd located last time. He flicked it on.

"Whoa!" Dr Drexler took a step inside. "I thought you said all their power supplies had been compromised."

"All except for this one, from what we found." Grayson sounded satisfied. "Like your lab, this pod came with its own battery power. Six, once you talk to the computer and get it all booted up and we figure out how to open the stack up there so this can actually get out 'stead of running into the shielding, then we just fuel it up and get the hell off this planet. It'll be close quarters, but way better than all of us gettin' dead."

[Grayson… I don't think this one pod will be enough.]

His brother didn't say anything. He couldn't, not without the others being able to listen in, but Mason could feel a new sense of heaviness in his mind, like someone had dropped a marble into the part that Grayson inhabited, pulling all his thoughts in toward it as it rolled down, down, down.

Dr Drexler was speaking. "…amazing find! Gosh, I see what you mean about the controls here, it really is intuitive, isn't it?" They sat down and reached for the thruster. "Wow, perfect distancing. Six, do you think it's possible that the Caridians who came here were already in contact with aliens? Not, like, just knowing that they existed, but actually working together with some of them? Would they have brought someone other than a Caridian along with them to Sik-Tar?"

"It is not impossible," Six allowed, his own eyes bright and assessing as he looked around the inside of the pod. "There have been a few instances of close cooperation between members of the Seethe and those of other species, but they are so infrequent as to be legends among my people." Mason sidled to the side, closer to his brother as the two of them continued to talk about the escape ship.

"Why don't you think it'll be enough?" his brother hissed.

[Weight limitations. We must err on the side of more fuel than less, even with a fairly thin atmosphere.]

"We're not *that* heavy altogether – surely we can squeeze in. Leave behind your legs, if need be."

[Liquid Xenium is heavy, brother.] Grayson's sense of lowness worsened. [And the question of livability is a viable one. The three of you have far more need to eat than we do, but there are very few rations. That means we'll have to use the pod's wormhole capabilities to get somewhere before you all starve to death, which means we'll definitely need to include excess amounts of fuel.] Mason paused. He didn't actually want to say this next part, but he was determined to be honest with his brother. [The easiest thing to do would be to leave the others behind.]

"We can't do that."

[We can. Neither of us *want* to do that,] – because they remembered the feeling of being thrown away in their childhoods all too well – [but in the end, saving you is the most important thing. No matter what, we have to stay together.]

Mason couldn't imagine life without his brother – he didn't want to. Having multiple minds was nice in that he was never exactly *lonely*, but listening to himself natter away wasn't the same as communicating with someone outside of himself. Someone who knew him, cared about him, and took the time to understand him.

Dr Drexler had done their best to understand him during this expedition, too. He was going to be very sad to leave them here and miss out on getting to know them better, but he couldn't see a way around it. Their importance simply couldn't compare to his brother's. [We still need to find the missing components for this pod before any plan can be enacted,] he reminded Grayson. [Perhaps we'll find something between now and then that will allow us to save more than ourselves.]

Grayson didn't reply to him, just nodded roughly, then cleared his throat and turned to talk to Six. "You ever flown one of these things before? You got any idea of what it's gonna need to get off the ground?"

"I have some idea, yes," Six said, "but there's no need to rely on my memory. There are surely schematics for these pods in the library. I shall translate the files and bring them to you, and we will discover what needs to be added to this one in order to make it work. I can already tell that several stabilizers will be required, and possibly an extra fuel storage tanker. Or perhaps not – I'll need to do some calculations on the amount of Xenium needed to get it off the ground."

"That sounds great!" Dr Drexler enthused, getting up from the pilot's seat and joining them in the doorway. Mason watched them from his right-hand camera, committing the picture of the three of them to his memories. It would help his brother later on if he could reassure him that he hadn't forgotten these two. Grayson, for all he liked to pretend he didn't have a heart, was the softer of the two of them by far. "We should–"

Taptaptap.

The noise was fairly soft, but in the vastness of the hangar it reverberated like someone was striking it with a hammer.

Dr Drexler whirled around. "What the hell is that?"

Taptaptap.

Six's antennae began to wave back and forth, like they were caught in a strong breeze. "I think it's coming from the door."

"But you sealed the door!" Dr Drexler turned their wide eyes toward Grayson. "You did, didn't you? You welded it shut."

"We did," Grayson said, "but–"

Taptaptap. Taptaptap... taptap... CLANG! The door that Mason and his brother had just finished repairing – where they'd laid down so many new layers of metal that it was twice as strong as it had been before – was suddenly ripped straight out of the wall. The tip of an enormous claw poked through the hole, swiveling around like it was searching for something. For them, perhaps?

Mason wasn't going to hang around and find out. He grabbed his brother by the collar of his EVA suit and threw him onto his back, then scuttled for the hallway that led to their one hope for salvation. He was slower than he liked, on only three limbs, but he still outpaced Dr Drexler and Six.

Maybe this was a blessing in disguise. Maybe those two would die now and save the Bane brothers the guilt of having to abandon them here.

The claw retracted, and a moment later several of the smaller revenant variations swarmed in through the hole. These ones looked the most like Six of any of them so far, slim and fast, except for the third one that entered.

That one was… odd. Bipedal, like the others, but not as tall, and it only had claws on its front limbs, not on all four of them. Its head was the strangest thing about it – oval, not triangular, and the eyes were around the size of the average human instead of the enormous orbs that seemed to come standard on the Caridians. The weirdest thing, though, was that the head itself was growing out of its stomach, like it had been decapitated and clumsily shoved back together.

Was this a new species of Xeno? Mason snapped a photo of it for later analysis but kept running. They were almost to the door. He waited to hear screams from behind him… but instead he heard a "Yeah, bitch, take that!" followed by a crackling *bbzzzztt!* He twisted the visual input sensor in his left leg around to take a look, and–

Saw the strange, gut-headed revenant that had been less than five feet from him and Grayson suddenly fall to the floor, its mold-covered body steaming from the force of the electricity Dr Drexler had fired through it. "Go!" they shouted, running at them even as they primed their particle detector for another shot. Behind them, Six was holding another revenant at bay with a flurry of surprisingly speedy blows, knocking it right off its pointy feet every time it got close enough to hit.

"Go, go, go! Get inside the lab, then we can activate the force field to keep them out!"

Mason got himself and his brother into the hallway. Dr Drexler and Six followed them a second later, and just after that, they triggered the force field mechanism that Six had discovered in the frame of the door.

Honestly, Mason wasn't sure how well it was going to work. Relying on ancient technology running on auxiliary power was dicey, and to be something that was supposed to keep out the vast kinetic energy of the revenants? How would that even work? Surely they'd hammer their way through after a few minutes.

He'd underestimated the Caridian tech. The force field didn't just hold them back – it literally fried the one that got close enough to touch it. More tried, and kept trying, but as the pile of dead – or re-dead – dead again? – grew to the point of obscuring the doorway, they finally pulled back.

"Yeah!" Dr Drexler said. "How do you like *that*?" They turned and looked at the rest of them with a smug look. "Perfect timing, wouldn't you say?"

"Not really," Grayson muttered, getting off Mason's back and onto his own two feet again. "Now how're we supposed to get anywhere, huh? Can't get the parts we need, can't access the shuttle to put them in place, can't even think about taking off when we'd have to get through a swarm of those bastards to do it."

Dr Drexler's smile faltered. "Ah. Right. I hadn't thought about that."

"Surely our earlier examinations of the ship must have yielded some ideas," Six said. "Tunnels or tubes that we could use to traverse to other areas, for example."

"None big enough for a fully grown person," Dr Drexler replied. "None connected to the lab, at least. Your people either built really big or really small – they didn't seem to care much for a happy medium."

"I'm sure they didn't anticipate the possibility of needing to give themselves backdoors to get through their own ship."

"Right. Well..." Dr Drexler ran a hand through their short, tangled hair. "I... I'm not sure what to do. We, um. We might... maybe we could..."

[I can do it.]

Grayson glanced sharply at Mason. "What're you talkin' about?"

[I can do it,] he said again. [I have three limbs left that are small enough to fit into those tunnels. One of my arms did it before as we were investigating the *Nexeri*, another one can do it again. They're mostly nonorganic. As long as I'm careful, they should be able to gather the parts and take them to the remaining pod. Once it's ready to go, we can use that arm as a distraction, the same way we did with the first revenant.]

"What is he saying?" Six asked. Grayson relayed Mason's message.

"That's a generous offer, but it seems awfully dangerous for you," Dr Drexler said. "The likelihood of you losing at least one more limb is very high. It's a lot to ask."

Mason shrugged. [It's that or die.]

"What choice do we have?" Grayson said.

"None," Six confirmed. "Come. Let's look over the schematic and ensure you know what to look for."

CHAPTER TWENTY-ONE
Grayson Bane

There were times when it was hard to keep up with Mason's brains. Grayson usually liked to ride shotgun, following along with the various little Masons' escapades and ensuring that everything was working well, but right now he felt his lack of energy like a lead brick had been grafted to his spine, pressing him down even as he fought to rise back up.

It was especially hard to keep up when all three of the remaining visual processors were functioning in different ranges: one in ultraviolet, one getting the best resolution in its heat-sensing mode, and the other's camera operating normally, which didn't help very much when there was little light to work with other than what it was generating itself. Not to mention the challenges of making it through ancient waste tunnels that were really too small for the arm's extensors to get through without serious modification, which made them so... damn... slow.

[Take a break.]

"Nope, I've got it," Grayson muttered, lifting his head up from where he and Mason were sitting in the mess hall. It had the biggest entrances into the tunnels, which so far seemed uninhabited by both revenants and mold. "M'fine."

[You're not. Go eat something. Drink something. Take a nap. Clear your mind. You're slowing us down more than anything else right now.]

"Who do you think you are, you pushy son of a bitch?"

[Don't talk about Mom that way. Go on.]

"Yeah, yeah." Grayson stretched and felt his neck crack in three places. "Fine, you brat. But let me know if you need another set of eyes."

[I do need another set of eyes, make me one.]

"When we're out of here." When he and his brother were on their way and everyone else was … doing whatever they were going to be doing at that point. Hopefully if they were revenants, they were back to being dead. And in the case of Dr Drexler and Six, they'd probably *also* be dead soon enough. If they were lucky.

Grayson was good at compartmentalizing. He had to be. He stood up and walked around, took note of how much food they had brought with them from Six's ship – he and Mason would be able to last about a month on it if they were careful – and finally went in to talk to Six about how to rev up the wormhole generator on the pod, because a month wasn't good enough and he didn't want to be surprised with any rusted but functioning Caridian booby traps or unexpected surprises once they were in space.

Six, per usual, was very free with handing over information. "It seems like it will be quite easy to operate," he assured Grayson. "Much like the wormhole generator on my own ship, all you need is to input the proper password and the sequence will initiate on its own."

"Yeah, but we don't have that password, do we? Or will the password that worked on your ship work for this one?" Grayson asked, vaguely aware of the first of his brother's limbs dropping down into the hangar. It did so slowly, every extensor used to soften its landing. None of the revenants milling about in front of the entrance to the hallway seemed to notice it, and Right-leg Mason headed for its target destination to steal a set of stabilizers for their getaway pod.

"Hmm." Six's antennae waved more vigorously. "That is an excellent question. The operational passwords for our ships are well known to all Caridians, as we are inherently loyal to the Glorious Hegemony. The passwords are to shield our technology from aliens, not from ourselves. However, they generally only stay relevant for a hundred years or so – once per the use cycle of each generation. After that we generate new ones for Seethe use. I will have to do some research to look this generation's password up."

"How's about you go do that now?"

Six left the lab for the library, leaving Grayson alone with Dr Drexler – and the creepy thing that used to be Dr Lifhe, who was looking less Centauran and more like a revenant by the hour. Almost all of his original skin had vanished now, replaced by carapace and shifting plates of moldy bone. His new eyes glittered, even in the low light, and his mouth moved almost constantly. Grayson wondered what he was saying.

"How can you stand to keep him goin' in here?" he asked Dizzie despite himself. He tried not to focus on how another one of Mason's limbs was coming out into the hangar. It had fewer extensors to give it swiftness, but Mason had let it down farther away from the crowd of revenants, where it was less likely to attract notice. "Doesn't he creep you the hell out?"

Dr Drexler sighed. "What am I supposed to do, just kill him?"

"Yeah, that's exactly what you're supposed to do." Grayson gestured at the testing chamber. "Pretty soon he's going to be too big to be held in there, and he'll start buttin' up against the force field. At that point you'll start electrocuting him bit by bit just by dint of doin' nothin'. Plus, don't think I haven't seen the shit you're spraying in there to keep his brain quiet. Better to finish him off before you run out, don't you think?"

"Maybe," Dr Drexler said. They sounded almost as tired as Grayson felt. "But I'm still learning a lot about the mold from him. Its rate of growth is impressive – I've been working on correlating it to visual data gathered from Dr Rigby's expedition, which makes me think that the mold that spread across PK-L7 has the same origin as this mold."

"Which is interesting why?"

Dr Drexler perked up a bit. "Oh, there are whole fields of astromycology devoted to the spread of spores through space! Think about how far Sik-Tar is from the PK-L system. If their mold has the same genetic signature, then that could feed into all sorts of theories out there about everything from gene seeding to the existence of a founder race, or even space mushrooms that can generate their own wormholes..."

"Bullshit," Grayson said, startled into a chuckle even as he was drawn back to watching Mason's progress. Left-leg Mason was trying to move a container of liquid Xenium into the pod now. It was slow going, but he was still good so far.

"Most of the people who push that theory are usually high on their own dissertation subjects, but it's out there," Dr Drexler assured him. "If it's true, then it tells us a lot about the original Xenos, too. They presented so differently than the revenants here – a lot more soft tissue, extensive growth of tentacles, that kind of thing, whereas here it's almost all clear variations on Caridian physiology."

"Except for that one."

"Yeah, except for that weird one. I have no idea what the basis for its anatomy is or why it's so different from the others. I don't want to theorize more without data, but I am *very* willing to call it creepy as hell." They shared a shudder. "Anyway, I'm taking constant readings on Corinus's mutations and–"

[Shit!]

Grayson leapt back into his brother's mind at the sudden swear word, blocking Dr Drexler out as he focused.

[One of these bastards found Left-leg Mason. He managed to get the fuel to the pod and hooked up to the tank, but it's punctured. There's some spillage, we can't say how much.]

"Where's Left-leg Mason now?" Grayson asked.

[In the process of being ripped to shreds,] Mason said grimly. [Don't try to access him, you don't want to experience that.]

Grayson swallowed. "Got it. What about the others?"

[They got their supplies to the pod and into position. As soon as we turn the power on in there, the stabilizers ought to take effect.]

"Good. Get them back here, then."

[Will do.] He sighed. [It's going to be weird trying to get around on one arm and one leg.]

"We'll make it work," Grayson promised him. Mason sighed and pushed him out of the group mind, and Grayson became aware of Dr Drexler looking at him curiously.

"News from your brother?"

"Yeah. He got everything fixed up on the pod, but the Xenium was compromised. Gonna be a rough takeoff if the takeoff generates enough heat to ignite the leftover liquid."

"I'll do some basic calculations on its rate of evaporation," they said, pulling out their tablet. "It might be less flammable once it becomes less volatile."

"Whatever makes you happy," Grayson muttered. He could vaguely sense the other limbs making their way back through the tunnels. Right-arm Mason in particular seemed very keen to get back, although his movements were a little jerky. His light was almost dead, making it impossible to gauge whether or not he'd taken extra damage out there. "You wanted to spray the limbs down with disinfectant when they got back, yeah?"

"Yes, absolutely." Dr Drexler reached for the palm-sized

mister they'd prepared earlier in the day. "Let's make sure we keep any more mold from joining us back here. This ought to kill the spores on contact, but I'd still wait a few minutes to make sure the limbs' nervous systems are clear before having them hook back up to Mason's main body. They make an actual neural connection, right?"

"Right."

"Then yeah, definitely wait a bit." The two of them headed for the mess hall and over to Mason, and a second later Right-leg Mason dropped down from the tunnel entrance in the ceiling. Dr Drexler immediately sprayed him down with the disinfectant. Right-arm Mason followed about thirty seconds later and was similarly sprayed.

"That's all that's left," Grayson said. "The left leg was caught by the revenants. It ain't gonna be joining us any time soon."

[Grayson ...]

"Aw, that's too bad," Dr Drexler replied. "Sorry about that, Mason."

Grayson shrugged, trying to put the loss behind them. No time for mourning the dead right now, after all. "Eh, I'll make him a better one."

[Grayson ... I feel like ...]

"And another left arm, I guess." Dr Drexler frowned in sympathy.

Grayson refused to feel bad about Lefty's disappearance. "He saved our asses. That's the most we can ask from any independently mobile, AI-controlled cybernetic limb."

Dr Drexler laughed. "Well said. Maybe ..."

All of a sudden, a lump of metal dropped out of the

ceiling. Grayson and Dr Drexler both startled. It was unrecognizable, hardly more than a single boxy piece of melted machinery and two awkward, pincerlike grabbers. It was unexpectedly fast, though, hauling itself over to Mason and attaching itself to the gaping hole on the upper-left side of his body before Grayson could stop it.

"No!" he screamed, but it was already too late.

[Lefty!] Mason rejoiced. [I missed you so much! Where have you beeeeeee...]

All of a sudden his voice began to fade out. His program's failsafes were kicking in, disconnecting his primary mind from all outer connections. That meant it had detected either a computer virus, or... or some other pathogen.

"Shit!" Grayson darted forward and grabbed the lump that was Lefty with his gloved hands, trying to pry it off his brother's body. It clung tenaciously, though, all of its former failsafes and releases burned away in the blast that Grayson had assumed had taken its life. "Disengage!" he shouted at his brother. "Disengage, you worthless son of a–"

"Back up!" Dr Drexler swapped their multitool over to its "zapper" function and hit the former arm with a carefully directed bolt. Lefty sizzled in place, but still didn't let go. "Shit, we'll have to–"

Grayson was already moving, adrenaline making him fast but jerky as he ripped off the rigid cover built over his brother's spinal nerves and pulled a special series of switches on his back. A second later, all of the limbs fell away, even Lefty, dropping Mason's head and torso to the floor. The limbs were all docile, except for that damn left arm, which was whirring and kicking even now as it tried to get up and reattach itself to Mason's body.

Looking down at the piece of his brother that was trying to destroy him, Grayson lost his mind a little bit.

"Goddamn piece of–" He grabbed the closest thing to hand, another of Mason's limbs, and began beating his left arm. "Coming back at the wrong time, always at the wrong time, couldn't have just died out there like you should have! You–" He lost his ability to speak but not his ability to beat the arm until it finally stopped moving.

"OK." Dr Drexler's hand on his shoulder pulled Grayson out of his violent fugue state. "OK, you got it. It's done. Take a few deep breaths, and don't worry, we'll figure this out."

"What's there to figure out?" Grayson panted furiously. Figuring it out was for people who had the luxury of time and not being threatened with their very existence getting ripped to shreds. People who didn't have to worry about their little brother – had Dr Drexler ever really worried about anyone other than themself? "Lefty found his way back, that little – and he's infected with the mold."

"Are you sure?"

"Positive. Mason's programming wouldn't have shut all his neuro functions down if it wasn't being threatened with something nasty. S'gotta be the mold."

"OK." Dr Drexler nodded. "Lefty is infected. That doesn't mean it got to Mason, right? We just need to run some tests and see whether or not–"

"He is infected."

Grayson and Dr Drexler both turned to stare at Six,

who'd spoken with calm assurance. The doctor replied first. "You can't know that."

"It is nevertheless the only conclusion we can reliably make at this time without more data on the spread of the mold," he said. "We must assume he is, in fact, infected until we can prove that he is not. That might take more time than we have."

"So what if Lefty is infected?" Grayson growled. "Mason's a bloody cyborg! Just chuck the limb and he'll be right. Unless of course you *want* us to leave him here. The three of us fly off into space using the pod *he* prepped for us and abandon him?" The thought of it filled him with fury. Never mind that he'd been planning for them to do that very thing to Six and Dr Drexler if they had to – it was the principle of the thing. Mason had done the work! He ought to be one of the ones to survive!

"I'm suggesting that we take sensible precautions," Six replied. "We must leave Mason isolated while Dr Drexler determines whether or not he truly is infected with the mold. We have no safe chamber for testing it right now, given the location of the former Dr Lifhe, so we should lock him in here in his current state while Dr Drexler endeavors to do these tests."

Dr Drexler turned to Grayson. "I can do it," they confirmed. "I've got some models to work off now, thanks to how closely I've been able to monitor Corinus. I think we should know within an hour whether or not your brother is infected with the mold. We can sterilize what's left of, well, Lefty with one of your welding torches and make sure it doesn't contaminate him any further, too, but… Six is right. We need him in isolation right now."

"Are you mad? There's no way I'm leavin' my brother while you–"

"Remember what happened the last time people started not listening to my plans?" Dr Drexler snapped. Literally snapped, like their voice was a rubber band that had been stretched to its limit. "It got us trapped in this undead hellscape, is what it got us! If you don't give a shit whether you get infected or not, then you can stay in here with him while I run the tests, but I *will* lock you in, and I *will* take measures against you if you try to get out before I verify that you're not infected. Do you get me? I'm sick of other people risking my life just because they're too busy or too angry or too dismissive to wait for some *goddamn scientific results*!"

Grayson blinked. He blinked again, and the rage inside retracted enough for him to realize that if he pushed right now, he'd only be making thing worse for himself. For both of them. He couldn't take on both Dr Drexler and Six, not without Mason, and he wasn't going anywhere without Mason either, so he might as well let them do their tests and confirm that his brother was all right.

Then they'd be leaving Sik-Tar as fast as they could come up with the right distraction, and screw these two if they tried to get in his way. "Fine."

"Good. Now. I'm going to go back to my experiments, you two are going to burn that arm to a crisp, and then Six is going to lock this place down." Dr Drexler turned and walked out of the mess hall, leaving Grayson alone with the Caridian.

"What're you staring at?" he asked, disconcerted to be the sole focus of the alien's large, all-seeing eyes.

"Everything," Six replied with a quiet clack of his mandibles. "More than you know. Now. Shall we get the fire?"

Creepy jackass. Grayson would be glad when he and his brother could leave this piece of work behind.

When. *When.* It had to be when.

Otherwise, he didn't know what he would do.

CHAPTER TWENTY-TWO

Dizzie Drexler

Running one experiment at a time was doable. Running two at a time was a challenge. Running three at a time, all on a massively condensed timescale, all alone, was almost more than Dizzie could handle.

It didn't help that they had Corinus staring at them the whole time, every move they made constantly monitored by his new, never-blinking eyes. Dizzie wanted to turn away and not deal with him at all, but they knew better than that. The injection they'd given him earlier would be wearing off within another hour under normal circumstances, and they weren't about to mess with a Centauran revenant that could control them telepathically. Hell, no.

Fool me once, shame on you – fool me twice, I might end up turned into an undead killing machine bent on consuming my friends and colleagues. Not gonna happen.

Instead, they continued to aerosolize the compound that blocked Corinus's telepathic abilities and released another dose of it into the testing chamber every hour. Dizzie wouldn't be able to keep it up for long, as Grayson so helpfully pointed out – there was only enough for four more doses – but if they weren't out of here by then, they'd have a lot more problems to deal with. The other revenants were still clawing away at the door, intent on breaking through to get to their prey despite the pile of charred bodies outside of it – most of which had renewed themselves with the help of the mold and gone right back to attacking.

They needed to get out of here; they needed to get to the pod before they were overwhelmed. Time was against them, but Dizzie knew that Grayson wouldn't budge until they figured out Mason's status. Plus – and they felt a little guilty about this, but only a little – this was probably the only chance they'd get to study the mold up close. They couldn't simply waste it.

If only we'd come better prepared. The things we could have learned… the experiments I could have run… It was both fascinating and depressing to think about, and Dizzie didn't have time to be depressed right now, so they pushed their feelings aside and focused on the tasks at hand. *First signs of appearance in soft tissue, around the eyes and mouth – eyes in particular, but Mason has no eyes, so–*

Bang!

Dizzie whirled toward the testing chamber, heart in their throat – had Corinus gotten out? Was he becoming too big for the chamber to contain? But no, Corinus was simply banging one of his claws – ugh, it was so strange seeing his hooflike appendages transformed into claws – on the wall loud enough for the sound to carry through the walls, not stopped by the force field.

Dizzie narrowed their eyes as he mouthed something at

them. What the hell was he trying to accomplish, distracting them like this? Did he just crave attention? Did the mold that inhabited him not like being alone? Too damn bad. They turned their back on him.

BANG!

"Shit," they gasped, turning once more to glower at him.

"What?" Dizzie demanded.

I have something to say, he mouthed slowly and distinctly.

Dizzie didn't want to hear it. They didn't want to hear anything Corinus could spout off right now, but they also didn't want him beating on the walls and maybe drawing the wrong kind of attention to the lab. Walking over, they changed the force field to allow for sound. "What?"

"How are the experiments going?"

Dizzie blinked, then narrowed their eyes. "That's it? That's what you want to ask me about, that's what you were banging on the wall for? Curiosity about the damn *experiments*? What the hell is wrong with you?"

"I want to help you understand, Dizzie," Corinus said, almost sounding like his old self again. Dizzie bit their lip as tears threatened to well up in their eyes. "That's all I've ever wanted, isn't it? It's why I sacrificed myself for you – to help you. The least you can do is listen to me now. I would say you owe me at least that much."

"You're not *him,*" Dizzie insisted. "I know you're not."

"I was him, though. Parts of me still are. I'm him enough to understand what you're interested in. Allow me to make a few useful scientific observations for you."

Dizzie glared at him. "Why bother?"

"Because you want to understand us," Corinus said.

Dizzie blinked at his use of the new pronoun. "And we want to *help* you understand us, before you join us. And you will join us, Dizzie."

"I won't." There was no way. Dizzie would rather be immolated than have any part of them end up ensnared by the mold.

"I think you will." Corinus tilted his head slightly. "About your experiments, though. You're working on a multi-containment model for gauging rate of adaptation, right?"

"Obviously." It wouldn't have been obvious to anyone else, but Corinus had known the experiments Dizzie was planning to try.

"Have you noticed any odd movements between cultures?"

Dizzie frowned. "What are you talking about?"

"Odd motions. Movements. Mirroring. That kind of thing."

"These cultures can't mirror each other. They don't have the sensory capacity for that," Dizzie said.

"So you haven't checked it then." Corinus shook his head. "Making assumptions, uh-oh. That's bad science, Dr Drexler. I think you should do a little experiment right now. Look down at your cultures and give the one on the left the same electrical stimulation you've been doing, but watch the culture on the right."

"This is ridiculous," Dizzie complained, but their heart beat uncomfortably fast now. Was it possible they'd made some sort of mistake, or…

"Please, for the sake of our former friendship. Humor me."

There was no friendship between Dizzie and a sentient, bloodthirsty, highly adaptable substance like the mold. Nevertheless, Dizzie bent their head to the microscope and applied a minor shock to the culture on the left. They gasped when they saw the cells on the right jump – not as much as they would have if they'd been directly hit, but enough that it didn't look accidental.

Verify, verify... They repeated the experiment the other way around. Then again. Again. Again.

"You can see that I'm right."

"Shut up," Dizzie snapped. Again. Again. *Again.* "Shit." It was possible... it was *probable*...

That the mold was telepathic.

Oh no. Oh no oh no oh no...

"Perhaps it will help to know that it is a very basic form of telepathy," Corinus said. "Very primal, guided by a superior collective consciousness. At least, that's how it is on this planet. We don't know what all mold is like – we are the universe's most adaptable organism, after all."

"Big claims," Dizzie croaked, then coughed to clear their voice.

"True claims. Corinus Lifhe's telepathy is much more highly adapted, but you have been blocking it from its purest use. However–" one of the tentacles coming out of his nose swiped over Corinus's right eyeball "–the parts of his brain used to direct his telepathy have been very helpful to us."

Dizzie slowly stood up, grabbing their pad and glancing incredulously at the data pouring into it. This was bad, this was so, so bad. "What do you mean by helpful?"

"Exactly what we say. We shall be much more effective at communicating from here on out, now that this body is joining the others."

"You're trapped in there, you can't–"

The door behind Dizzie opened. "Go and check the end of the hallway," they said to whoever it was – probably Grayson asking for more updates, again. "We need to check and make sure that the force field keeping the revenants out is still–"

The blow to the back of their head knocked Dizzie off their feet. They sprawled out on the floor, barely keeping their face from going into one of the table legs as the shuffling, clunking mass that was Mason Bane stumped past, heading straight for the testing chamber. Dizzie stared at him, half horrified by his appearance and half by the fact that he'd managed to get out of the room they'd been holding him in at all. His remaining leg and arm were back in place but growing out of both the sockets on the other side was a sluglike, bright green mass that connected the upper and lower parts of the torso. It moved the heavy metal body along with the help of what looked like a centipede's legs at first glance but, as Dizzie looked closer…

Oh, god. Bile threatened to come up as Dizzie realized that the mass was propelling itself with dozens of stumpy, misshapen hands and feet. They were small, perhaps a tenth what their size would normally be, but with so many of them flopping their side of the body along like flippers…

I have to get out of here. Dizzie turned and crawled toward the exit into the hallway. They were still ten feet away from the door when the testing chamber's force field was removed – the sound of it powering down was unmistakable.

Go faster, go faster, go faster! The only reason they were still alive was because Corinus was more intent on getting Mason to let him out than having him finish Dizzie off. And now that he *was* out, that was about to change. Dizzie knew they should stand up, should run out the door, but their body refused to cooperate. Their limbs seemed locked into their bent position, everything aching, their mind still reeling with confusion. It was all they could do to crawl, and so they did. Soon the sound of Mason's hideous little limbs joined theirs in another crawl, one that would end Dizzie.

Lucky for Dizzie, the ancient Caridians had decided the lab was the obvious other choice for a force field, in case of an experiment gone awry. As soon as Dizzie was in the hallway they grabbed onto the wall and used it to help drag themself to their feet, then activated the force field just as the first of Mason's tiny, tentacle-like feet slipped through the door. The scent of charred flesh filled the air, and the flipper feet writhed like worms at Dizzie's feet. They stared at the body of Corinus Lifhe, which was changing rapidly now that he was out of the confined space of the lab, then at Mason.

They checked themself, desperately making sure they didn't have any puncture wounds that would let the mold get through. Heavy breaths shuddered through Dizzie's lungs, breaths on the verge of becoming sobs. It was hopeless. There was no way they could get out of this now, no way. Not without–

"Mason?" From down the hall, Grayson shouted for his brother. He must have looked into the mess hall and found it empty. "Mason! Where have you gone off to? *Mason*!"

"He's here," Dizzie said faintly. Footsteps ran their way, but they didn't look over, couldn't stand to look away.

Grayson stopped next to Dizzie. He didn't say anything, which vaguely surprised Dizzie – they'd been sure he'd rage and scream, maybe try to open the force field and let his brother out, which… honestly seemed inevitable at this point. But he didn't. He just stood there, and after a moment Dizzie managed to tear their eyes away from the spectacle behind the force field and look up at Grayson's face.

He looked lost. Utterly, completely broken, like he couldn't quite understand what he was seeing but understood it all too well at the same time. It was a painful expression to see on another person's face, all the more painful because Dizzie knew how much the brothers meant to each other. "I'm sorry," they choked out.

Grayson cleared his throat. "I shoulda known it. Too good to be true, him escaping being infected after Lefty hooked in like that. Damn arm…"

Mason leaned forward until his face was level with his brother's. His former eyes hadn't regrown, but he had a series of round, lidless eyeballs on stalks popping up like mushrooms out of the plates on his right arm. He held the arm up so he could see Grayson better. He didn't speak out loud, but from the way Grayson flinched something was going on.

"Do you still have that mental connection with him?"

Dizzie demanded, getting to their feet. Their head ached sharply, but they weren't going to have a conversation this important lying down. Grayson nodded. "You need to sever it! Sever it completely, the mold is – it's telepathic! Corinus managed to guide Mason into the lab to set him free! This is serious, this is a complete disaster, this is… why are you smiling?" Because he *was* smiling – a dark, jagged thing, but a smile, nonetheless.

"There's no way to disconnect from my own brother," Grayson said after a moment. "Couldn't leave him if I wanted to, and you don't know how lucky you are that I can't."

"What the hell are you talking about?" Nothing about this situation was lucky, as far as Dizzie could see. "I'm serious, you need to cut things off right now, before he figures out how to use your connection to control you. We need to – I don't know, pick a room and barricade ourselves in it, because I'm pretty sure this field isn't going to hold them once they get big enough to break through the walls, and–"

"That is not a solution," a new voice said. Dizzie whirled around to look at Six and immediately regretted it when their head began to spin. "That would only result in all of our deaths." He turned to look at Grayson. "I am sorry for your loss."

"Sure you are." He finally looked away from his brother. "You already know the truth about the pod, don't you?"

"You are referring to the weight tolerances? Yes."

"Then you know what we were planning to do."

"Of course." Six's antennae waved vigorously. "I would not have let things get that far."

Grayson shook his head, laughing in a way that sounded painful. "Course you wouldn't. Eh, it's all academic now, anyway."

Dizzie looked between them, bewildered. "What's academic?"

"It don't matter. The point is, I'm not going anywhere. You two, though." Grayson glanced between them and shrugged. "You've still got a chance."

Dizzie was on the verge of shouting with frustration. "What chance?" they hissed. "We've got revenants battering the end of the hall, revenants in the lab who are growing themselves better weapons *as we speak* to break through the wall–" they gestured to the massive claw that Corinus was growing out of his right front limb "–and no exit! We wouldn't make it to the pod if we tried to run, there's nowhere to hide from these two once they break free… we're screwed!"

"No, you're not," Grayson said. "Or maybe you're not. Depends on how much of Lefty I can resurrect. Burned him out pretty bad, but I've always carried some spare parts for Mason around in my personal kit. Don't need the nervous system to be functional as long as I can work with the computer mind at this point."

"What are you talking about?"

Grayson bared his teeth in a rictus of a smile. "I'm talkin' about making you a distraction."

CHAPTER TWENTY-THREE
Dizzie Drexler

The "distraction" ended up taking half an hour and every tool left in their combined arsenals to create. Dizzie had stocked most of their own hardware in the lab – why lump it around from room to room when there were plenty of perfectly good places for it in there? Places which, of course, were now completely infested with mold, thanks to Corinus. They were lucky they'd grabbed their pad on the way out – if Dizzie survived this mess, the data they'd gathered so far would be enough to keep them busy for years.

There was enough to work with, though. Enough in the bag across Grayson's back and the kit that Six had stored in the library and the bits and pieces that had fallen down along the way that they could make the thing they needed to make, which was… well, to put it in Earth terms, Frankensteinian. Was that a word? Dizzie didn't really remember the story, but they did remember that the important thing about Frankenstein was that he'd made a monster. And this, Lefty in his latest form, was definitely monstrous.

What the hell wasn't on Sik-Tar?

"All right," Grayson said, pulling back and giving the arm a nudge. The new light he'd installed in its ocular array clicked to life. It had been cured of the mold, seared up one side and down the other, completely inoculated by fire. That had taken care of all the organic components to it, but the inorganic parts were a bit tougher. Tough enough, hopefully, to make it to a final self-immolation. Maybe, Dizzie reflected, the third time really would be the charm.

The plan was simple enough. Grayson, who had done some quick and dirty rewiring of his own neural implant to target Lefty and block out the rest of his brother, was going to send the battered arm back into the tunnels and over to the Xenium spill, where it was going to coat itself in the stuff. Then, he was going to make it crawl outside, get a good distance away, and blow itself up. That would hopefully be enough to lure the revenants out to follow it. Once they had, the three of them were going to make for the pod and get themselves the hell out of here. Or, at least, Dizzie and Six were.

This was the worst part of the plan, as far as Dizzie was concerned. "You can come with us," they insisted. "I'm sure we're within weight tolerances for it now, and if we're not we can get rid of some of the fuel."

"I'm not leaving my brother behind."

"It's not leaving him behind when he's not really there to be left!" Dizzie countered. "He's infected with the mold, he's a revenant, a – a Xeno! Xenos are *not* our friends! I had whole conversations with Corinus, but I never made the mistake of thinking anything he said actually came from *him*. The mold is… using his mind, using his *framework*, but it isn't him. And the thing that used to be Mason isn't your brother either."

"And I'm not me without him." Grayson shook his head. "I'm staying. It's fine. If I end up needing to be an extra distraction to get the two of you off this rock, that suits me well enough. The only thing the two of you need to worry about is getting to the pod without being seen."

Six clacked his mandibles. "That's not the only thing we must worry about."

They both stared at him. "What do you mean?" Dizzie asked.

"It has been shown now that the mold, when in possession of a body with advanced mental capabilities, can recreate the processes of that body. I'm not just talking about basic telepathy," he clarified, "I'm talking about being able to relate complex directions such as releasing the force field. Evidence suggests the other revenants are creatures solely interested in destruction – presumably because their bodies have been dead for so long – whereas the version that has evolved within Corinus, and presumably Mason, can communicate much more easily with each other."

Dizzie felt their headache worsen as the impact of what Six was saying sank in. "So we have to limit their chances to communicate with the other revenants. That's fine, they're contained."

"For now. If they breach that containment before we can make good our escape, they might be able to cause larger problems than we're anticipating."

"We don't know that the mold in *here* is capable of

communicating details like that to the revenants out *there,*" Dizzie argued. They had to believe this. They had to. If it was, if the creature that Corinus had become had some way of divulging everything it saw and heard in here to the swarm outside…

"Whether it has or it hasn't, we must be careful." Six tilted his eyes in the direction of the lab, where the *scratch-scratch-scratch* of claws against the walls could be heard more clearly by the minute. "Once Corinus and Mason escape, they will certainly come for us. It is best if we're gone by then. We should take pains to stay out of their sight, so that if they are free when Lefty explodes, they are also drawn to investigate it."

"Keep our heads down, get Lefty out there to distract everyone, do it fast," Grayson said. His lips twisted in a parody of a smile. "Anything else, guv?"

"Yes." Six stared directly at Grayson. "Find a method of destroying yourself and keep it close."

"Six–"

"Right," Grayson said before Dizzie could chide the Caridian. "Got that covered. I've still got that second vial of Xenium from when we did our first test." He patted a tiny pocket in the belt at his hip. "Got a mini-blowtorch from my touch-up kit for Mason, too, so it'll go off when it needs to. I'll be right. Now." He pointed to Lefty, then to Six. "You're the tallest, and Lefty's only got the two extensors now. You lift him up to the tunnel, and I'll see what I can do about getting him out into the hangar."

CHAPTER TWENTY-FOUR
Lefty

As far as microcosms of a larger collective went, Lefty was working off relatively few instructions. The problem was that the instructions he had left were battling each other out in his programming. The mind itself was gone, but the computerized support structure of that mind remained, and it was conflicted.

The primary initiative was to return to wholeness – that had yet to be accomplished. Whole was not whole; complete was yet incomplete. They hadn't checked in, and their battery power was under ten percent. They had to recharge soon or face potential permanent separation from the main, and that was not allowed.

The secondary initiatives, more recently programmed into the processors, were louder than the primary initiative. They instructed "disregard, disregard, disregard" over and over again, and "follow new guidance, follow new guidance, follow new guidance." They were insistent, urgent, and loud. In the end, they were the commands that won out, and Lefty shared his ocular sensor with the far-mind that was Programmer and followed his lead.

Being back in the tunnel was slow. It was filled with obstacles, and Lefty's measuring devices had been damaged during his… well, his *everything* that had happened lately, which meant he had to estimate the right spot to exit from rather than know it. His exit took the form of a drop from a hole out of a vent just two feet from the ground, which was good. He didn't have enough extensors left to lower himself down softly.

It was bad, however, in that he was a good fifty meters from the spill of liquid Xenium that was Step B.

Movement was slow, and as quiet as Lefty could make it. Many more revenants had crawled inside the ship, and the hangar was filled with the noise of a hundred scuttling, ancient gray corpses turned bright green with new, single-minded life. A faint whisper of another initiative ghosted through Lefty's programming for a moment – to seek out. To rejoin. To become whole with something other than the central body, something bigger. The compulsion to be more was… was…

The Programmer returned control to the secondary initiatives, and Lefty made it to the Xenium. He rolled himself in it, coating ten percent, twenty-three percent, fifty-eight percent of his exterior. The minimum standard was met, and now Lefty had to enact Step C: getting out of the hangar.

The door to the outside was small. Removing himself through it without being detected had a zero percent chance of success. The tunnels that led outside were high up, and hard to navigate even when Lefty had ten times the extensors he did now. That chance of success was untenable.

There was only one solution – make a new hole. The initiative could not be denied. Fortunately, Lefty had a basic understanding of the properties of liquid Xenium thanks to his learning algorithms, and could estimate how much of it he needed to explode, and where, in order to increase his chances of creating an egress. There was, after all, a very big door in the far wall already. It was sealed, but it was still weaker than the solid sections of the wall. The proper explosion in the right place ought to do it.

The most challenging thing was getting enough of the liquid Xenium into the proper place, and not leaving a trail of it that would return the fire to Lefty and blow him up prematurely. Once he had the appropriate amount in position, Lefty attached his Programmer-made explosive device to it and removed himself to the far wall, creeping slowly beneath crates of Xenium and around abandoned pods in an effort not to draw attention to himself. None of the revenants had noticed the new pool of Xenium so far.

Problem: without his explosive device, how would he blow himself up once he was at an appropriate distance outside?

Solution: to be considered more fully after the accomplishment of Step C.

Lefty hunkered down next to the pod, calculated that the odds of setting off the rest of the liquid Xenium stockpiled in the hangar was less than twenty-five percent given the distances involved and concluded that was satisfactory, then set off the explosive.

The blast was small but hot, reverberating through the hangar with a dull roar that even drowned out the grunts and cries of the revenants. For a moment Lefty determined that he had fatally miscalculated – the heat might be enough to trigger the explosion of the liquid Xenium that he himself was coated in, and if it did…

It did not. Moreover, he had been correct in his assessment that the blast would be enough to contribute to creating a new way out. There was a crack in the wall now, large enough for Lefty to slip through with room to spare as long as the revenants didn't take advantage of it first. He scuttled over as fast as he could under the cover of dust, dodging several freshly severed revenant limbs on the way, until he reached the new crack.

Ah, Lefty fit through. Excellent. He crawled out into the dusky light and began to work his way across the wet, gritty plain, doing his best to blend in with the bigger rocks when he saw them. The connection with the Programmer's secondary initiatives thudded away in his programming again, skipping lines and pushing to the top over and over and over – there was a new Step D waiting for him to apply once he reached the appropriate distance from the structure. It looked like–

Oh, well, all right. That was simple enough. Even with just two extensors, Lefty should be able to manage that.

His rate of speed was slow, less than a foot per second. It took nearly fifteen minutes to reach the required distance, and then another two to find an appropriate rock after the Programmer kept rejecting the ones brought into ocular range.

Finally, one was approved – dark black, with a sharp edge. Lefty read the instructions being sent to him from the Programmer, incorporated them into his action log, and proceeded to remove the casing covering up his sensitive AI circuitry. All he needed, the Programmer said, was a spark. One spark. Hit the redundant sections until spark was achieved, then be rewarded with completion. *Completion.* The most vital primary programming objective. As much as Lefty could look forward to anything anymore, he was looking forward to that.

One spark. Lefty picked up the rock, poised it over his computerized brain, and brought it down with all the strength his extensors could manage.

One spark. *Smash.* One sparrrr… *Smash.* On… spa… onspa… one… *Smash.*

Heat. Light.

Spark.

CHAPTER TWENTY-FIVE
Grayson Bane

Grayson rubbed at his eyes, doing his best to dispel the afterimage that had been seared onto his retinas in Lefty's final blast. "Damn thing finally managed it," he said, voice hoarse with emotions he wasn't going to dare consider right now. What kind of idiot felt sorry for a computerized *arm*, after all? Not him. He sniffed, then asked, "Any movement from the end of the hall?"

Dr Drexler slowly stuck their head around the edge of the doorframe still protected by the force field. "I think they're leaving," they whispered. "I can't see any more movement from the bodies stacked up there."

"Give them a moment to regrow and move away," Six advised. They waited for another painstaking five minutes before the last of the revenants who'd been burned into stillness after trying to break in regenerated with the help of the mold and dragged themselves toward the newer and more interesting locale. Apparently whatever consciousness was at work here, Lefty's explosion had been enough to tempt it into a foray outside. Just what they needed, and honestly more than Grayson had thought they'd get after the stupid little thing set off that bloody Xenium spill inside. That was what programming fast got you, nothing but a big mess that you had to clean up later, and–

Crack! Crack!

"Oh shit," Dr Drexler said, retreating back into the mess hall. "Mason and Corinus are almost through the wall next to the lab." They wrung their hands. "If they connect with the rest of the revenants, do you think they'll be able to turn them around and set them on us again? What if the way to the pod isn't clear? What are we going to do if–"

"Do you ever stop asking questions?" Grayson sighed and pushed to his feet. "I'll take care of distractin' 'em. You just make sure you're ready to run when the coast is clear. Got it?"

Dr Drexler frowned. "Grayson, really, I think we could all make it."

"And I've already told you, I'm not goin' anywhere without my brother," Grayson said. "As soon as he was infected, I knew I'd never be getting off this rock. It's fine," he added, holding up a hand to forestall any more of their pointless pleas.

Never mind that it did, actually, feel kind of nice to have someone care what happened to him apart from his brother. Never mind that he'd been prepared to leave Dr Drexler here like so much flotsam on the edge of a bright blue Martian tide. Never mind any of it. Intentions were nothing, actions were everything, and Grayson was running low on time for both. He needed to make what he did next count.

He joined Dr Drexler at the door and looked down the hall. "Yeah, the revenants are almost out. All right. Time to do this. Don't worry, I'll get their attention." He shooed Dr Drexler and Six back into the mess hall. "You stay here and worry about yourselves, eh? Don't wait too long to leave."

Don't make all of this shit we've gone through be for nothing.

Dr Drexler still looked like they wanted to argue, but Six nodded firmly. "We will be ready," he said and, hoisting both his and Dizzie's bags over his shoulder, he took them into the library. Eh. Wherever he wanted to hide, it didn't matter to Grayson. The only thing that mattered now was–

Crash. Chunks of ferrocrete, supposedly too tough for anything that wasn't laser-powered to cut through, fell to the ground. A pair of claws followed the last of it out, and a second later Mason stepped into the hallway. Or what *had* been Mason.

He was almost unrecognizable now. All of his skin was swallowed by the mold, and another pair of large, alien eyes jutted out from the holes where his human eyes had been, in addition to the ones still bobbing on his arm like ichorous flowers. He'd grown new limbs on top of the old ones, his torso held upright by multiple centipede-like, chitin-covered growths coming from his leg holes. He looked ghastly, like a nightmare from the Bane brothers' childhoods come to life. Not like Mason at all, but Grayson felt the pressure of his mind on their connection and knew that, no matter how he looked, this was still his brother.

His brother. His birthright. His burden.

Grayson threw his burden the finger, then turned and ran for the end of the hall. Deactivating the force field took less than three seconds, which was good because Mason was already coming toward him. It was time to move.

The hangar seemed completely empty of revenants, all of the crawling, creeping, clicking assholes off to check on Lefty's big boom, no doubt. There was a new big damn hole in the wall, too. Plenty of room for Grayson to escape through, if he felt like leading Mason and Corinus on a merry chase across the plains.

Ugh. Chases weren't his thing. Grayson was too squat and out of shape to be much of a runner; less than a dozen yards from the hallway he'd just left he was already getting out of breath. *Better to hide yourself away somewhere safe and wait to strike than to run around flailing and hope.* He didn't have a choice if he wanted to clear a path for the others, though, so he–

"*Augh!*" It felt like he'd just taken a knife to the calf. Grayson staggered and fell onto his good knee, the bad leg stretched out behind him like a piece of strip steak. He glanced behind him and saw Mason just a few feet away, his new left-side claw gleaming red in the low light.

"Oh, you little bastard," Grayson breathed. "You want to kill me now? Do it! Just do it!"

Mason didn't move, though. He just stared with those awful new eyes, more terrible than any adaptation Grayson had ever seen on his brother before because *he* wasn't the one who put them there, and waited for Grayson to get up.

So he did.

It was hard to take a step forward, his Achilles tendon nearly severed, but Grayson made it one foot. Then two. Three. Fo–

"*Shit!*" Another slice, this time across his other leg. Not the tendon, no – higher up, through the meat of his hamstring. Grayson turned and screamed at his brother, "Don't you goddamn play with your food, you little shit! What the hell is wrong with you? Just finish me!"

Again, Mason didn't move, leaving Grayson to wonder what the creature would do to him next. He'd broken out into a cold sweat, his mouth going dry as he lost more blood to the floor beneath him.

A *snap-pop* came from the hallway he'd left behind, making Grayson wonder what the hell was going on with Six, Dr Drexler, and the former Corinus Lifhe. Eh, not his problem – his problem was this pile of mold and metal in front of him that had the balls to play with him, like he was some sort of toy.

"You wanna be rough?" Grayson said through gritted teeth. "Fine. We play rough." He opened his brain to the section he'd abandoned the moment he knew what had happened to Mason, reached out for familiar circuitry buried in among the mess of his brother's mind, and *twisted.*

The right arm and leg, the ones that still retained Mason's original mental core, suddenly buckled, sending the entire conglomeration of parts that was revenant Mason into a tilt, then a fall, and finally a lopsided collapse to the floor. Grayson had never directly controlled his brother like this before – he'd never had to – but he'd put the system in place so that if things got bad and Mason couldn't control his own limbs for some reason, Grayson could take over and save him.

Funny how now he was using this failsafe to save himself.

Or, really, not funny at all. He knotted the limbs up as tight as he could, then put them into a holding state and disengaged. He wasn't going to be able to run now, but he still needed to keep Mason's attention away from the route to the pod…

Ah, the refinery, the one that Dr Drexler and Corinus had taken cover in when they ran from their very first revenant. Grayson could heave himself up into that, give himself and them some time to get things done. He turned over onto his hands and knees and began to crawl toward the conveyor belt.

He risked a glance over his shoulder only once, and wished he hadn't. Mason had given up on trying to straighten out his hopelessly tangled right side and was pulling himself across the ground after Grayson using only the limbs on his left. All those awful little feet and hands, scrabbling through the gory trail of Grayson's own blood as his brother fought to catch up to him… Grayson shuddered and looked away.

He reached the refinery and hoisted himself up and onto the conveyor belt, thankful that his arms hadn't been injured along with his legs. Grayson crawled along the crushed pieces of old bone and carapace, all roasted in place so that the mold didn't get the chance to regenerate. This whole planet needed to be firebombed, blown to atoms by the power of its own stores of Xenium.

The belt behind him shifted and clanked, and Grayson knew without turning around that Mason was following him in. Fair enough, he'd expected it. He ignored the frisson of fear that shot through him and kept crawling, determined to make the furnace at the back of it before his brother caught up to him. If Grayson was going to go out, he was going to do it head-on, not dragged to his death like some sort of sniveling snitch.

He got to the chamber at the end and fell down into it. There was a big piece of claw still in here, moldy once more but not regrown into its own hellish version of a revenant yet. Grayson grabbed it and held it tight as he listened to Mason. His brother grunted with effort as he forced himself farther down the chute, closer and closer to Grayson. Grayson wondered if he shouldn't just cut his own throat with the claw and be done with it.

"No," he muttered. He'd said he wouldn't leave his brother behind – that included leaving him like that.

Not for the first time, Grayson reflected that his life would have been a lot easier if he'd just let Mason die when he was twelve, and so badly burnt by the fire that had raged through the slum they'd grown up in that the hospital had labeled him "inert" and put him in cold storage to turn into crop fertilizer later. Grayson had broken his brother out, stolen enough credits to pay for his therapies, and designed an entirely new system of custom cybernetics for him. He'd made the best version of Mason he possibly could from the ruins of the old one, and now that person was coming to kill him.

Better him than anyone else.

Grayson sighed and threw the claw away, then settled with his back to the scarred, patchwork metal wall of the furnace and stared at the dropout of the chute. Bits and pieces of exoskeleton preceded Mason's arrival, pushed out of the way by the massive bulk of his body, almost too big for him to fit it through the relatively narrow entrance. When he did emerge, it was face-first, his blank human bits straining through, followed by his new, unsettling eyes. Grayson steadied himself in his position, one hand on the vial of Xenium in his pocket, the other on the torch. As soon as Mason was close enough, he'd light a fire that would burn them both out of existence.

But now that he wasn't running away, Mason seemed happy to draw things out without actively cutting into him. "Ha," Grayson grunted. "You what, wanted to punish me for trying to run from you? Little brat. Where was I gonna go, huh?" He gestured to his legs. "Never been able to move fast on these, no need for you to cut into me."

"Nnnnnn…"

What? Mason was… speaking? How, how could he be speaking? His body didn't have functioning vocal cords anymore!

"Nnnot. Run."

"Oh my god," Grayson whispered, dropping both the vial and the torch. He held a hand out toward his brother. "You're talkin' to me. How are you talkin'?"

Had the mold literally regrown his voice? Grayson couldn't remember what his brother had sounded like all those years before, but it had been nothing like the deep, guttural bass that was coming out of him now.

"Nnot rrun," the voice – someone's voice – said through Mason's open mouth. "Nnot let another ttake you." He crawled closer, and lifted his foremost claws up to frame Grayson's head. Ever so gently, he pressed his sharpened thumbs right into the divots at the top of Grayson's eye sockets.

Grayson wanted to blink, to rear back, but he couldn't. He was captivated by the sound of his brother's voice, and those big, luminescent eyes staring down at him from above.

"You'rre minnne firrrst." Mason began to press, and Grayson screamed as he felt the tip of the claws pierce his eyeballs. One sharp *rip* later and he was blind and shrieking, the pain overwhelming his brief period of hapless mesmerization.

The last thing he heard was the sound of crunching, like grapes popping against molars, before his throat went hot and slick and then everything, even that, faded away.

CHAPTER TWENTY-SIX
Dizzie Drexler

It was hard not to reach out and pull Grayson back as he marched off to his death. Dizzie knew they couldn't do it, knew that Grayson was making his own choice and that nothing they said would deter him, but… It didn't seem right. It felt too much like Corinus all over again, someone sacrificing themselves so that the rest of them – Dizzie specifically – could live. Why were *they* the worthy one, though? Why weren't *they* doing the sacrificing? The guilt of living did battle with the visceral fear of dying until they fought each other to a laborious standstill in Dizzie's mind, leaving them exhausted by their own emotions.

Dizzie almost envied Six's cool, unemotional response to the whole thing. They might have raged at him over it, demanded answers, demanded that he teach them how to put up such a perfect distance, but there was no time for that. All they had time to do was hide in the farthest corner of the room as the revenant that had been Mason went storming past, chasing his brother down with claws akimbo.

Holy shit, Mason was fast. Dizzie and Six were going to be lucky if they made it out of this hallway before Grayson was caught and killed, never mind them getting all the way to the pod. Maybe the best thing to do would be to stay right here and wait for Corinus to come and find them – or better yet, to go to him! He was waiting, after all; he'd been waiting patiently for Dizzie for hours now, so it really was time to come together again and move on to the next stage in their personal evolution as a tea–

What the hell? Dizzie gasped, clutching their head as they forcibly wrenched their thoughts back to reality. What the hell was that? There was no way Dizzie or Six were going to Corinus! And he shouldn't care about them, either – now that he was free, he should be going to join the rest of the revenants, not skulking around here.

Except… Corinus was different from other revenants. Different from other Xenos entirely – after all, how many of those infected with the mold had maintained their ability to speak? How many, if any of them, had been psychic?

Damn, but Dizzie wished they had more data on the shapeshifting Empusa who was rumored to be part of the original expedition to PK-L7. It would at least give them a baseline for comparison and… and…

And Dizzie loved comparison. Loved it so much that the best thing to do right now would be to infect *themself* with mold and then compare their changes to those of the other people in their crew. It would be fascinating, and give them a firsthand experience of how the mold could literally reshape an entire body. They couldn't wait to discover the rush of that initial infection, and the characterization of the pain scale alone would be–

"No!" Dizzie hit the side of their head with one fist,

ignoring Six's murmurs of concern from the other side of the room. "Stop it! I don't want that!"

But *Corinus* did. And he had finally learned how to make his telepathy work *with* the mold, rather than having to work around it. The serum Dizzie had been dosing him with had long since worn off, and now... now he was free. Now he was apex, the cleverest mind in the collective. He was prime, center, master, and would be even more once he had everything he wanted. And what he wanted was...

Dizzie pushed to their feet, stumbling clumsily toward the door at the end of the mess hall. They turned once, just once, managing to gain enough control of their own body to look back at Six. They knew there was desperation written on their face, clear in their eyes even if they couldn't voice it on their own.

Help me! Save me!

But Six simply stood up and watched Dizzie stagger out into the hall, his antennae waving wildly but the rest of him remaining completely immobile.

Dizzie walked on unstable legs down the hall to the laboratory, so briefly a place of hope and excitement before descending into despair. The wall beside the door was a mess, completely destroyed thanks to Mason. The force field itself was turned off now, and just within the door of the lab was Corinus. He was barely recognizable now – his eyes were as big as the rest of his head, and he had two extra legs growing from his torso and supporting him in an upright position. When he saw Dizzie, he smiled.

"There you are. I knew you would come to me if I asked nicely."

The confirmation was bitter. Dizzie gritted their teeth and managed to get out, "You're… in… my… head."

"Yes. My telepathy isn't back to its full strength yet, but that won't take long. Come inside." He stepped back and made room for Dizzie to enter the lab. They tried to make their feet drag, tried to slow down the seemingly inexorable advance into death that they were making, but it was impossible. All Corinus had to do was think, "Come," and Dizzie came.

"Good." He tilted his head slightly, big eyes twitching on their stalks. "Hmm. Even with the mold's help, I still can't penetrate the Caridian's mind. No matter, of course. I'll do so in person soon enough. But it's frustrating to be denied something I want."

"So… sorry… for… you," Dizzie gritted out between their teeth.

"I know you're not, but that's all right. I want you far more than I want him, after all." Corinus gestured to the testing chamber in the back of the lab. "You and I were both scientists not so long ago. This mind retains its scientific training and curiosity. There is much *I* would like to learn about the mold, and how best to ensure its successful spread across the galaxy. Just as you restrained me within this chamber for your tests, now I shall run tests on you."

"But why?" The pain of fighting Corinus's control was enough to make their head throb, but Dizzie was determined to know the truth before they lost all self-control. "Why bother? You're so smart – why do you need me?"

"Because I want to know what it's like to be you," Corinus said, the fascination clear in his voice. "You are more than merely something to be consumed; you are precious *data*. Data is what we need. We are more than we appear to be, too, and with your mind on our side and whatever I find from my experiments, we shall all become more and more." He tilted his head. "I think I will run growth-rate experiments on each of your body parts. How long different concentrations of mold take to fully consume different pieces of your flesh. I will save your head for last, so you can watch the procedure and appreciate what I am doing."

"I won't... appreciate... my own torture," Dizzie snapped. They fought the power of Corinus's telepathic control with everything they had, but he was too strong – their legs took them into the testing chamber with barely a pause. The walls and floor were coated with mold, and Dizzie went from fighting back to holding very still, so they didn't fall into it.

"That's all right," Corinus said, his eyes moving side to side as he reached one foreclaw toward the control panel on the left of the testing chamber. "I will appreciate it enough for both of us." He touched the panel, and the force field snapped into place between them. His control over Dizzie's mind eased, but it didn't even matter now that they were trapped inside this awful place with no way out. He fully faced Dizzie, looking pleased.

They hoped that Six had made it, at least – he must have taken his chance and run for the pod, and Dizzie couldn't blame him. This was going to be terrible in ways they'd never imagined before, but if one of the expedition, just one of them, made it out, then at least it wouldn't all be for nothing. Six would be able to warn others about Sik-

Tar, he could try to prevent people from coming back and disturbing this deadly planet any further, he could–

"I believe I will start with a paralytic," Corinus said, backing up toward one of the tables but not taking his eyes off Dizzie. "It is simple enough to manufacture and can be turned into a gas and pumped into the chamber. I'm looking forward to you experiencing the same thing I did every time you took my telepathy away. Then, I will – *hkk*." His brief, tense exhalation was immediately followed by the brutal *SNAPSNAP* of another force field turning on...

Only this one was held in place by Six, and its components framed each side of Corinus's neck.

Corinus's mutated head slid off his shoulders like hot grease off a spatula, landing with a lugubrious *splat* less than half a meter from the edge of the new force field. His body collapsed to the ground far more slowly, the mold inside it working to keep it going even though the host's central processor had been removed. Undoubtedly *some* kind of head would regenerate soon enough, but for now–

For now, Dizzie looked at Six, who stepped out of the shadows behind the table holding the force field he'd probably cannibalized from the end of the hall. He'd hooked it up to a battery with a series of messy connective cables, the sort of thing that should have been impossible to hide, and yet neither Dizzie nor Corinus had noticed him arriving until he'd sliced Corinus's head off. "You have the most amazing timing," they told him, awestruck. "I didn't even hear you coming. Are all Caridians this sneaky?"

"I wish I could have been here sooner," Six said with polite avoidance, setting their awkward weapon down on the nearest table, then stepping daintily over Corinus's body to release the force field. "It was surprisingly challenging to create access to a power source large enough to provide the – oof!"

Dizzie cut him off as they stepped out of the testing chamber and went straight into a hug. Six startled as they gripped him, then relaxed enough to give Dizzie a tentative *pat pat* on the shoulder before stepping back.

"We should go. Our location is severely compromised, and Dr Lifhe will be regenerating soon."

"Have you seen any sign of Grayson?" Dizzie asked, knowing to expect the worst and yet hoping against hope that perhaps, somehow, he had…

"I'm afraid I have not. I think that it would be… unwise to linger," Six said, and Dizzie didn't have to read between the lines to know that Six figured Grayson was already dead, or worse – assimilated.

"Right." Dizzie looked around the lab quickly, triaging what they had and what they could carry, before grabbing a few instruments off the tables. "Do you have the bag with our–"

"It is in the hallway. We should go," Six repeated as a sudden piercing scream echoed through the hangar. *Oh god, that's Grayson.* "Now."

Dizzie nodded numbly. "Yes. We – yes." They followed Six out into the hall, but not without a backward glance at Corinus's body. Jutting up from his severed head, one of his eyeballs twitched, turning toward Dizzie and Six and following their movements before they finally moved out of sight. "We need to go *right now*."

They picked up the pace, Six leading at a steady jog down the hallway and out into the hangar. There were no revenants to be seen – Lefty had done his job well – but there were plenty of *sounds* coming from one of the refineries. Dizzie followed the trail of bright red blood and felt their stomach curdle. Grayson must have run in there, tried to take refuge, and Mason had found him.

Was still finding and *dealing* with him right now, apparently. Ugh.

They wished for the ten thousandth time since they'd started this cursed trip that they'd thought to bring a gun of their own, something that they could have used to defend themselves more deliberately than a scientific multitool, a jury-rigged pair of force field generators, or an unstable, highly flammable chemical compound worth a ridiculous amount of credits. But regrets were useless right now. Grayson had given his life for them to escape.

Corinus had also given his life so that *Dizzie* could escape. Whatever he'd become, the person he actually was had cared for them enough to make the ultimate sacrifice to save them. That needed to be honored.

"Let's go," Dizzie said, and resolutely tuned out the slorping, crunching sounds coming from the refinery as they worked their way through the messy hangar, past the storage containers still full of precious, deadly Xenium, to the one pod that might be their ticket off this dark, hopeless world.

The repairs that had been made earlier were perfunctory, but probably enough to get them into orbit. Dizzie let Six worry about filling the fuel tank – he was stronger, and the last thing they needed was another spill right now – while they sat down at the controls and tried to figure out how to start the thing up.

It was actually… oh, gosh. If Dizzie hadn't been sure this was an alien ship, they might have assumed that a human had designed parts of it. It was so *understandable*. Right hand here, managing the throttle, while the left hand worked the control wheel. Even the computer interface was exactly the right size for a human hand. There were additional controls that looked perfect for Caridian claws, but these pieces… they were just…

Power suddenly flooded the pod with a gentle sighing sound, and the door, which had been hanging open up until now, slid closed. Soft yellow light filled the tiny cabin, and a second later the control panel in front of them lit up bright blue. A series of Caridian numerals scrawled across the screen, followed by–

"What the–" Dizzie knew they were gaping, but they couldn't help it. They turned toward Six. "Why are there commands available here in *English*?"

Six looked over Dizzie's shoulder at the panel. "Oh, there are? That simplifies things quite a bit. I was almost sure before, but I'm pleased to have my suspicions verified."

"What suspicions? Verifying what?"

"That is a question to be answered once we're off Sik-Tar," Six replied. "It is asking for a–"

"Password, I know, but you're the expert when it comes to Caridian passwords," Dizzie replied. They moved to get up from the seat, but Six shook his head.

"There is no need to displace yourself. Let me try this." He tapped a series of symbols on the panel. The screen flashed black. "Hmm. That one worked when we restarted power to the rest of the larger ship."

"Well, it's definitely not working now, and – *aaaah!*" Dizzie couldn't stop the scream that bubbled out of their chest as a sudden impact hit the door of the pod. It was…

Holy shit, it was Mason, only…

Dizzie stared. They couldn't help it. The picture he made was horrific, stomach-churning, yet at the same time it was impossible to tear their eyes away. He had become an abomination, the sort of hybrid mess that had been outlawed by the Coalition generations ago – a crawling, chimera-like cyborg with two heads sprouting from its metal shoulders. One was Mason's original head, complete with big Caridian eyes, and the second…

That was Grayson. Just his head, but it was him, *he* was in there, somehow… and he was screaming. Whatever had happened to lead to his decapitated head being fused to his brother's neck like a parasite, it was clear that the mold was the only thing keeping it alive. But it hadn't yet managed to overcome Grayson's control over his own thoughts. He had no eyes, but he seemed to know what he was looking at anyway, and his voice sent chills down Dizzie's spine.

"…o! Go already! Get off this goddamn rock, you idiots! *Fly the hell outta here!*"

"Oh my god." Dizzie's hand clenched spasmodically on the throttle before they forced their attention back to Six. "We need a password to activate this thing, *now*. Before he–" The sound of claws scrabbling at their door, so recently closed, was almost loud enough to overwhelm their voice. "Password!" they shouted.

"Try one of yours," Six suggested, far too calmly.

"Why the hell would one of *my* passwords work?"

"Take it on faith, Dr Drexler," Six said. "What have we got to lose?"

Well, put it that way... everything about this pod was weird. Maybe this would be just weird enough, too. Dizzie tried their standard tab password, the most common anagram of Doctor Vivian Rigby they used for devices – Byronic gator vivid. No good. They tried the anagram they'd used on their old lab – cordy orbiting viva. Still nothing. *What else, what else...* Finally, they tried the version of her name they used specifically on their Xenium-related research: arv dicing ivy robot.

The panel came to life under their hands. It was in *English*, it was in a language that they could read and understand, and the commands it functioned with appeared to be nearly identical to the ones they'd learned to use for operating the *Telexa*. How... what...

"I would please ask that you get us into space as soon as possible," Six said, his mandibles clacking as he stared at the mutated Bane brothers trying to break through the pod's door.

"Yes, right! Yes... OK. Um..." *Shit, shit, how do you fly a ship again? Engine check, um, boosters and thrusters and – wait, no, those are the same thing...* It took some fumbling, but the pod responded like it was supposed to, and in no time they were ready to initialize the launch sequence. As soon as they did, a fiery blast should propel them up one of the long spires that led out the top of the ship and up through the atmosphere until they were free.

Free. Unless…

Countdown to launch. Ten… nine…

"There's liquid Xenium on the floor out there," Dizzie muttered, then glanced at Six, who was strapping himself in beside them. "What if it throws off our launch?"

"That is possible," Six said. "But I think we'll make it."

Dizzie's head snapped around to look at him. "But how do you–"

"*Dizzie.*" He reached out and put a gentle claw on their shoulder. Behind him, the scrape of other, far less gentle claws got louder. "Against all odds, we have made it this far. I believe we're destined to survive. Trust in fate, just this once."

Four… three…

"Fate," Dizzie said miserably. But then… there was "fate", fickle and unscientific, and then there was the only logical action to be taken in order to survive. If they happened to coincide this time, well, Dizzie could ignore that. They nodded.

One… zero.

The little pod's booster rockets fired, and Dizzie almost fell out of the seat as the ship began to rise off the *Nexeri*'s floor. Almost simultaneously, the pod was shoved hard to the side, so hard that it scraped against the wall of the chute guiding them upward with a sound like metal against glass. The liquid Xenium in their fuel tank was fighting to outrun the spill on the floor, which was probably soon going to ignite the *rest* of the store of Xenium in the room any second now, and then they'd really be–

FOOM! Dizzie was flattened back against the seat so

hard it made their neck hurt as the explosion from below rocketed around, and then past them, engulfing their pod in white-hot fire even as they soared out of the ancient ship and into the sky. Alarms blared, bright blue warning lights blinked, and for a few seconds they were sure that it was over. They'd lost, they'd been caught by the incredible explosion of all that Xenium; they and every revenant on Sik-Tar were going to die, for real this time, with no mold left to resurrect them. This was the end. This was... this was...

White flames were abruptly replaced by soothing blackness. A moment later, a claw reached out into Dizzie's field of view and shut off the blaring alarm. They just sat there and watched, breathing hard, too adrenalized and battered by their stupidly rapid ascent to realize what had just happened until–

"Oh my god." They were alive. They'd made it, they were in space and they were alive! Dizzie turned to look at Six, wincing as the pain in every muscle in their upper body made itself known but able to put it aside as the endorphins of pure, triumphant euphoria rocketed through their body. "We're alive! We made it!"

Six spread his mandibles wide, giving Dizzie an expression that was as close to a human smile as they had ever seen on him. "So we did." His antennae waved gently. "Well done."

Well done? *Well done?* Damn straight it was well done! "We just survived an apocalypse!" Dizzie pointed out. "I can't even begin to calculate the odds of us being able to live through something of that magnitude! The Xenium alone was bad enough, when it came to the take off, but to make it through the revenants and the mold and – the mold!"

They let go of the controls and dove toward their pack, pulling out a bottle of decontamination spray. "Stand up," they ordered. "Right now. We can't take any chances with the mold hitching a ride on us. We need to decontaminate immediately."

Six came, as mild as he always was, and stood still while Dizzie hosed him down with mold-killing spray. Then they handed the bottle over to him. "Now you get me."

Dizzie still wasn't satisfied until they cranked up their battered particle detection unit – also thoroughly decontaminated – and ran a check on the pod's small cabin, then their belongings, then themselves. The small percentage of mold stores that still registered on the machine were diminishing as they watched, down into the single parts per billion. After another anxiety-inducing five minutes and a second check, there were no active reads of mold anywhere in the pod.

"Finally." Dizzie dropped the nearly empty bottle of spray onto the floor and slumped back against a wall. They hadn't realized until now just how tired they were. The comedown from what had to be the longest day in the history of the universe – had all of them really been together just that morning, it seemed impossible – was hitting, and hitting hard. That plus the sudden plummet of their adrenaline and the fact that they hadn't eaten or drunk anything in hours was enough to take the shine off their miraculous survival.

A tear slipped down Dizzie's cheek. They wiped it away, clumsy and angry at their own clumsiness, the way their fingers felt thick and rough and everything from their toes to their ears ached. More tears followed, though, and some of them pooled in the corners of Dizzie's lips, the salt taste a sharp change from the disinfectant that suffused the air.

"It's not fair," they whispered, which – what a stupid thing to say. Of course it wasn't fair – what about life was ever fair? Humanity had fought for centuries to instill fairness into society and failed at every step along the way. Nature wasn't fair; the universe wasn't fair. Why should Sik-Tar have been any different?

The dream that Dizzie had held close in the back of their heart from the beginning of their voyage to this dark planet was finally ripped away, like pulling a bandage from a particularly nasty wound. The dream of discovering a usable source of Xenium, of making their and Corinus's reputations, of bringing him home safely and securing funding for bigger and better expeditions and finally contributing something to the study of the mold and the Xenos that would make Dr Rigby's memory proud… all lost. All gone.

What was the worth of data that had such an incredibly dear price? The deaths of two-thirds of their expedition was undoubtedly an affordable price to those in power who had no soul and no conscience, but Dizzie wasn't like that. Couldn't *be* like that, especially not in the wake of so many people dying so that they could live.

If they could have changed places with Corinus right now, if they could have spared his life and given theirs in turn, they would have. That thought was nothing but a funnel for their despair – useless, what good was dwelling on it? What good was dwelling on *any* of it? But Dizzie couldn't help it.

They buried their face in their hands and did their best to stifle the sound of their own crying, even though they knew it was futile in such a small space. If Six was kind, he would turn around and look the other way.

He wasn't kind, though – or at least, not kind enough to ignore Dizzie's breakdown. Instead, he was cruel enough to acknowledge it by sitting down next to them and offering a hard but warm shoulder to lean against. "The loss of your friend, and of all our companions, is sad," he said. "There is no shame in acknowledging that."

"But I don't want to… I can't…" Thinking about it made it more real, and Dizzie wasn't *ready* for it to be real. They wanted to bask in the warm glow of survival, not look around them and see everything that they missed, everyone they wished was there. Corinus had been their fellow researcher and best friend for the past three years. They'd shared every triumph and every failure, and now… now, to have to face the ultimate triumph that was survival and couple it with the terrible failure that was losing him…

"I, too, am sad." Six leaned his shoulder against Dizzie's. "Perhaps you will permit us to be sad together."

That was it. It wasn't the support they would have gotten from Corinus, but it was the valuable, incredible reminder that they weren't alone that sealed the deal for Dizzie. They leaned over against Six and let the tears come, let out the fear and angst and pain that had been haunting them ever since the first ancient corpse came back to life, and cried until their eyes itched and they could barely keep themselves upright.

Six sat with them through it all, a staunch support through the tears and shivers and shakes. He handed them water when they were done, a clean cloth that they could wet so that they could clean off their face, and finally made up a little berth that Dizzie could lie down in.

"Don't we have to... shouldn't we..."

There were so many things left to do, so much to figure out. Where the hell were they even going to go now? Could they make it back to the Coalition with the fuel they had left? What would the reaction of their superiors be when they got there? This trip had been an unmitigated disaster in every sense of the word – the faint hopes the Coalition brass had held for their expedition turning into something profitable not only hadn't panned out, they'd lost valuable personnel as a result of it. Dizzie would be lucky if they weren't packed off to some corporate lab to do scientific scut work for the rest of their life.

And it wasn't going to be any better for Six, either. For an alien associated with an aggressively expanding empire to be one of the last people standing, when everyone else who'd died was a Coalition citizen, wasn't a good look for him. He would probably be subjected to interrogation, to imprisonment, maybe even to death as a result of this awful expedition.

"Whatever you're worrying about, it can wait," Six said, his voice a dim whirr against the backdrop of anxiety and fatigue. The heat of his body was real and present, though, a comforting press against Dizzie's side. "It can all wait long enough for you to rest and gain some peace. Rest now. You will not be alone."

Not alone. That was probably the best that Dizzie could hope for right now. They closed their eyes, not sure they'd be able to sleep but willing to try – anything to escape the sensation of despair that was doing its best to envelop their brain.

It worked. Darkness turned to nothingness, and in Dizzie's last moment of self-consciousness before they fell asleep, they were grateful for it.

CHAPTER TWENTY-SEVEN
Ix-Nix-Six

Caridians didn't require the same sorts of creature comforts that many other species did to survive and thrive. He had watched with a vague sense of fascination as the other members of their expedition, even the stalwart and haughty Thassian, had succumbed to the need for something more than basic subsistence over and over again. More food and water than was needed purely for survival, entertainments to keep their minds removed from the present, conversation to feed their spirits and the pleasure of enjoyable companionship to feed their hearts… it had all seemed so odd, and yet so *right* at the same time.

Six truly had done the inconceivable, but not in the way his Seethe-mate had warned him. Or rather, not *just* in that way. Over the course of this journey, he had found common ground with a disparate group of Coalition aliens, had enjoyed their presences and learned from their experiences and, in the end, guarded himself successfully against their treachery.

He had known such treachery would come – as soon as

he verified his initial hypothesis about where he was and what they'd found, Six had known the outline of what was going to happen. It was merely a matter of surviving long enough to ensure that history repeated itself, and that Dr Drexler survived as well. It had certainly been a challenge, but now here they were, together in space, with the fuel Mason had hauled on board and enough food for a human – Six himself could go without for up to three Coalition-standard months – to survive the trip as they flew this pod back to Coalition space and faced up to their mistakes.

Or…

Or they could do what Six knew that they *must* do. What he would have to persuade Dizzie that they needed to do. The odds of a ripple in the space-time continuum were, for once, firmly with him – Six knew it would happen the way he needed it to. He just needed to make sure Dizzie was ready for it as well.

Right now, the human scientist didn't seem ready for much at all. They were exhausted, yet capable of the most interesting feats regardless of that exhaustion. They had woken up twice in the past seventeen hours, once to drain a thermos of water in one long, unbroken series of gulps before staggering to the waste facilities, and again five hours later while crying out from a nightmare, saying their colleague's name over and over again before they fell back into a fitful sleep. Six hadn't even had to *do* anything that time, just watched as Dizzie self-soothed enough to drop back into slumber. Fascinating, truly fascinating.

Soon, if the twitches that were coursing with more frequency through their body were any measure, they would be waking up again. Hopefully this time it would be for longer. Six was ready to talk.

Ready to talk. How very alien you've become. In the Seethe, one was ready to do their duty – no more, no less. The Queen Minds dictated what that duty was, and relied on each member fulfilling it to the best of their ability. Six knew he had been fortunate to shape his own path the way he had in the past; he would be more fortunate yet to direct his future the way he hoped it would come about.

Hope. Fate. Future. You think of things that are truly perverse, for one of your kind. How are you better than any other renegade Caridian?

Well, Six liked to think he was at least better prepared than most of those who evaded Seethe orthodoxy.

"Mmm..." Dizzie mumbled something to themself, then slowly pushed up onto their forearms and looked blearily around the pod's small cabin. "What the..."

Six picked up the thermos he'd prepared for them and held it out. "Here. Don't be afraid to drink it all. The pod has a very advanced water recycling program."

Dizzie laughed hoarsely. "That's a nice way of saying that it'll make my pee drinkable again."

"It is," Six agreed, pleased that they understood him.

"You... never mind." They stared at him for a long moment, then sat up, took the thermos from his hands, and sipped pensively at the water. "Where are we now?"

"Still above Sik-Tar," Six said. "I didn't want to leave orbit without talking to you about our destination. In truth, it's been interesting to keep an eye on the conflagrations happening below."

"Confla – what do you mean?"

"The planet is on fire," Six replied. Dizzie scrambled to their feet and joined him in front of the tiny viewscreen. He adjusted their heading so that their former landing site on Sik-Tar was just below them. "You can see it, lighting up the clouds from below," he said, pointing.

Dizzie stared in wide-eyed silence, perhaps in a state of awe but more likely in one of some level of distress. Distress seemed to come to humans with astonishing regularity. How did they function with so many challenging feelings cluttering up their minds so frequently?

"Still on fire?" Dizzie said at last. "But the clock says I've been under for more than half of a Sik-Tarian day. That's twenty-two hours, that's… for it to still be burning…" They glanced at Six. "Have you calculated how far the burn has spread?"

"I believe the distance is contained to the single Xenium field we were located on," he said. "However, the *depth* of that fire is quite impressive. It appears that the mining operation at hand penetrated nearly to the center of the planet. The vein of Xenium was quite narrow, but very deep. This fire could burn for days. Perhaps for weeks."

"Incredible." Dizzie stared down, a hint of their old liveliness in their eyes. "And all of it gone to waste…" The liveliness dissipated, and so did their energy. They slumped down into the pilot's seat, seemingly oblivious to the way it perfectly fit their much shorter body.

Will I have to bring it up, or will Dizzie know? They're smart – surely they must know. But knowing and acting on knowledge were two different things.

Six decided to try his claw at being comforting again. "I'm quite sure that the force of the blast that helped propel us into space was more than enough to atomize our former companions. The Bane brothers and Dr Lifhe are surely free of the mold now."

Dizzie chuckled and passed a hand over their eyes. "Yeah, I think you're right. All of Sik-Tar might be free of the mold now, but it's also probably going to be free of all its Xenium, too, the way things are going." They tilted their head as they stared down at the fiery clouds. "I guess that's for the best. Given what happened after *we* found this place, I wouldn't want anyone else to show up here unprepared." They sighed, then looked at Six. "That's not what the Coalition is going to want to hear, you know."

Six nodded. "I do know that," he affirmed.

"They're not going to be happy with our losses."

"None of us are happy with our losses."

"No," Dizzie agreed somberly, "but they'd be tolerated if we were coming back with more than just a single tankful of Xenium and some data that's probably going to be shoved into a Guild-locked black box the second I try to present it."

"That is true," Six said. He realized he was treading on delicate ground now. "Perhaps it would be in our best interests to consider a… different destination."

"A different destination." Dizzie's eyes narrowed. "Like your own home planet? Knowing what I know of your people, Six, I seriously doubt I would be welcomed there."

"Our home planet is strictly off limits to those not of Caridian origin," Six admitted. "There is another location within the territory of the Glorious Hegemony that I had in mind. One that is more favorable to ideas of science… and outsiders."

"Hmm." Dizzie stared at him for a long moment, their expression unreadable – oddly so, for them. Six had learned a great deal about reading the thoughts and emotions of aliens off their faces since joining this expedition, and Dizzie had been his best teacher, if an unwitting one. Now he realized that there were depths to their mind that he didn't understand.

He might, Six acknowledged, be on the verge of admitting to something that would make Dizzie despise him. He hoped otherwise, but he had to be honest with himself – try as he might, he couldn't see either the past or the future with a clear lens.

Rather than begin the interrogation that Six knew was coming, though, Dizzie turned their face toward the back of the pod. "I need to clean up. Is there a…"

"There is a sonic cleanser," he confirmed. "And a fold-out curtain for privacy."

Dizzie chuckled. "How polite. I didn't know that Caridians even felt the need for that sort of modesty."

"We don't," Six confirmed, feeling his antennae wave more briskly as the pulse of his ichor quickened. He calmed as Dizzie merely nodded, then got up and rooted through their bag until they found a fresh set of clothes.

"Give me a few minutes," they said. "Then we can talk. And eat, too. I'm starving."

They probably wouldn't be technically starving for several more days, but Six supposed it was possible they felt that hungry, given the level of exertion they'd endured. "I'll prepare some food."

"Thank you." They went over to the corner where the sonic cleanser was set into the wall, found the notch where the hard plastic curtain was located and pulled it out, then set about renewing themself.

Six pulled several meal bars from his own pack for Dizzie's consumption. Provided by the Coalition, they were dry, flavorless, and suitable for providing sustenance for ten different alien species. He filled another thermos as well, then turned his eyes back toward the planet and tracked the distant billows of flame, edged with burning blackness that dissipated quickly into the red mist of Sik-Tar.

What a beautiful place it was, truly wonderful to experience. If only he had looked far enough ahead to anticipate the dangers they'd faced.

And yet… in a way, he had. That "way" was what he would have to justify to Dizzie in a moment. He found himself looking forward to it.

Dizzie returned five and a half minutes later, hair frizzed from the sonic cleanser and wearing clean clothes. Their feet were bare. It was the first time Six had ever seen human feet before. He marveled silently at their strangeness, then looked up at Dizzie as they cleared their throat.

"So." They unwrapped a meal bar but didn't bite into it. "This pod is equipped with personal amenities a Caridian would never want, isn't it?"

"It is."

"You don't need a toilet. You don't need a shower."

"I do not," he confirmed.

Dizzie nodded. "And yet this escape pod was part of a ship that is at least a thousand years old."

"It is," Six agreed.

"Which leaves me with two choices," Dizzie said. "The first is that your ancestors were close enough to another species, a species with needs completely unlike your own, that this species' comforts were taken into consideration in the design of the mining ship's escape pods. This one I doubt, since you yourself have said your species is very insular."

"That's very true." Six knew he sounded too excited for such a solemn moment, but he couldn't help it. He was about to share a revelation that defied all logic and yet couldn't be denied.

"But that doesn't explain everything, up to and including the fact that the password that got this particular pod moving is one that only *I* would guess. *Me.* As if the computer system knew that I, out of all the beings in the universe, was going to be the one to pilot it." Dizzie's dark eyes glittered with curiosity. "How could that be?"

"How do you think it can be?"

"Time travel." The words fell from their mouth with reluctance, but once they were out there more explanation followed quickly after. "I couldn't stop wondering about how weirdly *comfortable* the lab was, like it had been set up to a human's standards. Even the height of the tables in there was something more ideal for the average human's use, not a Caridian, which didn't make *any* sense until I began considering perhaps your species lived through different stages, one of which might be shorter."

"We do have a larval stage," Six said, revealing one of his

people's deepest secrets without compunction. It didn't matter at this point – Dizzie wasn't going to betray him. "However, once we emerge from our time of transformation, we are already at our fully adult size. Subsequent molts are infrequent and usually the result of healing trauma, not further growth."

"I knew it!" They slapped the table. "That lab was set up with a human in mind – maybe even with *me* in mind, considering the password thing. But how is that possible?" Their eyes narrowed. "Did you know this going in? Did you know that Corinus and the others were going to die? Because if you did, so help me I will make you–"

"I did not know," Six said firmly. "I had no idea of what this place truly was until I saw it up close, and even then I didn't understand the dangers it represented until Dr Lifhe was infected. If I had, I would certainly have shared that information."

Dizzie looked only slightly mollified. "When did you understand what the *Nexeri* really was?"

"Once I got inside it and discovered its purpose as a combined research and mining vessel," Six replied. "The truth is, I have seen the *Nexeri* before. It is currently in skeletal form in the shipyards of my home planet."

Dizzie's jaw dropped, and the skin over their cheeks flushed a shade darker. "I knew it," they whispered. "The tech, it – it seemed so advanced even though most of it wasn't working, and the readings I was getting about the materials used in its construction – those had some serious biophysical engineering properties. I know Caridians have been spacefaring for a long time, but some of those molecules were just… they were so familiar, things I think I've read about in papers before."

"Indeed," Six said. "Caridians are an advanced species, one of the most advanced in our galaxy. But that doesn't mean we aren't constantly improving our own technology, and that includes gathering intelligence on the latest Coalition advancements. Indeed, I would be surprised if you *hadn't* recognized some of those molecules – the materials for this ship are partially based on advancements spearheaded in Coalition science labs. Your military keeps a fairly closed mouth about this sort of thing, but your Guilds…" His antennae waved from side to side. "Their security is much more easily penetrated. Caridians know many things that the warring factions of your Guilds are desperate to understand, and have shown themselves willing to make inauspicious trades because of it."

"Is that how you learned to interact with Coalition species so well?" Dizzie asked insightfully. "Because you've been, what, working as a *bribe* dealer within Coalition space?"

"It is one of the ways," Six said. He felt no remorse or regret for the role he'd played in gathering intelligence – being a spy was an honorable job among Caridians, noble even, given that they had to put up with so many "outside influences". "I've always been a little quirky."

"Quirky." Dizzie nodded, their lips quivering a little at the corners. "Yeah, I can see it. So. This ship, then, it's being built right now?"

"It's slated to be completed in approximately another two decades," Six confirmed.

"And is it going to, what, run on liquid Xenium? Do your people already have a store of the stuff? Have you been mining Sik-Tar for centuries already?"

"Not at all. This ship is being designed with standard fuel resources in mind." Six paused. "I cannot say exactly how it ended up on Sik-Tar, when its current destination is an asteroid belt on the other side of the galaxy. Wormholes are excellent transports, but there is always a slight possibility of a time fluctuation while using them."

Dizzie held up a hand, and Six snapped his mandibles shut. "Are you saying..." they began in a trembling voice. "Are you saying that a ship that's not due to launch from your home planet for another twenty years ended up traveling back to the *past* and crashing onto Sik-Tar? That it was actually an accident, like we thought originally?"

"That is exactly what I'm saying." Six was pleased Dizzie was understanding the situation with such clarity.

"But... but the pod! The lab! The *password!*" Dizzie gripped their hair in their hands and pulled on it with a groan of frustration.

Maybe they were having a few more issues with things than Six had initially assumed.

"If I was on that ship – if *we* were on that ship when it landed in the past, why the hell would we go back to Sik-Tar? Why would we even *assume* we might go to Sik-Tar, when you said your people expect it to end up in an asteroid belt? How would *we* get on the *Nexeri* in the first place? What would we–"

Six held up a claw. "You must understand that I simply can't answer most of these questions at this time, because neither of us have lived this future yet. We have lived through something that *influenced* the future, but there's no way to know for certain that it is you and I who are destined to return to Sik-Tar someday, whether on purpose or by accident."

Dizzie stared at him. "But the password, the– the–"

"Twenty years," Six reminded Dizzie gently. "Twenty years between now and when the *Nexeri* is destined to take off. That is a long time to spread your knowledge and your passion to others. Perhaps there *was* another human, or several, on the expedition that led the ship to its destruction. Perhaps they shared your love for the science of Dr Rigby and used that password to honor both of you. There is no way to know for certain that either of us ever go back to Sik-Tar right now."

"Why would we even want to go back?" Dizzie snorted, but their expression was thoughtful. "And yet we do. We, or someone who will know us, does. Whether they meant to or not, they go back in time and… and they thrive on Sik-Tar. For a while, at least."

"Indeed," Six agreed. "For a while." Not forever. His mind conjured up the vision of the wet, rocky plain, pieces of his people collecting in every crevice and notch. *Certainly not forever.* "Perhaps we end up living on a Sik-Tar before it evolves into the planet we have just experienced. Perhaps we end up studying the liquid Xenium, and the Xenos. Perhaps we discover whether you can have one without the other. This ship, this pod, is designed to run on Xenium, while its mothership is not. When is that change made? Who makes it?" What was the human physical movement that would help him get across his – ah, right. He shrugged.

"It is simply impossible to know all of this right now. Paradox is the nature of time travel. We could ask the Council of Queens, but they generally do not share their secret knowledge."

"They must know something about all this," Dizzie muttered. "We must bring back some kind of knowledge that proves useful to them. Otherwise, why would they let an outsider into your culture?"

Six's antennae straightened with pleasure. "You are amenable to returning to my people with me, rather than to the Coalition?"

"Are you kidding me? What choice do we have? Do you want to be tortured and interrogated and–" Dizzie went off on a rant, listing off a dozen different ways the two of them might be treated upon their return to Coalition territory, none of them good. If Six could have smiled to indicate his warm feelings, he would have right then and there. As it was, he resisted the urge to stretch his mandibles apart – he knew the gesture didn't quite go over right to those without similar facial features.

"So there's no way we can go back there, not if we don't want to get flayed alive and hung out to dry," Dizzie finished. "But are you really sure that your people will be any better? They have no reason to be kind to us either."

"They have no reason to be unkind," Six said. "As the sole surviving offspring of a once-great hive, I have resources that make the rest of the Seethe treat me with more respect than perhaps I deserve, as long as I use my resources in the name of the Glorious Hegemony."

"The *Nexeri*..." Dizzie pointed an index finger at him.

"Wait, is the *Nexeri* something that *you're* building? You're responsible for making it?"

"The version we saw on Sik-Tar had clearly undergone numerous design changes since I first signed off on the funding, but–"

"How could you not tell me any of this sooner?" Dizzie demanded. "How could you not – and you spent all that time in the flipping *library*, you must know so much about what happens next! So… what happens next? Do we go back to Sik-Tar? Do we die there next time? It's not just the pod that makes me think at least one human died there," they added. "I know you saw the revenant with the *skull* tucked into its guts. That was human bone structure – adulterated, definitely, but human all the same. That could have been me!" They blanched. "Odds are that it was me, aren't they, not some other human. Even after we escaped this time around, are we fated to die on Sik-Tar?"

"We weren't this time. Perhaps we never will be," Six replied. "Like I said before, time travel is rife with paradox. Everything I read in the library – and there was much of interest – is thrown into flux by the fact that we now know of that potential future. Even once the *Nexeri* is running and ready to go out on its first expedition, does that necessarily mean we'll be thrown back into the past on that initial trip? It could take years, decades, before the rift in the space-time continuum that sends it back into the past comes into existence. And I discovered nothing that makes me believe it must be you and I who lead that particular expedition. There are so many other things for us to do right now: ships to build, Xenium and Xenos of all types to study. There is time to improve our understanding of what might be the most desperate threat our galaxy faces."

Six stared intently at Dizzie. "What you discover in the next phase of your life could be used to save entire systems before the threat that Xenium and the mold poses progresses any farther through Coalition space than it already has."

That the mold *would* progress eventually, that much he was certain of. Whether Dizzie ever came back to Sik-Tar or not, what Six had read in the library had confirmed his suspicions that the data they had gleaned during this ill-fated expedition was going to be immensely useful, at least to the Caridian people. Probably to the Coalition and the Guilds as well, if they ever got the chance to trade it.

The losses they had taken still saddened him, and he could see that they weighed heavily on Dizzie's soul. But the eagerness he felt at what was next for their future was even stronger. *The universe has the ability to surprise even the wisest of us, and I am far from that.*

Dizzie finally broke the silence. "How much farther is Caridian space from the Galactic Coalition home system anyway? I know you don't need to eat and drink the way I do, but we don't have unlimited resources here, and ion drives aren't *that* fast."

"Ah." Six was happy to be able to present good news in this case. "This pod is equipped with its own wormhole activator. With the amount of Xenium that made it into the tank, I should be able to return us to my home planet with no difficulties."

Dizzie's eyes widened. "Wow. That's pretty convenient."

"Very," Six agreed.

"Well, I guess…" They shrugged with far more ease than Six had managed it. "I guess that's the best course of action for us. Do you want to send a message ahead, let them know we're coming?"

"It won't be necessary. The queens will have no difficulty with our passage, I assure you."

Dizzie smiled, small but genuine. "That's great. I… I can't believe I'm actually looking forward to this." They rubbed their hands together. "Once all the introductions are made and we're getting set up, can I have my own lab?"

"Of course." They would be given everything they needed, much like Six always had been. He turned to the controls to ready for their departure, but his mind was able to keep working away on other things as the navigation system, which could have felt so unfamiliar, came alive with ease for him.

He hadn't shared everything with Dizzie. Not yet. He wasn't sure if he ever *would* share this next part with them – the part where the *Nexeri* had gone back in time to Sik-Tar more than once. If everything really had gone as he'd read – if the ship that he was in the process of building had successfully traversed the space-time continuum multiple times, a fact that should be impossible but perhaps wasn't with a fuel source as powerful as liquid Xenium to help control the probability fields… Then it was possible, even likely, that the great minds which ordered the Seethe knew far more about the issue of Xenium, and its Xeno threat, than Six could understand.

Perhaps the queens knew even more than he *wanted*

to understand. Six thought for a moment of the specter that Dr Lifhe had become, the intelligent being who was nevertheless no longer himself, fully ruled by the alien mold and intent on increasing his knowledge.

Was it possible that... that Six had already brought the mold *back* to his home? Based on what he had learned from the *Nexeri*'s library and the experience they'd just had, was it a probable hypothesis that the consciousness that controlled the mold had worked its way up through the ranks of his people without killing off the *entire* Seethe, just parts of it?

Six thought about the devastation of certain hives throughout the last millennia, how even without the pressure of external warfare or internal strife some of them had simply... combusted. Broken down. Immolated themselves.

Was the mold even now ruling the Glorious Hegemony?

"Six." Dizzie's voice broke him out of his surprisingly dark reverie. "Is everything OK?" they asked as they strapped into the seat next to him. "You look like you might be having second thoughts."

Six had, in fact, briefly considered the wisdom of dropping their pod straight back down onto Sik-Tar and consigning them, and their potentially devastating knowledge, to the flames. But the look of hope in Dizzie's eyes stopped him.

Surely we can control enough variables to prevent societal contamination by the mold. Surely we're wiser now than we were when we first arrived here. "Not at all," he said. "Are you ready to go?"

Dizzie pressed their lips together and nodded firmly. “I’m ready.”

“Then go we shall.” Six turned on the generator, and a spark of blue-white light began to swirl and expand in front of them, blocking out the fiery inferno below them.

Surely they were ready for this. It was time to move on, into the future… and eventually, into the past.

“In three,” the nav system announced. “Two. One.” The wormhole opened, and as Six guided the pod inside, he was able to pretend for a moment that his claw wasn’t trembling.

Surely…

The wormhole swallowed their pod. Sik-Tar, and its dying secrets, was left alone in its own cold, remote corner of the galaxy, to burn out like a candle in the foreseeable future.

Its past, however, was something else entirely.

ABOUT THE AUTHOR

CATH LAURIA is a Colorado girl who loves snow and sunshine. She prefers books to TV shows, has a vast collection of beautiful edged weapons, and could totally survive in the wild without electricity or running water, but would really prefer not to. She loves writing speculative fiction of all genres, and has a long list of publications under her belt as romance author Cari Z.

authorcariz.com // twitter/author_cariz

SCOUNDRELS & SOLDIERS BAND TOGETHER TO SURVIVE THE ONSLAUGHT OF ALIEN-ZOMBIES SPREADING ACROSS THE GALAXY

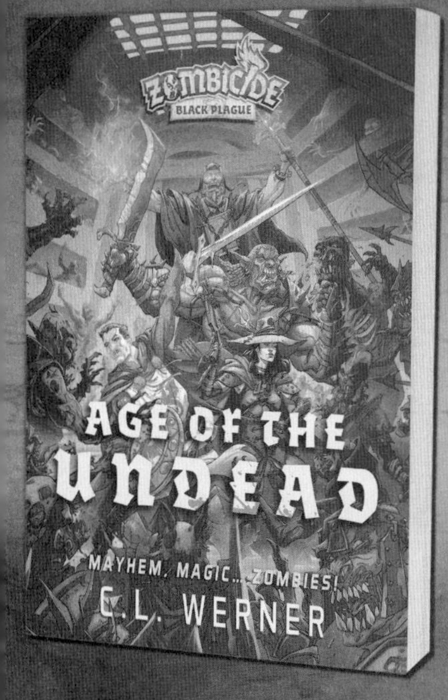

A BOLD KNIGHT ENLISTS UNLIKELY ALLIES WHILE DISCOVERING THE SOURCE OF UNDEAD CORRUPTION!

ZOMBICIDE

ZOMBICIDE
ALL OR NOTHING
YOU THOUGHT ZOMBIES WERE BAD... TRY BEING ONE.
JOSH REYNOLDS
ZOMBICIDE
LAST RESORT
TRY NOT TO DIE.